Read by Dawn
Volume One

Hosted by Ramsey Campbell

First published 2006.

Published by Bloody Books™.

9 8 7 6 5 4 3 2 1

Contents

Acknowledgements

Thanks to Simon Petherick at Beautiful Books for creating an imprint that allows me to indulge my passion for sharing the nightmares around.

Grateful thanks to Tony Makos, Lara Matthews and John Treadgold whose invaluable insight helped shape this collection.

Finally, my very special thanks to our host Ramsey Campbell whose stories have long fed my nightmares.

Adèle Hartley, Curator, Bloody Books

Introduction

Ramsey Campbell

I n Edinburgh on certain nights, folk out late or up early have observed a strange phenomenon at the Filmhouse Cinema. Throughout the darkest hours shrieks have been heard from within, of people or of power tools. More monstrous noises have troubled the night, and as the sun comes up, the etiolated audience staggers forth glassy-eyed and inarticulate as zombies. What secret rite may have taken place beyond those locked doors? None other than the annual Dead by Dawn horror film festival, an event capable of outraging the good burghers of Edinburgh. Well, better read than dead, and this book offers its own varied festival of horror.

It's going to be a long night, but the day is not yet done. To begin, David McGillveray holds "The Colour in the Jar" up to the light. The setting may be familiar enough – an ordinary urban daymare – but it's entered by an enigma that hints at something greater and more magical. So does Jeff Jacobson's "Last Day on the Job", in which details so everyday that most of us would hardly find them worthy of remark turn out not just to presage but to conjure up an alien apocalypse. If those aren't gods that first make the people of Chicago mad, they're certainly out to destroy them or at least to enjoy a late lunch.

Michele Lee depicts our world after a different catastrophe in "Bloodwalker", a tale that revives that useful category, science fantasy – fiction in which fantastic elements are taken for granted because they've set the rules of their environment. Its bewitched society has its own grim laws and logic, and the worst attitudes are uncomfortably human. The future is also involved in Brian Ross's

1

"The Face in the Glass", but although the sunlight shows it, that proves tragically unilluminating. We may be glad to join Scott Brendel on "The Seventh Green at Lost Lakes" for a little light relief, although his humour is satisfyingly grisly. Golfing horror is a teeny genre – H. Russell Wakefield contributed to it, as did the H. G. Wells adaptation in the Ealing Dead of Night – but this may be its most gruesome example. It's the kind of fun in the sun Sam Raimi might have had in his less respectable days, and so is "Zombie Fishing Trip". Brian Rosenberger's blank verse wriggles with imagery as witty as it is disreputable.

But the night is looming, and darker things are to come. In Rayne Hall's "The Bridge Chamber" a child leads others into darkness in an attempt to outmanouevre routine cruelty, but if nothing is waiting down there except dark, how terrible may that turn out to be? "Lessons" traps the reader with a vision turned in on itself, blinded with horror. When religion yields to superstition, Katherine Patterson suggests, the result can be nasty, brutish and short. Compared with this, the gross-out toothless zombie antics of Justin Madison's "Popee" are unthreatening; they even lead to a moment of tenderness. You won't find much of that in "Before You Say Anything", but Amanda Lawrence Auvergine has a horrid joke for us, and also a succinct study of affectless behaviour. Brian Rosenberger is back with "The Bride Wore Black", and so is his wit, spiked with poisoned puns and acid alliteration.

Now the evening is upon us. It arrives with deceptive gentleness in the form of David Hutchinson's "The Sutherland King", the kind of dark or at least twilit joke that ladies baking cakes might tell one another. In Bryce Stevens' "Payday" the urban sunlight seems close to malevolent, and perhaps nightfall brings the best it can for its haunted hobo. Day turns to night again in "The Little Girl Who Lives in the Woods", Rob Moore's suburban legend of child abuse and childhood innocence at its worst. What is done in daylight brings consequences after dark. In Stefan Pearson's "The Kylesku Trow" day and night are indistinguishable. If the story recalls fairy tales at their cruellest, its subterranean urban madness is still grimmer, and we'd be well advised to guess that final riddle while we have time. The night in Patricia MacCormack's "The Bloom of Decay" glows with a lurid linguistic illumination. The tale yearns for darkness, but it's immured in its own prose or borne helplessly away by a flood of language. By contrast, Joel Kuntonen's "Final Girl" brings on a supernatural nightfall, just one of the ways in which the characters are trapped in genre. The prose even reproduces the experience of a tracking shot. The effects of the monster's eternal return seem inescapable, but at the end a hint of humanity flickers and dies. As for Lavie Tidhar's "Eine Kleine Nachtmusik 1943", with its echoes of Lewis Carroll and Dorothea Tanning, who can blame the protagonist for seeking the wonder that may lie beyond horror?

Night is here with a vengeance. It gives cover to the evangelist – a distant relative of Robert Mitchum's preacher in Night of the Hunter – and his activities in Andrew Wilson's "Evangeline". A religious man using the services of a brothel? Surely this must be a feverish dream with no basis in the real world. He's tortured not just by his own guilty desires but by a reminiscence of Dr Xavier and his X-ray eyes. Stephanie Bedwell-Grime might be remembering the anthologies of Herbert Van Thal in her tale "For a Steal"; at any rate, it's where horror fiction intersects with fantasies of punishment – in this case, of protecting one's property and meting out one's own version of justice. Matt Wedge's "Frankie" suffers the terror of everybody's endless night – the kind of waking nightmare that troubles many imaginative children. Religious thoughts can turn black in the dark, and if daylight brings him worse, his last night is the worst of all.

The unlucky central character of Sam Minier's "Stuck" is plagued by nocturnal regrets and unhappy replays of her life. Those are traps in themselves, but there's a physical one to exacerbate matters, and her escape proves to be more hideous than her plight. Replaying of a different order is the basis for James Reilly's "House Broken"; on Christmas Eve – that night of maniacs and the malevolent, at least as far as horror is often concerned – who will be the ultimate victim as the genre loops back on itself? I should think any burglars who read this anthology would want to think twice.

Another thief is dealt with by David Turnbull's "The Woman Who Coughs Up Flies". She's immersed in loss and disappointment like treacle that attracts the insects, but in this tale of unnatural anguish love finds a way, though hardly a comforting one. The narrative is pitilessly lit until the sun comes up. John Probert's "Special Offer" also leads us towards dawn by way of the most desperate time of night; here it's desperate in terms both of the kinds of broadcast the sleepless may stumble upon and of their rash response to it. Readers may be additionally disconcerted to learn that this unsettlingly contemporary nightmare was written by a doctor. A further dawn is promised in Chet Gottfried's "Body Hunt", a glimpse of a future not unlike the one Michele Lee threatened, although his characters have recourse to even grimmer methods, however everyday these may seem to the perpetrators. When the world has been so overrun by predators, humanity might see fit to give up. In my own tale "The Place of Revelation", night yet again yields to daylight, which renders at least one of the teller's visions more transparent. Last and most succinctly among the stories, Joel Jacobs' "What Betty Saw" calls up the brightest light of all.

The Colour In The Jar

David McGillveray

The Smiling Man had the wickedest trainers the kids had ever seen. Hypnotised by his designer labels, they followed their piper into the shadow of the tower block.

"You won't walk out of there with those on your feet, mate."

"You might not walk out of there at all."

The kids laughed. The Smiling Man continued across the cracked concrete, trainers grinding on broken glass. Wheelie bins and abandoned cookers looked on in silence.

"You won't be laughing for much longer, mo'fuckah," shouted the leader of the pack. She was eleven.

The Smiling Man stopped and turned his smile on them. His hair was long and golden, tied back behind his ears. His beard was clipped to the latest design and his eyes were clear cobalt crystal. But the kids only saw the smile. There was something in it that flayed away years of the street, peeled away all that protective bravado.

The kids scattered.

The little girl stayed a moment longer until she could bear it no more. Then she ran after the rest.

Old Jeb sat dead in his chair, a crust of dried spittle on his lips. The stink of his corrupted body filled the room. Net curtains grey with years of cigarette smoke filtered the light to a subterranean fog and the television prattled without pity.

Two young men stood in the kitchen. One drank Jeb's whiskey

from a chipped coffee mug. The other stuffed stolen things into a sports bag.

"You look in the bedroom and I'll check the bathroom. Old people have always got pills," said Vitals.

Skinny slurped at the mug and coughed. "You turned over other places, then?"

"No, my Dad lived with his old man for a bit. I know about pensioners. They've always got more cash than they let on. Make sure you check under the mattress as well. They like to hide things under mattresses."

"What, like porn?"

"No, knobhead, like money." Vitals hefted the bag in one hand. It was full of ornaments and knives from the kitchen drawers. "Quick sharp, before anyone else comes. We've got first dibs on this trick."

⁕

Trash lay in piles against the walls of the lobby: chip papers and Coke cans and polystyrene burger boxes and syringes with orange needles. The air smelled of stale lager. A bass thump echoed from somewhere higher up in the tower.

The Smiling Man enjoyed it all, drinking it in with unremitting pleasure.

He had never been here before, but he had been to countless places like it. He knew the address, the floor and the apartment number. It had been foolish of Jeb to think he could play games. The Great Employer *hated* deal-breakers – they caused him to thrash and rage in his pit with a fury as old as the world. But to the Smiling Man, the hunt and the harvest were distilled joy. And then there was the bounty: the approval of the Great Employer and the elevation of his own soul.

The elevators stood open, reeking of piss and thick with teenage glyphs to love and revenge. Yes, the Smiling Man had been to many places like this and not in a single one had he ever used the elevator. He walked past and found the stairs. He held the door for an old Asian woman in a colourful shawl, smiling down at her as she scuttled past without a word or a glance.

Unhurried, he began to climb.

Skinny pushed open the door of the bedroom. It was dark and stank of old man and unwashed sheets. He flicked on the light and looked around.

A single bed lay pushed up against the wall behind the door, along with a small table and a bedside lamp. A huge standing wardrobe dominated the opposite wall, its oak front secured with a metal key.

Thick curtains cut off the view of the next tower. Skinny walked over to the window and peered around the curtain to see if he could see his Mum's flat, but it was the wrong side of the building. He jumped and then froze at the sound of breaking glass and swearing from the bathroom. Then the sounds of rummaging continued. He let the curtain fall back into place and opened the wardrobe.

Skinny wrinkled his nose as a draught blew the whiff of moth-balls in his face. The wardrobe was full of ancient suits and shirts. Skinny smirked at the carefully folded piles of long johns. Half a dozen pairs of leather shoes lay in a neat row in the bottom, all shone to perfection. He grinned when he discovered four plain gold wedding bands hidden at the back of a drawer. Skinny put them in his pocket.

The bed was next. Skinny remembered what Vitals had said and lifted the mattress. He smiled. Vitals had always been the clever one.

A brown envelope sat there waiting. Skinny snatched it up and unstuck the flap, emptying the contents on to the bed. He began going through it, spreading it over the sheets with his fingers.

"Fuck it."

Photographs and letters, that's all. Some of the pictures were in colour; most were black and white, a few yellow and brittle with age. They showed people in weird clothes that called across the decades and made Skinny giggle. In all of them the same young man looked into the lens with haunted eyes. There was writing on the back of some of them, and a few dates, eighteen hundred and something: testimony to a long, long life. Skinny didn't try and read the letters. There was nothing for him here.

"Fuck it," he said again.

He kicked over the bedside table in frustration. A phone book flopped out like a fish from a bucket.

He made for the door, hand automatically going to the light switch. His mum always screamed about the electricity when anyone forgot to turn off the lights. Something he had not noticed before made him look back into the gloom.

A glow came from the far side of the bedroom, the faint rectangular outline of a small cupboard set in the wall. He went over to it. Light shone from behind the door as if God, sorely injured, had crawled there to die. Skinny searched for the latch and blinked.

Inside was a single shelf and on it sat a jar. It was an ordinary jar, with the peeled remnants of a label on the side and a screw top lid. Skinny stood and stared for a full minute.

It was all he could do.

Inside the jar danced liquid light. Undersea colours of aquamarine and turquoise and azure swirled together in mesmeric patterns, as if driven by ever shifting currents. Indistinct images formed and reformed, tickling memories and desires inside of Skinny. It was beautiful. He could not bear not to have it. He wet his lips and took up the jar, holding it before his eyes so that he could see deeper into the light inside. Things glittered there, tiny shards of emerald and gold. The jar was warm to the touch, like the skin of a girl.

Skinny put it inside his jacket.

A black guy and a white guy in matching puffer jackets blocked the way to the fourth floor. The Smiling Man stopped three steps below, looking up at them with inexorable good humour.

"Got a light, Sonny Jim?" asked the white guy, eyeing the new arrival's couture leather coat. He held a stubby rollup in fingers heavy with tattoos and chunky jewellery.

The Smiling Man's grin widened a little further, to better display two rows of Hollywood-white teeth. He leaned forward and clicked his fingers so that his thumb stuck upwards. A blue flame that matched his eyes flickered from the tip of his manicured thumbnail.

Confusion drifted across the man's face, but he leaned forward reflexively and lit his smoke. The sweet smell of marijuana filled the stairwell.

"Who the fuck are you, David Blaine?" demanded the black guy. He wore an ugly scowl under his baseball cap. "I ain't seen you before and I don't think I like your face."

The Smiling Man took a step up the stairs and the two highwaymen took a step back, as if choreographed.

"You don't come by here unless we say so, Sonny Jim. We require something for our trouble, or you'll get something for yours."

"Yeah."

The Smiling Man stepped forward again and once again the two men moved back. The black guy reached inside his jacket but the Smiling Man raised an index finger and shook it from side to side once, twice. Puzzled, the man let his arms drop to his sides.

"Listen asshole, you take one more step and you're fucking dead. Don't you know who we *are*? We *own* this estate, and if you don't –"

The Smiling Man winked at him. The white guy's mouth continued to move but the words stopped coming. The man's hands rushed to his throat, jaws working. Fear took him for the first time and his eyes widened in panic.

The Smiling Man smiled his farewells. He stepped on to the landing with them and walked by, trainers scuffing a little on the concrete as he began to climb again.

They didn't even watch him go. Someone had...something had...it hadn't happened.

"What happened to you?" asked Skinny. He felt like giggling again and he could feel his cheeks going red, but he knew the look on Vitals' face. Vitals had several tiny cuts all over his hands and was wiping shards of non-existent glass from his jacket.

"Fucking medicine cabinet fell off the wall, didn't it."

"Was there anything in it?"

"Medicine, Skinny. Funny that, innit? Medicine being in a fucking medicine cabinet. It's in the bag."

"But why did it fall off the wall Vitals? It scared the shit out of me."

"Look, shut up all right? It was an accident. You're always scared shitless of something anyway. If it had been up to you, we wouldn't have come in here in the first place and then where would we be?" Vitals narrowed his eyes. "Now, I know you found something. I'm reading the headlines off your face."

Skinny cringed under his companion's interrogative stare. "Rings, I found some rings," he said.

"Oh yeah? Let's have a look then."

Skinny brought the jewellery from his pocket and put them in Vitals' outstretched hand. Vitals peered at them, turning them over in his palm.

"This is all right, mate. I can get us a decent bit of wedge for these, Deano knows a bloke. Nice one."

Skinny could feel the weight of the jar in his jacket, could feel sweat prickling at his hairline. He didn't like lying to Vitals. He didn't want Vitals not to be friends with him. But the colours in the jar were so beautiful, and it was his, he had found it, not Vitals.

"And the rest."

"What?"

"You think I'm soft? You wouldn't make much of a spy, Skinny. Your lying just ain't up to scratch."

"But Vitals, you've got the other stuff. It's nothing, honest."

"Listen, you little shit, you wouldn't have anything at all without me." Vitals twisted a handful of polyester from Skinny's jacket and shoved him roughly against the wall of the flat's cramped hallway.

"So show and tell."

Skinny looked away miserably. "It's not fair," he whined.

"It never is," said a cultured voice, a newsreader's voice. The two boys whirled as the front door was pushed open. They had left it as they found it, unlocked. A man with a smile stood in the doorway.

"Nice trainers," Skinny blurted as Vitals released him.

"We were just leaving," said Vitals, picking up the sports bag at his feet.

"No need to go just yet. I feel we could have things to talk about." The man's voice was genial, gentle, irresistible. He stepped into the hallway and carefully closed the door behind him. "The door was open when you found it, I take it?"

"We heard the telly. It was on loud."

"Shut up, Skinny. Listen, mate, we got the wrong place. Like I said, we're leaving." A steak knife appeared in Vitals' hand. It had a wooden handle and a serrated edge.

"Is Jeb in at all?" asked the Smiling Man. He nodded at Vitals encouragingly, as if trying to reassure a scared child that it was all right to tell.

"Don't make me have to go through you, mate," said Vitals. His voice was edged with panic, his eyes were everywhere but that smile.

"Everyone's so unfriendly here. Is this the world you live in, where people wave knives like this at strangers? It's all so adorable," enthused the Smiling Man. Vitals looked at his empty hand in disbelief. The Smiling Man wagged the steak knife at them like a matron's finger and sniffed the air. "Into the front room, I think."

Jeb still sat in front of the television. The Smiling Man went over to him and bent down to look into the old man's eyes. He grabbed his jaw and turned the head from side to side, then used his thumbs to pull back the eyelids. He sniffed. He licked his lips. He stopped smiling and Jeb's head rolled onto his chest.

"Too long dead," he said. "Oh Jeb. So clever, so naughty."

"Was he your dad or something?" said Skinny.

The Smiling Man looked at the young man and then turned abruptly and drove his foot through the television screen. The thing fell over backwards in a crunch of sparks and shattered glass.

Vitals bolted for the door, still clutching his precious bag of booty.

"This one's a real handful." The Smiling Man made an apparently casual gesture with one hand and Vitals froze. Skinny stared. It was like that time he went to Madame Tussaud's as a kid, only this time the waxwork looked like who it was meant to look like. Vitals' eyes had that look, like they were seeing beyond the walls. He rocked very gently in place.

"What . . . what's going on with that?" Skinny stammered. He shrank back against the wall.

The man was grinning again, all traces of anger gone. He stepped around Jeb's body and took the bag from Vitals, peeling back each stiff finger until it came loose. He looked inside, shaking it a few times. Crockery and metal clinked together. He dropped the bag and began going through Vitals' pockets. He found the wedding rings and tossed them aside with a snort.

"I know it's still here. I can taste it. But Old Jeb's tried to hide it and your friend doesn't have it. You've got it, haven't you, boy?" The Smiling Man's eyes seemed to glow in the bad light.

"I don't know what you're on about."

"Don't be dull-witted now. The door open? The television on? It was an invitation. Problem is, you two weren't as quick as Jeb would have liked. He should have known better. I mean, round here theft is a certainty but it doesn't work to timetables." He glanced at the body in the chair. "Close, but no cigar, old man."

Skinny cowered as the man came closer. He badly wanted to piss.

"It's mine," said the Smiling Man, "and it's caused me some trouble to reschedule my appointments."

"I–"

"Pretty, is it?"

Skinny's eyes widened and his mouth formed an 'O'. The

Smiling Man held out his hand.

Skinny was compelled to reach for the jar. When he saw the colours, though, he hesitated. He fell in love all over again and the room, Vitals, even the Smiling Man fell away. He was enveloped in the warmth of it: it spoke to him on some level of human kinship that he could never articulate.

The Smiling Man took it from him and to Skinny it felt like a sudden bereavement, all pain and injustice and helplessness.

"You don't really want this," said his tormentor, shaking it before Skinny's eyes. He removed the lid from the jar and Skinny stared at the colours, agonised. "Now, Jeb's rather tired old chassis is unfortunately too far gone. I'm unhappy, it's not ideal but it's his own fault. There really was no cause to bring others into this."

It was a trick of perspective, tunnel vision in the filtered sunlight. The Smiling Man stood over Vitals. One grew and the other shrank away, like headmaster and schoolboy, a lopsided camera zoom.

The Smiling Man held Vitals' jaw in one hand as he had done with Jeb, forcing his mouth open. Then he brought the jar to Vitals' lips and tilted it forward so that the liquid began to pour. No, not pour, *flow*. None of it dripped or dribbled down his chin. Every beautiful, scintillating drop went inside, sucked through an invisible straw, blind and hungry for life again.

Vitals did not blink or choke or cough. He absorbed the liquid from the jar in unnatural silence as the Smiling Man administered it with fierce concentration and gratuitous satisfaction.

At last, all of it was gone. Skinny breathed again, and so did Vitals. It erupted out of him in great wheezing gouts. His reanimated body sagged and seemed to shrink in on itself. He bent over as the Smiling Man stepped back, a thin strand of bile unrelated to what was in the jar hanging from his mouth.

The Smiling Man turned to Skinny. "Laters, my pretty soul," he said. "Maybe I'll see you again."

Skinny jerked and was out of the flat and running before his dawdling and battered senses retuned.

"Take a moment." The cultured voice was soft, understanding.

13

Vitals eventually stood straight, chest rising and falling. The muscles of his face fell into unfamiliar alignments in response to instructions given by someone other than Vitals. He stared into the vastnesses of the Smiling Man's eyes and saw what waited for him there.

"The boy's heading the same place you are, always was. But I couldn't let you go without saying goodbye, Jeb." The Smiling Man smiled.

Last Day On The Job

Jeff Jacobson

"So. Gonna join 'em, huh?" Amy asked, raising her dark eyebrows and taking a drag off her cigarette. "Just march right up and volunteer to let corporate America suck out your soul through your wallet?" She exhaled, forming her mouth into a delicate "O" shape, creating a perfect smoke ring. We were sitting in a window booth in an empty coffee shop at the corner of Jackson and Franklin. The place smelled of meat cooked too long in a microwave and it was giving me a headache.

I watched as the smoke ring broke apart on the tiled ceiling and shrugged. Working as a bike messenger in downtown Chicago hadn't been much fun for a long time. My fingers were acting on their own, twisting and twisting my napkin into ragged knots.

Amusement flickered in Amy's eyes. Her right eye was circled in heavy black mascara; she looked like Malcolm McDowell in A Clockwork Orange – except Amy was a hell of a lot cuter. Her hair was black as well, cut into a tight bob, and a black choker encircled her slender white neck. She was wearing a dark, short sleeve dress that barely reached her mid thighs. There was a pair of tight biking shorts under that. Tiny scars crisscrossed her pale knees – a detailed history of her battles with cabs, other bikers, and the pavement itself.

To me, she was a dream in black boots.

And of course, she had a boyfriend.

A small television on the wall babbled quietly to itself about the devastating rainstorm that had rolled across the nation two days ago, leaving floods and chaos in its wake. Sheets of dark water had covered the streets of Chicago's Loop, filling basements, flooding the subways, leaving behind a slippery, dark slime that coated the concrete.

Amy continued, "You got a choice here, right? Why would anyone choose to be a... a fucking robot? Wear a nice little power tie, a plastic smile, like all the other corporate clones. Sit in a little box all day, breathing recycled air, thumb up your ass. I'd rather breathe bus exhaust than that motherfucking recycled air."

Our walkie-talkies lay silently on the table between us like two dead pets. It was 10:30, and midmorning was usually the busiest time of the day. But we hadn't heard anything in over two hours.

Amy leaned in close. "The 'Rat Race' doesn't even come close. It's too kind." I glanced out the greasy window. The street was empty, quiet. "Those corporate robots, they're more like ants... They're just a bunch of ants, crawling around the hive. We're all turning into the same thing. Nice little consumers." She grinned, an empty, scary expression. "Gotta keep that economy growing."

I shrugged again for the hundredth time that morning.

"Besides, if you quit, who am I going to ride with? Just think about it, okay?" She reached across the table and briefly touched my hand, and I found that I was able to stop twisting the napkin.

"Let's get out of here," I said.

She nodded. "Yeah, this bullshit is getting old. I'm gonna call the office."

I wondered where the waitress was and tossed some money on the table. Outside, the heat hit me like a soft, wet wall. I wiped at my forehead and my hand came away wet. Every movement seemed to leave ripples in the air.

The street had an eerie, abandoned atmosphere.

Behind me, Amy kicked the door open. "Phone's fucked," she announced. "Wanna head back to the office, see what's up?"

A quick, slapping sound echoed off the pavement. A man wearing a black suit was running down the sidewalk on the other side of the street, leather soles slapping the concrete. He wasn't doing the usual Executive-I'm-in-a-hurry-but-I-don't-want-to-look-like-I'm-in-a-hurry-Shuffle either; this man was not late for a meeting. He was flat out sprinting.

We watched him run past the tourist entrance to the Sears Tower. He stumbled as he flew off the curb, nearly going to his knees on Wacker Drive. But he caught himself, raced across the Chicago River bridge and disappeared.

"What bug crawled up his ass?" Amy asked, locking her front tire into place.

I laughed. The air felt thick and oppressive. A featureless gray haze covered the sky about fifteen stories above the ground. It seemed almost solid, obscuring the buildings, the sky, the sun.

Across the street, the door to some ridiculously expensive clothing store opened and a wheelchair appeared. A blue mask covered the lower half of the old woman's face. A tube ran to a small oxygen tank at the back of the chair. A stooped, frail old man slowly nudged the wheelchair out onto the sidewalk. He looked confused and cautiously edged out to the curb, as if he was afraid of what he might find. He looked up and down the street, then raised his hand.

A taxi swerved around the corner of Jackson and Clark, and stopped near the old folks. The driver, a thin guy with a face like a blunt nail, pretended not to notice the wheelchair. His fingers drummed impatiently along the top of the passenger seat. The meter was already ticking. He turned and glared at Amy and me, sucking at his teeth. We glared back.

The driver finally shook his head and climbed out of the taxi. He made a big show of stretching, then walked around to the back of the cab and opened the trunk. The old man and his wife couldn't figure out how to get the wheelchair off the curb.

The sound of shattering glass came from far away, then it was gone.

Amy leaned forward and spit her gum as far as she could, her whole body rigid, tiny fists clenched, several knuckles wrapped in band-aids, up on her tiptoes in those black boots. The wad of chewing gum bounced off the windshield. I grinned, proud of her, and bent down to tighten the quick release lock on my front tire.

I heard a quick crunch and looked up to see the driver flopping and twitching on the pavement in erratic, staccato patterns. I wondered if he was having some sort of seizure. But then I saw that the top part of his head was caved in. He sucked in a ragged breath, drooling thick blood. One eye blinked. Around him, the street was wet, but not with blood. It looked like just plain water. Slivers of glass were scattered across the pavement.

Three small goldfish lay amidst the shattered glass. One of them slapped its orange tail weakly against the pavement. I finally got it. Someone had dropped an aquarium.

The driver's breath came out slowly in a bubble of black blood. He didn't take another. Amy tried to light another cigarette with a shaking hand. The air felt heavy, threatening to burst into liquid at any moment.

A sheet of paper floated past my face and landed gently on the street. I picked it up. It was blank on both sides and looked like an ordinary piece of copier paper. Another sheet drifted into view. Then another. I whipped around. Hundreds of sheets were falling slowly through the air. More paper followed, thousands of pages drifting down through the gray haze. Manila envelopes and folders began to fall as well.

Amy's jaw was clenched so tight that she bit the filter of the cigarette in half. The burning end dropped to the pavement, landing between her boots. "How –"

She was cut off by the gut-crunching sound of a computer monitor suddenly landing in the middle of the cab's hood. The yellow steel erupted around it like some heavy metal flower, flinging yellow paint chips and sharp pieces of plastic into the air. The entire cab bounced, rear tires almost lifting completely off the pavement.

The sky began to rain glass. I grabbed Amy and pulled her close, dropping to our knees next to the cab, trying to protect her back with my own. Cold fire crawled up my back as the shards of glass sliced into my skin. The deadly rain slowed to a trickle and stopped.

I stood up slowly, trying to ignore the needles of pain in my back. My shirt stuck to the warm blood. Glass crunched under my feet. The cab looked like it was covered in sharp chunks of ice.

Office equipment began crashing into the pavement. A filing cabinet smashed into a parked car. A chair landed near me and shattered. Computers rained down by the hundreds. I yanked the open the driver's door and shoved Amy into the front seat and fell on top of her. We curled up, grimly hanging onto each other on the wide bench seat as the cab rocked and shuddered under the onslaught. Something hit the windshield and a thousand cracks zigzagged across it, but the safety glass held. A coffeemaker exploded through the back window. Amy whimpered and wrapped her strong arms around my left shoulder and upper right arm. Her fingers clamped against the some of the glass stuck in my back, but I didn't mind.

The cab stopped shaking and the crashing sounds receded.

I lifted my head and listened, but couldn't hear anything else. I slowly slid out of the cab, staying low. Mangled and crushed office equipment had transformed Jackson into a long stretch of some corporate junkyard. The mist was down to the fifteenth floor. I reached out for Amy, and heard a wet thud.

A woman abruptly appeared on the pavement in front of me, right in front of the open cab door, face down. Her left arm was tossed casually out to the side, as if she had just waved. I couldn't see her right arm. I wished I couldn't see her head. Blood trickled slowly from her nose to the corner of her mouth, slipping past the conservative lipstick into darkness. Her tongue protruded slightly from the lips, hanging limp and still. The wet tip rested on the asphalt. One pale eye stared directly up at me.

Amy shrieked and scrabbled backwards inside the cab. I couldn't tear my eyes away from the dead woman. Her silk shirt was pulled up around her midsection, revealing skin stretched so tight it looked like a thin, clear plastic bag barely holding in wet meat. I couldn't move my arms, my legs.

Until a man slammed into the pavement, bounced, and landed on Amy's bike. I thought I had blinked. One instant, there was Amy's bike, near the back of the cab, resting on its side, surrounded by shattered keyboards and sheets of blank paper. The next, a man was lying on his back, brown wingtip next to his ear.

The left handlebar jutted out from his chest; it looked like part of his ribcage was caught on the brake lever. Blood suddenly started pouring out of his nose and right ear as if someone had turned on a faucet.

Amy clawed at the passenger door, but it seemed stuck. "Wait," I shouted. She kicked at the door. "Wait!" I shouted again. The passenger door popped open with a grinding scream. "Wait!" But then the air began to vibrate. The street, the actual asphalt under my feet started to shake. I blinked and looked up.

The gray sky was full of bodies.

For a moment, silence.

When they hit, it sounded like thunder.

I flinched and scrambled backwards. People kept falling out of the sky. An overweight bald man smashed face down in the street beside me and his stomach burst like a rotten tomato. A foul smelling, warm mist suddenly enveloped me, and my hand and arm came away a reddish green. No one screamed except me.

I fell crawled onto the sidewalk and pressed my back into the V-shaped wedge of a revolving glass door. Bodies were landing on bodies now and the pavement was slick with blood. They kept falling; some not moving on the way down, others pinwheeling their arms and legs. Some glanced off the sides of the buildings and tumbled through weightless cartwheels. Many of them bounced when they hit the unyielding concrete.

The thunder increased.

The sheer volume made me realize this was voluntary. On the street, the bodies were now four and five deep and rising. I somehow understood that everyone up in the gray mist, from the CEO on down to the janitors; they were all lined up, waiting for their turn. I realized that they'd broken the windows with the office equipment, clearing the way, preparing to jump.

A burst of static exploded out of my walkie-talkie, still strapped to my side. I flinched, thinking the building was falling down around me. But then I caught my breath and shouted, "Amy!" Harsh, frantic breathing came out of the tiny speaker grill.

Then – "Jack! Where are you?"

"I'm here, on the other side of the street," realizing as I said it how stupid that sounded. "Where are you?"

The seconds ticked by. Nothing. I stared at the walkie-talkie, clenching it in my fist, willing it to work. Finally, her voice broke through. "– Sear's Tower...the tourist –" More static. "– glass roof, oh god, people are coming through, just crashing through the glass –"

"Get under something. I'll find you. Just stay there!" I took a deep breath and held it, then scrambled forward through the swamp of warm meat. Someone bounced off a car and impaled himself on a parking meter. But that was all; the rain of bodies was slowing.

I hit the button of the walkie-talkie again, shouting, "Amy! Amy!"

Then Amy's voice. "I'm here, next to the elevators...the air – it's different... but I'm feeling... better." Something cold crawled up my back and the tiny hairs on the back of my neck came alive. Her voice sounded wrong.

And then it hit me. She was next to the elevators. The elevators of the goddamn Sears Tower. People, everyone, everywhere in the city, were leaping out of tall buildings. And Amy was inside the Sears Tower. Tallest fucking building in the world.

"It's safe in here..." her voice floated out of the speaker.

"DON'T!" I screamed, even though she still couldn't hear me. "STAY THERE! Oh please Christ, don't go into the elevators –"

The Sears Tower was just across the intersection, on the far corner. The mountain of bodies filling the streets was at least twenty, thirty feet high. I put one foot on somebody's broken arm but stopped. The air. Amy had said something about the air. I knew with a sick dread that once I was inside, and got a taste of that air, all thoughts and hopes of finding Amy would be gone. I could see myself calmly climbing aboard the elevator and riding to the top floor...

So I aimed for the clothing store across the street. The cab was gone, buried under thousands of bodies. Before I thought about it too long, I started climbing. The flesh was still warm. Torsos and limbs shifted under my hands and feet, threatening to suck me into

21

the spongy, tangled mess. Near the broad top of the mountain, my left foot sank into someone's chest and caught on the ribcage. I uttered a short shriek and jerked it free, then tumbled headfirst down the other side. I landed on my side in the warm blood, and a glistening, shattered bone scraped my cheek, but I wasn't hurt.

The wheelchair was there, half crushed, but the old woman was gone. I spotted the edge of the blue tank underneath more bodies near the curb. It came free with a wet, squelching sound, trailing blood and chunks of meat. The mask was still under the bodies. I decided I didn't need it.

I slung the tank over my shoulder as I moved, ignoring the pain from the glass stuck in my back. It was getting harder and harder to catch my breath. The air felt wet. Slimy. I climbed across the pile of corpses on Franklin until I was in front of the tourist entrance.

The walkie-talkie produced nothing but static. I grabbed the tank and, just for the hell of it, grasped the ragged end of the tube and put it to my lips. I swallowed, then slid the tube between my teeth. Cold, cold oxygen blew into my mouth.

The air tasted clean, sweet, and wonderful.

I picked my way through the shattered remains of the tourist lobby. The room was now just a battered steel frame with pieces of glass sticking out from the beams like jagged, irregular teeth.

Warm, humid air washed over me as I pushed through the spinning doors. The hiss from the walkie-talkie warbled slightly, and suddenly Amy's voice was there, sounding like she was right next to me.

"Jack...where are you?" She sounded drunk, or stoned maybe. I'd talked to her once when she was high, at a messenger party. At the time, her voice had gotten this lilting, mischievous tone that made me ache for her even more. But something was missing now, something that I couldn't figure out. "Where are you, Jack?"

I took a deep breath, shouting quickly into the walkie-talkie, "I'm here! I'm downstairs –" another quick inhale on the tube – "come down, please!"

"Oh Jack..." I realized she hadn't let go of the button, and still couldn't hear me. "I'm in the elevator...going all the way..." A quick giggle.

I found a wide corridor, lined with elevator doors. All of the doors were open – except one. I couldn't help but feel the open doors were waiting patiently for me. I gritted my teeth, then stepped inside. The controls were simple. Just two buttons. UP and DOWN.

I pressed UP. The doors slid shut.

"THE BOTTOM FEEDERS ARE IN CHARGE" was scrawled across the inside of the door in thick black ink. With a slight lurch, the floor started vibrating. I felt like throwing up, so I set the oxygen tank on the floor and stared straight ahead at my blood soaked image in the shiny metal walls. Amy's voice filled the small room. "It's okay, Jack…Everything's okay…You should come on in, the water's fine."

"AMY! AMY!" I hissed, tube still clenched between my teeth.

Amy kept talking, murmuring into the walkie-talkie. "…it's okay, Jack. It's okay. I'm at the top now… And it's beautiful…" Then nothing. No static, no hiss, nothing. I threw the walkie-talkie at the floor. The elevator shuddered. My ears popped.

The doors slid open and thick, hot air rolled into the elevator. It felt like I had just fallen into an oven. Only a few of the fluorescent bulbs were working, and these flickered on and off sporadically. In the flickering light, I could only see wisps of mist that clung to the floor like hazy snakes. Glass shards reflected the fluorescent lights onto the walls and ceiling in surreal patterns.

I desperately wanted to press DOWN. Instead, I put my hand on the edge of the door, bit down hard on the tube and stepped out into the moist air. Sweat instantly beaded up on my forehead, rolling down my face, down my neck, down my chest and back, stinging as it slid over the dried blood and glass.

Every single window had been shattered. The skies beyond the windows were utterly black. No other buildings, no Lake Michigan, no lights, nothing, as if the sky itself was gone.

My foot sent something sliding across the floor. At first, I thought it was just a large piece of glass, but then I saw it, under a curling tendril of gray mist – a walkie-talkie. I broke into a shuffling run, oxygen tank heavy at my side, praying that I would find her, that I wasn't too late.

And there, standing on the high window ledge in the flickering flashes of light, was Amy. She faced the darkness, a tiny figure with pale skin in a black dress. She turned her head slightly, looking back over her shoulder, but I don't think she saw me. Her eyes were empty and dull; they didn't reflect light. I remembered this one time when some asshole cab driver had nearly knocked her into one of the El's steel girders. She caught up to the cab at the next light and planted a small footprint of dripping mud and melted snow on the driver's window, cracking it in the process, belting out "Pencildickmotherfucker" in one tremendous howl. Her lips were pulled back, bright teeth bared in a savage, defiant grin. Now, whatever strength that had lived inside of her had died.

I was ten feet from her when she slowly took one step forward off the ledge and out into the darkness. I got a quick flash of her white neck and her pale, wiry arms as she fell, and that was all.

I screamed something and stumbled towards the wall of windows until my knees slammed into the ledge. Mist flowed down the side of the building like some vaporous waterfall in slow motion. But Amy was gone.

For a moment, I thought about pulling the tube out of my mouth and just dropping the tank over the edge, letting it tumble away into darkness. I'd just have to take one deep breath, just one. It would be easy. Quick, painless. And everything would be over.

No. Amy might be gone, but I'd be goddamned if I was going to die like this.

I got a better grip on the tank, bit down harder on the tube, and stumbled back to the elevators. I felt positive that the elevator doors would never open, as I jabbed the DOWN button again and again. Deep booming thunder cracked, rattling the fillings in my teeth. Red lightning crackled across the black sky, like veins under an eyelid. In that red flash, I caught a quick glimpse of dozens, maybe more, of long coiling tubes, tornadoes of mottled flesh, squirming out of the dark clouds above the city, snaking into the skyscrapers. They seemed to be coming out of nowhere, a whole forest of them. Then the image was gone, swallowed by the darkness.

I smashed the glass face of a long red box and pulled out the fire axe. I didn't think it would help me much, but the weight made me feel a little better.

The elevator doors slid open. I fell inside and banged the DOWN button with my axe. For a second, nothing happened. I backed into a corner, watching the open doors. Nothing moved but the mist, drifting patiently along the floor. Then the doors slid shut. And the metal box began to drop.

Amy had been right. "Nice little consumers," was what she had said. We had all been too much alike. We had been conditioned. Groomed. Prepared. Altered. And when the time was right, something had come to our world from somewhere… else. Maybe something had gotten into our atmosphere, seeped into the clouds, the air itself, waiting and feeding off of our pollution, off of all the television and radio waves, off of all the fucking cell phone conversations, everything. Then, when the clouds were fat and pregnant, it had started to rain.

I'm not sure how long the doors were open. Eventually I crawled out onto the warm marble floor and found my outside. I could see only by the streetlights. They must have been light-sensitive, automatically switching themselves on, responding to the darkness. I staggered forward into the foggy, silent streets filled with mountains of corpses.

I thought I heard something move quietly behind me.

I brought the axe up, keeping it ready, but I didn't turn around and look. I had to get out of the city. Some open place. Somewhere. I kept moving forward, heading west.

Way off in the distance, the streetlights began to go out, one by one.

I heard sounds. Wet sounds. Crawling. Slithering. Slurping. Like someone trying to suck the last drops of a thick milkshake through a straw. I thought about the tubes coming out of the sky. And all those corpses.

The dying streetlights got closer.

I listened to the things that were now all around me and clutched the axe tighter. But I refused to stop and look; I just kept moving forward towards the bridge that the running businessman had crossed. In my head, I could see the things slithering out of the sewers around me, coming out to a meal. An easy meal. A nice, tenderized meal. A nice, wet meal. A nice, soft meal of the mountains of meat.

The last streetlight went out.

Darkness claimed the streets.

I raised the axe and kept moving.

Bloodwalker

Michele Lee

I t wasn't in my job description. Nowhere near it actually, but lots of people confuse Forensic Specialist with Detective. Of course once we heard a child was involved it changed everything. No police officer, regardless of position, wants to hear about lost or abused children. Unfortunately we usually see the worst of people.

Jennifer Rice sat across the desk from me, a slight woman, very business like. Her black hair was chopped short, chin length, her pale blue eyes looked professionally made up, then they filled with tears. Her navy jacket and skirt had been perfectly pressed ten minutes ago, before sheer desperation entered her voice. I hadn't seen what was in the canvas bag she clutched, but I had a bad feeling that I would soon.

"Technically this isn't my job," I said, pretending not to notice the fanatic gleam in her eyes.

"But everyone else told me to come to you," she said, slightly panicked.

I pulled a travel pack of tissues from my desk drawer. Sometimes allergies are useful. "I'm not saying I can't or won't help. I'm just not sure why everyone seems to think I'm perfect for the job."

"My son is missing," Rice said, fumbling with the bag. "I went to pick him up from the babysitter's and he wasn't there. No one was. All the furniture was still there, but the clothes, the pictures, the toys, all the things that make a house a home were gone."

"Ms. Rice we have an excellent Missing Persons department. The best in this half of the continent," I reminded her.

"And they told me to talk to you." She pulled something fuzzy, red and green from the bag. She threw it onto the desk. "That's why."

I opened the bundle. It was a soft, pastel green blanket, the gender neutral kind they give out in hospitals. The middle of the blanket was stiff and dark red. You didn't need my powers to know what dried blood looked like.

"How do you know this is your son's?" I asked quietly. I couldn't take my eyes off the stain. I felt it, once it left the bag.

"My son and I are lycanthropes. I'd know his scent anywhere," Ms. Rice said, rubbing her arms. Legends said lycanthropes didn't get cold because the fur, when they were in human form, stayed just below the skin. It was a silly legend.

"I'll help, but only if the case is officially filed with Midguard Missing Persons," I said, still unwilling to touch the blanket.

"Oh thank you, thank you so much Miss Hall."

Blood tells many stories, if you have the training, or gift, to listen. Pure training told me this much blood from an eight year old boy was bad. Once I stretched the blanket out on a desk under a good light I saw a pattern.

"It was wrapped around a wound," I said aloud. The pattern was a lack thereof. It looked like the blood seeped into the blanket. Bruce Singer from Missing Persons sat in one of the vinyl chairs, dutifully taking notes. His face remained blank but I knew it bothered him. You'd think a guy with three kids would avoid cases like this. "It was tied like a bandage, around a wound to stop the bleeding maybe. See the points where it changes. That's where it was tied or bound. Mother 'thrope confirms the blanket and blood are her son's but let's get some typing to back it up."

That's the thing about all the supernatural powers popping up these days. Legally reports from telepaths, 'thropes and witches of all kinds have to stand in court if the source is reliable. But 'beyond a reasonable doubt' is much easier to attain with numbers than with words. People seem to trust science more, though any scientist can tell you it's just as easy to lie with facts and figures.

I used the blunt edge of a scalpel to scrape off a few flakes of the blood. Here came the fun part. Bruce slipped the blanket into an evidence bag and Daniel Temps, one of the lab guys, slid a chair under me.

"Do you need a glass of water?" Daniel asked. He was the only one in the room not looking away uncomfortably. Even outside of the office Daniel knew blood. He looked like the typical kid straight out of college, bright hazel eyes, sandy blond hair that always fell into his eyes and a darker red mustache and goatee. But Daniel was one hundred percent pure werewolf. The first to work in the lab.

"No, just hand me my sunglasses," I said sitting. Daniel's beefy hands passed them to me. I took the few flakes and put them on my tongue, pulling the glasses on to hide my eyes. Normally an ordinary brown, once the power activated my eyes filled with blood and tended to seriously creep out anyone watching. The burn started slowly, sliding from my tongue down the back of my throat and travelling, creeping through my body. My muscles tensed, out of my control. Under the glasses the heat filled my eyes and my forehead burned.

He woke up tied in the bathtub, arms behind his back, and gagged. One of the girls, Mandy, poked her head into the room. When her eyes met his she slammed the door and ran down the hall.

Something was wrong. He couldn't see straight and for a minute everything went black again. How could he fall asleep tied up in the bathtub?

Mrs. White came in a minute later. Jeremy realized he'd woken up again, because he didn't remember her coming in. Mr. White came in then, he remembered that much, in ripped jeans and a stained white shirt, something Jeremy had never seen him in before. Mrs. White still looked all proper and clean, like TV moms. Except for the bloodstained apron.

Mrs. White sat on the toilet. Mr. White took the edge of the tub. He stretched one of Jeremy's legs up, holding the rest of him down. Mrs. White pulled the big shiny butcher knife from the sink. Jeremy struggled. The blood surged suddenly to his head and he blacked out again.

He woke up to a horrible pain in his leg. He looked down to see blood moving slowly down the white porcelain of the tub. His blood. Mrs. White shushed him, holding his head and rocking him while Mr. White wrapped a blanket tightly around his leg. On a plate on the sink sat a red, bleeding chunk of muscle and skin. Beneath the blanket his leg looked wrong.

The screams stopped when my lunch burned its way out of my mouth, which meant they were mine. Most of the people in the room, male and female, made a colossal leap as far from me as they could. Many fled the room all together. Daniel already stood beside me, holding a wastebasket between my legs.

I didn't blame the rest of them, even though it hurt a little every time I saw that look on someone's face. The basket held much more blood than the few drops I ingested. IHF, Infectious Hemorrhagic Fever to the professionals, hadn't been found in a human in over fifty years. But a generation still remembered it, text books still boasted graphic black and white photos and occasionally some one still bore the scars. Growing up in the horror of a blood borne disease that killed an estimated six billion people had its effect on people. To be truthful the statistics were still being debated. When they witness me ingest blood to use my power most people cringe. They also avoid me, just in case. If anyone is going to come down with IHF, they assume, it'll be me.

"Are you alright Raven?" Daniel asked as I sat back up in the chair. The kid knew me. He offered me a tiny bottle of mouthwash.

"No I am definitely not alright." My hands shook.

"What did you see?" he asked in a hushed voice. As was legally required a tape recorder ran in the background.

"They drugged him, probably, because he couldn't regain consciousness and while he knew something was wrong he didn't try to fight. He was disoriented, fuzzy headed," I began.

"Which means they're familiar with therianthropes," Daniel said, taking notes on a yellow pad on his table.

"Very. They drugged him, tied him up when he was unconscious. When he woke up he was in the bathroom. They came in, notified of his consciousness. But he passed out again, and they cut off the muscle from the back of his thigh. That's what was missing when he came to." I paused. "It wasn't missing. It was on a plate on the sink. That's where I lost the vision."

"It's probably the pain. Hard to defy the human instincts to avoid pain." Daniel patted my arm and rolled over to the glass door. He opened it and yelled out, "Whoever's going to the White house check the bathtub drain and look for a used…"

He looked at me. "White with little blue flowers."

"…Plate that's white with blue flowers."

"And look for the butcher knife," I said. "Don't forget to look through the trash, even the dumpster."

He yelled it, then looked back to me. "What are you thinking?"

My training kicked in, turning the information from a first person horror movie into a scene of clues. It was hard looking through someone else's memories for clues that would be useful to me. "The Whites are clean, immaculate. They'd have taken out the trash and washed the dishes before they left. They wouldn't like to leave a mess for anyone else to clean up. So, time to relax the kid, drug him, carve him up when he's regaining consciousness, clean up… Maybe two hours on us?"

Daniel nodded. I swigged my mouthwash. With as much of the stuff as I used I should be turning green by now, or have a higher alcohol tolerance. I stood. "I've got to get to the scene, so they don't miss anything."

"But you were just supposed to do a reading," Daniel said, already analyzing the blanket.

"Yeah, I know. But I can't just leave it there if I can help."

"So you going to tell the mother then?" Daniel asked, almost smiling. I was a workaholic, not a sadist. We paper-rock-scissored for it. I lost anyway.

"So why do we always do this part again?" I asked, dumping and rinsing the bucket in the stainless steel sink.

"Because everyone else are cowards," Daniel replied. This time he did smile. I left the bucket in the sink to dry and left Daniel to his grisly details. I went back to my office. They said they gave me the privilege of an office to myself because of exemplary service to the force. Truthfully, it's because most people were scared of me. It gave me a private place to use my gifts.

Midguard used psychics, or the gifted, more than any other police force on the northern continent. Officially it was NA16, but as we were the city in the middle of the continent, Midguard. Psychic testimony saves a ton of time by keeping the cops headed in the right direction. Midguard Police Corps only hired psychics with seventy five percent accuracy or better. The certificate in a black frame on my wall said ninety seven percent.

Ms. Rice watched me as I moved past the teetering piles of papers and folders on my desk. Her coffee sat untouched on the opposite edge. I sat down. "The lab needs to keep the blanket to scientifically verify that it is indeed your son's blood on the blanket." I held up my hand as she opened her mouth. "Scent verification by an unlicensed, distraught, emotionally involved therianthrope won't count in court. Anyway, I'm here to update you before I go to the scene. The Whites knew what they were doing. They knew how to physically restrain your son."

"Of course they do. That's why I chose them. They have three therianthrope daughters of their own," Ms. Rice said. I kept my jaw from hitting my desk. Of course, the little girl.

"Are the White's shifters?" I started taking notes.

"No, they adopted their children," Ms. Rice said.

"Don't shifters fall under Amber's Law?" The code, sentence according to some people, gifted children to government run orphanages and forbid any person, other than a family member, from adopting or fostering a gifted child. It hadn't happened here, but across the sea several psychics had gone criminal because their parents raised them to it. Or used them for it. One had only been fourteen. It raised so many questions of who was responsible that most continental counsels imposed much stricter laws to prevent the abuse of gifted children.

"No, we're a race, not gifted. We slip through the cracks."

Daniel tapped on the door. Without waiting for a word from me he poked his head in and looked at me. "They're calling me in for scent."

"The Whites have three other kids," I said at the same time.

"Sniff a trail?" Ms. Rice asked. I was already pulling on my coat and throwing the notebook into my bag.

"Dogs have difficulty tracing shifters. Sometimes they're scared and almost always the scent changes if the person shifts. Until we find a way around it, we use shifters." I nodded to Daniel. "He's our scent hound."

Daniel grinned. "Registered and ready."

"I'm coming with you," Ms. Rice said, grabbing her coat.

"It would be better if you stayed here," I said automatically. "Crime scenes are busy and I wouldn't want to disturb you further."

She snorted. "I'm the one who found it. Going there again won't disturb me any more than it did then. Their apartment is above mine." She looked between Daniel and I. "And I know their scents. I could tell you which is which."

"You can't come on site. Not even if your apartment is considered the scene."

"I have to go. I have to do something," she said, closing the door as a sort of silent affirmation behind her.

❧

The Whites lived in the top left apartment in a building with wood colored shingles. The neighborhood was restored, but two blocks down you could see empty, dilapidated buildings, proof of what we'd lost. In other sections of town restorers gutted abandoned buildings for supplies, leaving skeletal beams and concrete in their wake. What would they do when they ran out of houses to dissect?

Ms. Rice and her son lived on the bottom floor. For now the whole building and grounds were roped off. We left Ms. Rice in my car outside the watchful pair of guards in their vehicles. She didn't own her own car. Part of me didn't understand why she wanted to come back. Most of me knew exactly why she waited.

Daniel opened the door for me and we walked up the stairs to the second floor. The apartment was one of the nicest I'd been in. The living room was painted pale yellow with white trim and golden or pale wood furniture. It still filled the place, the copper colored couch, large television and stereo inside a blond wood entertainment center. I shook my head. Beyond the crowd of cops and experts I saw a pale blue walled kitchen and white doors down the hall on the opposite side of the room. Not really the kind of place I ever expected to see.

"Change warning," Daniel said. It was kind of like yelling "Fore" before hitting a golf ball. As soon as the words left his mouth fur broke out over his skin. It didn't so much replace the skin as fill it up. His knees reversed themselves with pops, his nose pulled back against his face while his mouth, ears and arms lengthened. Muscles thickened around his bones, moving strangely under his skin even though he stood still. He didn't seem to notice, or care about, my gaze, or any of the other outright eyeballing that came from the rest of the room. I never really got used to seeing him change. I found myself watching, trying to pick out each individual change as it happened.

He wasted no time, burying his nose in the couch, then the carpet. The he stood up from his crouch and snorted. "Cleaners," he said. "Chemicals, everywhere."

"Clear the way," I yelled, because he probably shouldn't. "Try the bedroom," I told him.

Rice was right. The place was furnished, but empty of all the things that made a house a home. No dirty dishes, no smears on the glass, no dirty clothes or scuffs on the walls. This place seemed more showroom than home. I looked out of the patio, down to an expanse of dead grass and empty gardening containers. Daniel moved back out from the bedrooms and to the front door. After a sniff in the hall he moved down the stairs. I followed him, head forward, hands in my pockets.

Outside Daniel almost made it to the street. Ms. Rice stood at the curb, trying to push past two policemen to Daniel. She was doing it politely at least, not using any of that wonderful supernatural strength against them. "I can smell them," she screamed to us.

I nodded to her, but my attention was on Daniel. He shoved a city-issued trash can over and dug through it. I really hoped the kid wasn't in the can. I ran over, crime scene kit in hand to gather and label whatever he found.

He put four things aside from the pile as it spilled out into the street. Two brightly colored plastic plates, a soiled cloth napkin and a piece of something almost white. It felt spongy, maybe rubbery, when I picked it up. Each of the items went into a separate bag, all nicely labeled in permanent black ink.

"Anything else?"

Daniel's wolfy head nodded. I opened another bag and he carefully placed a small plastic food storage container into it. Then he became human again. "Her son's scent isn't on that one, but one of the other girls in the house is on it."

I looked closer at the contents of the bag. What was unmistakably old blood, dying to a dark purple, crept around the plastic and pooled in one corner of the bag.

"What did you find?" the mother cried, coming up to us. The trash bins were outside the police rope. I hid the bags in my scene case.

"We don't know yet," I said levelly. "Could be nothing. Please, Ms. Rice, remain calm and let us do our jobs. Trying to help is admirable, but you could not only get hurt, you could ruin evidence, and even be brought up on charges."

I let Daniel take the case, he was the lab tech after all, and led a trembling Ms. Rice back to my car. She hunched over on herself again, power suit and bold business woman lost to frantic, worried mother. "Now we have to wait. Lab work takes time, and that is where our biggest clues will probably be. Do you need to tell us anything else?"

"No, I've told you all I know. They took a report and everything."

"Then please try to take it easy while we work. If you're the religious sort, a little praying never hurts."

We left Jennifer Rice sitting alone on the doorstep of her apartment building while we drove back to home base. Daniel and I rode in silence, because there was nothing we could say to each other. Daniel was the only lab tech today, but the safety of not one, but four children was a higher priority than the line of corpses waiting to be bagged, tagged and investigated. The infamous they estimated the northern continent's population at sixteen million, split almost entirely into four main cities. One on the eastern seaboard, one to the west, us, then one much smaller city in the northern part of the continent. So many people in one small area made for a lot of cramping, and crime.

We finally made it back to headquarters. I sat in a black chair in the lab, with only Daniel as a witness this time, and took in some of the dead blood from the mystery container.

It had no intelligence, because it had been cut off from that. But the blood still had memory. In the memory it burned. It sat in heat until its juices ran out, a silver fork stabbed it and placed it in the container.

I didn't puke this time, but only because there was nothing left in my stomach to come up. I went down to Missing Persons and fought the police record keeper for the Rice file. Someone up there didn't want me to have it. But the supervisor overruled whoever it was and I got the file in the end. I sat in the lab, listening to Daniel muttering and reading the file. The only thing I learned was that the Whites owned a car.

Fuel wasn't available in steady flows so owning a vehicle was an investment which could be a loss for months at a time. Until some great scientist out there came up with an alternative to fossil fuels anyone who owned a gas burning vehicle or product, cops included, just had to deal with shortages and price gouging.

Asking if anyone was looking for the car seemed like a stupid question. But it wasn't my job to assume some one else had done something that made sense, so I asked anyway.

"Anyone looking for the White's yellow station wagon?" I asked one of the radio monitors. "I didn't see it on the scene."

"I was just about to call you," she whispered. "Bike patrol on the edge of the city just called in wanting a confirmation of the regis-tration number on a canary yellow wagon." She turned back to the microphone. "Number is KL562C. Confirm please."

"Number matches," came the cracking voice from the speaker. "Send an arrest team. Units 506 and 508 will keep location secure."

I didn't wait for any more of the message. I ran for my vehicle. I slammed into Daniel, coming out of the lab, along the way.

"Okay, some preliminary tests are done," he said.

"They found the White's car," I said cutting him off.

"Then I'll walk with you. The food container is a shifter, but not Rice's son. The blood is thinned, well, to be more accurate...it's cooked, Raven," Daniel said jogging along side me.

"Cooked?"

He nodded. "Heated to a boil at the least. And the white substance? It's fat. There's a small piece of skin on it. I'm running the test to match it to the Rice kid, but it smells like him, so I'm almost positive it will be a match. It was a clean cut, not torn, looks like a serrated knife."

"Serrated?" I thought, feeling slightly sick. "Like a steak knife?"

Daniel nodded.

"So what you're saying is?" I asked, not really wanting to hear the answer, but having to. I slid into the car and pulled the door shut.

"It looks like the Whites are serving filet of werewolf."

"Dammit. Don't tell his mom. Not until after we get them." Before he could say more I peeled out, radioing for directions to the site.

When they said on the edge of the city, they meant it. Midguard ended suddenly forty-five to fifty miles from its center. I passed a general style store, a grocery, a gas station, then pulled into the hotel parking lot. Beyond I saw only empty, broken foundations and far off, the tree line.

I made a beeline for the knot of uniformed and plain clothed officers, bikes, cars and horses near the motel office. They broke through the door as I broke into the crowd.

"Hall, what are you doing here?" Detective Arr, probably scene commander, asked as I ran up. He towered over me, lanky body, head, face and hands hidden by a shapeless hooded trench coat and fuzzy gloves.

"Preliminary reports suggest the Whites are cutting off meat from the children and cooking it," I said, trying to catch my breath.

"Why would they be doing something like that?" Arr asked, trying to keep his face calm.

"All four children are shape shifters. They heal faster than a human would." I sighed. "So they have four renewable meat sources in there."

A look flickered across his face and disappeared. "Alright, let's go."

I followed Arr and his officers in, squeezing into the packed room. Jeremy and one of the girls sat on the far bed, looking terrified, but being looked after by a small female officer. The back of Jeremy's jeans showed spots of blood on one leg. As I watched a paramedic cut off the pants and began dressing the wound that was the back of his thigh. I knew the cut originally went to the bone, but I didn't see it as the medic worked.

A tall, angry looking blond man talked in big angry words as the police, four of them, pressed him against the hotel wall and read him his rights. "What right do you have coming in here and scaring my family like this?" he said.

On the near bed a small, pretty voluptuous woman broke into tears. Jeremy was right. She did have perfectly shaped brown hair, small, delicate features in a small triangle shaped face and wore a spotless navy dress. The old fashioned kind with the sweeping knee length skirt. I walked over to the stove in the tiny kitchenette, turned the burner off and removed the pan, with its two browning lumps of meat from the burner.

I went into the bathroom and found the two remaining girls, naked and dripping in the shower. I found two standard hotel issue white towels and helped them both wrap them around themselves. They both had long flowing scars down their buttocks and thighs. The littlest one was six.

"Are you okay?" I asked. They nodded shyly, seemingly unconcerned by their scars.

"Are you a real police officer?" the youngest one asked.

I nodded. "I'm here to help you."

When all four children sat on the bed together, each one receiving a thorough going over by medics and a crime scene photographer, I followed Mr. and Mrs. White out into the lot.

"What have we done?" Mr. White raged.

"Eating your children isn't legal anywhere," Arr said. "You're being charged with kidnapping, child abuse, and anything else we can pile on there."

White laughed. "Don't you mean animal abuse?"

"They're children," Arr said quietly.

"They're animals. Dogs. You have no right to arrest me for eating dog meat. Other people do it all the time."

"They are therianthropes, a legally recognized race here," Arr said, the quiet becoming dangerous.

"Why did you do this to me...them?" I asked, quickly correcting myself.

Mrs. White, descending primly into the back seat, said, "You don't expect us to trust our health to the meat the government provides? It's filled with additives, growth hormones and other cancer causing agents."

Arr slammed the door on his side. It was lucky Mr. White hadn't been leaning out. I slammed the little missus's door. Arr looked over at me.

"Younger ones are more tender, he says. And younger ones heal faster." He looked away from me.

"It will be okay now."

"No, it won't. Those four children will be scarred mentally, if not physically for life."

"But they won't be abused anymore. They can start to heal," I said quietly. I wasn't sure I believed it, but it was the kind of thing someone has to say. I didn't know when I became the optimist. "Some people see them as animals, not humans."

"Regardless, they're kids, Raven."

"I know." I did know. I knew better than Arr or any other rescuer there. I knew exactly how human, and how young the White's victims were. What I didn't know was if there was any fair amount of punishment that could be dealt to the Whites.

We charged the Whites with four counts of kidnapping. A background check revealed that none of the children had been adopted, they just disappeared one day like Jeremy. We also charged them with three counts of child abuse and four counts of endangering a minor. There should have been something more, something greater we could have charged them with. The degree of the abuse was so heinous. I felt that I had failed them by not being able to punish them further.

The children, for better or worse, returned to their parents to heal.

And me? Wrapped up in the dark at night, I dreamed of cooking meat for weeks.

The Face in the Glass

Brian G Ross

S quatting on Italian tile, Laura polished the glass door on the oven until it sparkled like the day she had bought it. She smiled into the mirror-like shine, satisfied with her work, only this time the face in the glass was not her own.

She fell back – from her haunches to her denim ass – and the spray gun clattered to the floor. It was her face staring back at her, no question, only with deep stress valleys on her brow, and hair that was beginning to grey and fray at the temples. From the floor she turned her head this way and that, but in the glass her reflection was fixed forward as if frozen.

There was a blackness under this woman's eyes – a depth of pain – that was more than just too much make-up or a trick of the light. In those dark pools she carried a sadness that the addition of a simple smile would not have erased. It was the melancholic face of a woman she barely recognised as her own.

The happy summer scream from outside stole her from her daydream. Jesmond, Laura's three year old son, played in the sandpit she had built for him the year before. Spotting her curious glance, he waved – his hand almost disengaging at the wrist in his enthusiasm – and went back to his imagination. Laura stared. It was amazing how much fun a kid could have in four square feet of store-bought sand.

She turned back to the oven door, but now the haunted porcelain stare had been replaced by the dishevelled look of a single mother with too much housework and too little time. She cracked a smile, which proved difficult, and to her glass reflection she told herself she was working too hard.

"Jes, mummy's just popping upstairs for a minute. I won't be long." She rubbed her temples, anticipating the headache that was, even now, calling her name in block capitals. "Will you be okay out there?" Without waiting for a reply, she took herself upstairs, head between her hands.

Jesmond looked up, his thin blonde hair laced with white sand, but all he could see was his mummy's bottom as she left the kitchen. He scrambled out of his sandpit, leaving his castle only half built and his moat only half filled, and padded across the hose-damp grass towards the house.

Once inside the kitchen he went to the open door that led to the stairs and listened to his mummy pottering about on the second floor. By the time she started making her way downstairs, Jesmond had already found his hiding place.

Laura came back into the kitchen, half-filled a glass with warm kitchen water and, taking a deep breath, knocked back the two pills she had retrieved from the bathroom. Convinced she was just tired, she slammed the oven door closed and turned it on.

"Hey Jes!" Laura rinsed the glass and put it on the drying rack. "You want lasagna tonight? Mommy's special recipe."

Jesmond stifled a laugh and, in the growing warmth, waited for his mummy to find him.

The Seventh Green at Lost Lakes

Scott Brendel

My father always had some mangled folk wisdom to offer when the shit hit the fan.

"Don't stick your dick where it don't belong," he'd often say from the bar stool from which he'd fall before noon. A pearl of wisdom, God rest his soul, which fell from the broken necklace of his insights before the swine of an unaccepting son.

He was right. But it was a lesson I learned the hard way the day I took Arthur C. Levant to Lost Lakes.

I drove Mr. Levant to Lost Lakes on a day in early October. He sat quietly in the back of the car, reviewing papers he'd assembled for the visit. Some deal he planned to close.

It was by chance – or, if you believed my mother, the hand of the devil – that I started working for the guy. He was a man of drive and ambition who gave me a chance when no one else would, a man who made a fortune by buying things and perverting them for profit.

And my role?

"Persuasion," he explained one day after I snapped the thumb of a man unwilling – or unable, I couldn't remember which – to make a loan payment. "Your goal is to persuade clients not to do something stupid. Your mere presence should suffice. Often, the best bat is the one not swung."

It wasn't until later I realized he wasn't talking about baseball.

I left the interstate at an exit in the middle of nowhere and turned onto a well-kept road that wound its way into the trees. This road leads to someplace important. The thought popped up like the hand of a zombie digging itself out of its grave.

"Are we there yet?" Mr. Levant asked, sounding like every kid with an itchy ass that ever took a car trip. "He said there'd be a sign."

Sure enough, there was, hidden in the trees. The Lost Lakes at Shadow Mountain, it said.

"Pay attention," he told me.

"I was."

"You missed it."

"No biggie."

We sounded like an old married couple at times.

I backed up, then turned onto the invisible road beside the sign. Small trees and bushes pressed against the car then retreated, until we found ourselves beneath a canopy of trees facing a gigantic gate.

Like Jurassic Park.

"There's an intercom," Mr. Levant said.

I drove up beside it. "Won't work."

"Why not?"

"The wires are loose."

"Try it anyway."

Feeling stupid, I pressed the button. "Mr. Arthur C. Levant to see Mr. Eldritch Gore."

I let go of the button and waited. "See? It's broken."

The screech made me jump. The gate opened, its hinges screaming as if they hadn't been asked to do anything so arduous in years.

"What the fuck?" I said, staring at the loose wires.

"Paul. Language."

"Sorry."

"Look out!"

I looked back at the gate as something huge flew over the hood of the car. I dove sideways onto the seat, but whatever it was missed. When I sat back up, it was in time to watch the ass end of a buck race into the woods.

Like it was trying to escape.

The narrow drive twisted through the trees so you couldn't see very far ahead. As we rounded another bend, something darted into the gloom.

"What was that?" I said.

"What was what?"

"That thing. Jumped into the woods."

"Another deer?"

Or friggin' Big Foot.

"I didn't notice," he said.

There were a lot of things he didn't notice. Mr. Levant had no sense for the undercurrents of a situation, and there were times when I figured my job was to protect his naiveté.

The woods fell away, and that's when we saw the estate house. It looked like a castle plucked from an isle off the coast of Scotland – not just old but ancient, as if it had been here since the beginning of time.

"Incredible," Mr. Levant said.

The place gave me the creeps, even before I saw the two figures standing by its entrance. Both stood at parade rest, as still as the trees in the forest. I pulled up beside them, then got out and held the door for Mr. Levant.

The larger of the two men wavered like a statue coming to life, then stepped forward.

"You must be Mr. Levant," he said, extending a hand. He was a tall, gaunt man whose flesh seemed shrink-wrapped to the bones beneath it. His hooded eyes made him look either sleepy or poised to strike, and he smiled without revealing his teeth. "I'm Eldritch Gore."

I wouldn't have touched the man's hand if it held the key to the vaults at Citibank. But Mr. Levant did. The two men shook, then Gore turned to me.

"And you are...?"

"Paul," I said, reluctant to tell him anything more than the basics.

From the way he looked at me, I could tell that he knew who I was – first name, last name and every ill-tempered thing my mother had hurled my way. Gore smiled, and this time the teeth came with it. Just the uppers. But that was plenty.

"Paul is my assistant," Mr. Levant said.

"And a man of many interesting and useful talents," Gore said, as if recognizing my untapped potential. "This," he said, of the man behind him, "is Oxenberg."

My first instinct was to laugh. Oxenberg was a short, runty man with dark eyes so bulbous I expected him to snap flies out of the air with his tongue. No threat, I decided.

"You'd like to play?" Gore asked Mr. Levant.

"Love to."

"Will Paul be joining us?"

"He'll caddy for me."

"Splendid." Eldritch Gore smiled at me again, and it was all I could do not to shudder. The guy gave me the willies. "Oxenberg will ready the clubs. This way, gentlemen."

It was dark inside the ancient house, and the polished floor made our steps echo. Great chandeliers hung far above, in such deep shadow that I honestly thought they held candles rather than light bulbs.

"No one playing today?" Mr. Levant asked.

"Just us."

"Is it always so quiet?"

Gore cocked his head. "Not always. We do have special events, but not as often as we used to."

He led us past a huge fireplace with blackened logs on the grate and piles of ash beneath it. Mixed in the ash were lumps of white. While Gore and Mr. Levant walked ahead, I bent to examine one.

It was a vertebrae. From the broken back of some sizable creature.

"Something of interest?" Gore stared at me. There was nothing sleepy about those hooded eyes.

I slid the bone beneath the grate and out of sight as I stood. "Lovely floor. Marble?"

"From Italy. You know marble?"

"No. Just what I like."

"And what, pray tell, is that?" He displayed those upper teeth again, and the sight set me off into a momentary agony of images: of things crawling inside that mouth, of a long reptilian tongue that forced its way past my lips –

"Paul," Mr. Levant said. "Are you all right?"

I swallowed and nodded, fighting the urge to vomit.

Oxenberg waited on the first tee. I took my place beside him, wondering how he'd gotten both sets of clubs here so quickly. The little man stared at me with those shiny orbs. I reminded myself that my mere presence should suffice. Oxenberg didn't seem to think so.

"It's the little ones what you gotta watch," my father once told me. But I could have broken Oxenberg like a wooden matchstick.

"Mr. Levant, would you like to start us off?"

"Certainly. Tell me about the hole."

"A long par 4. Two hundred thirty yards to the dogleg, then another two hundred to the green."

"Any hazards?"

"Oh my, yes," Gore said, staring at me. "They're all about."

I shivered, as if Oxenberg had slid an ice cube up my back.

Gore looked back at his guest. "Water on the inside of the dogleg, sand around the green."

Mr. Levant nodded.

"Then there's the woods," Gore said. "They can be hell."

You'd never mistake Mr. Levant's style for that of a pro. He had an angled, sideways swing. It was the only way he could get the club moving around his own girth. Setting the head of it behind the ball, he drew back and swung. The ball flew through the air, hit the fairway and rolled.

"Well struck," Gore said.

Then our host was up. He hit the ball with an elegance and precision that might have landed him on the tour. Despite the difference in style, however, he achieved nothing more nor less than his guest. His ball came to rest beside Mr. Levant's ball, as if out of courtesy he played to his guest's level.

Oxenberg and I followed the two players down the fairway to the bend of the dogleg. Mr. Levant hit a three-wood that bounced to the fringe. Then, coincidentally, so did Gore. As we headed for the first green, there was nothing to see but the rest of the hole and the trees that surrounded us.

"Beautiful course," Mr. Levant said. "So peaceful."

"It can be, yes."

Too peaceful, I realized. There was no sound whatsoever, beyond what little noise the four of us made. There were no birds clattering about the brush, no geese flying overhead on their way south.

Both men chipped onto the green. Mr. Levant dropped his putt for par. Gore missed his and settled for a bogey.

I watched him pull his ball from the cup. The blown putt had all the hallmarks of a host letting his guest win. He caught me watching and flashed his teeth.

The two men chatted as they played the next three holes without incident, and we walked further into the woods of Shadow Mountain.

The funny stuff started on the fifth hole.

"This one is tight," Mr. Levant said.

Gore nodded. "A par 5. Narrow chute through the trees and sand traps around the landing area."

Once again, Mr. Levant selected his driver. But this time, there was trouble. He hit a respectable shot, but it faded as it rose and vanished into the woods.

"Damn." His shoulders sagged. Then, to my surprise, the ball popped out of the woods, bounced softly, and came to rest in the middle of the fairway.

"What luck!" Gore said. "You must have hit a tree."

Bullshit, I thought, feeling that ice cube sliding up my spine. A ball hit that hard would have come rocketing back out. If it had come out at all.

Mr. Levant looked up, surprised. "What a break!"

Gore smiled, as if pleased he'd been able to ensure his guest a good time. Then he hit his own tee shot. His ball landed in a sand trap.

"Tell me about the members," Mr. Levant said, as we walked down the fairway.

"They are a prominent few. Wealthy and powerful."

Once again, the two balls were close together. I handed Mr. Levant his three iron. His shot tore a patch of turf the size of my hand from the ground.

Divots were normally the province of caddies, but to his credit, Mr. Levant always took care of his own. Which is why I saw what I did.

While Mr. Levant retrieved his divot, Gore took an iron from Oxenberg and stepped into the trap, where his ball sat like an egg in a little sand cup. Mr. Levant handed me his iron, then bent to fix the divot. As I watched Gore, I saw – had it not been for the subsequent events of the day – the strangest thing ever.

Ripples ran across the surface of the sand as if something swam beneath. Ripples that smoothed out the dent in which the ball sat.

I blinked and looked again. The ripples were gone – if they'd ever been there in the first place. Gore took his position as if nothing unusual had happened, then glanced up, as if sensing my stupefaction, and cut me a crooked grin. I was so startled I stepped back and bumped into Mr. Levant.

"Paul–?"

"Sorry, sir."

"Be careful," he said. Then: "You sure you're all right?"

Gore raised his eyebrows as if wondering the same thing, while Oxenberg stared, his moist eyes glinting with fever.

Like a matchstick, I thought. I'll break that little bastard.

"You found the water, I'm afraid," Mr. Levant said. He could afford sympathy, since his ball sat high and dry on the grass.

"On these next holes, it's hard to avoid." Gore handed his club to Oxenberg, who holstered it with a flourish. "The Lost Lakes."

"Excuse me?"

"The club was named for them. A series of spring-fed lakes. All interconnected, we discovered, when we noticed that some of the things that lived in one lived in the others."

"What kinds of things?" Mr. Levant asked.

"Some unusual forms of marine life. Fish. Frogs. Other things."

"What made them so unusual?"

"Their features. Odd little mutations. And their size."

"What about their size?" I asked.

Gore gestured to Oxenberg, who nodded and trudged over to the lake where the ball had disappeared. Then Gore dropped another ball. "Oxenberg found a rather large tadpole once. The size of a carp."

Gore hit his shot. It bounced on the fringe of the green, then rolled close to the cup. It appeared that routine capitulation to the guest had ended.

"Imagine the frog it would grow into," Mr. Levant marveled, humoring his host. I could tell by his smile that he thought Gore was yanking his chain.

"Yes," Gore said. "Imagine."

They walked on to Mr. Levant's ball, while I debated about helping Oxenberg search for the lost ball. I couldn't imagine he'd find it, since the lakes were covered with scum.

Oxenberg, however, seemed determined. Then he must have seen it, for he walked straight into the water, Gucci loafers and all. Before I'd had the chance to consider him stupid, he was up to his knees in slime and staring down at something.

Then more funny stuff.

He pulled the cuff of his shirt and jacket back to the middle of his forearm, as if suddenly concerned for his apparel, and reached down into the water to his wrist. After a moment, he pulled his hand out of the water and shook it daintily, like a cat that has missed the goldfish. Except there was a ball in his hand.

No way, I thought. You can't stand knee deep in slime and pluck a ball from the bottom when you're only up to your wrist!

Oxenberg marched toward shore, then stopped suddenly and teetered as if his foot had become stuck in a hole. He tugged and tugged, frustration clouding his face, then pulled a club from Gore's bag and slammed at the water behind him. Water flew everywhere as he beat the lake in anger.

I loved it. The little turd had completely lost his cool and, with any luck, his hand-sewn loafer. And what did he do? He whaled away at the water.

Then his foot popped free. Oxenberg steadied himself, then resumed his march to shore. I watched with quiet glee to see if he'd be hiking in a sock for the rest of the round. I grinned with anticipation. Then the grin froze.

As he stepped onto shore, something came with him. Something long and shiny and black that let go of his ankle and slid back into the lake. Something with suckers.

"With a choice between shittin' a brick or hittin' the bricks, I generally go with the latter," my father once said. "Listen to your sphincter."

Mine felt ready to let go, but I battened down the hatches. Meanwhile, Oxenberg stamped up the fairway, water sloshing from his loafers and cuffs, leaving a slime trail like an oversized slug.

"Why exactly have you come, Mr. Levant?" Gore asked, as I rejoined the group.

"Didn't your attorney explain?" Mr. Levant hit a superb shot, then handed me his club and winked. He led the way to the green.

"Mr. Thornton was unclear," Gore said. "In fact, he seemed strangely agitated. Insisted I meet with you. Something about your interest in the club."

"Yes. My interest."

"I hate to disappoint you. But membership at Lost Lakes is very closely held. The club is not accepting new members."

Mr. Levant smiled. "It's not membership I'm after."

We reached the green, and the two men assessed their lies as they conversed. I took up my position beside Oxenberg.

"Then what? What is your interest?"

"A financial interest. In Lost Lakes."

It was Gore's turn to smile, and it was the kind of patronizing smile I knew would delight Mr. Levant. The dim-witted look of a steer coaxed to the slaughterhouse floor with a bucket of feed.

"Please pardon my bluntness, Mr. Levant. But why would a club unwilling to bestow membership sell you a stake in its property?" Gore stroked the air with his putter, then stepped up to his ball.

"I'm not asking to buy a stake," Mr. Levant replied. "I already own one."

The putter in Gore's hands seemed suddenly seized with life. Instead of tapping the ball into the cup, Gore drove it off the green and into the weeds. He straightened slowly and stared at Mr. Levant. Oxenberg stiffened beside me, but the froggy little dude remained where he was.

"What do you mean?" Gore asked.

The silence grew oppressive.

"Taxes. Actually a tax lien, to be more specific."

"We pay our taxes."

"No." Mr. Levant smiled again. "In fact, you don't."

"We leave that to our attorneys."

"You should have been more diligent. About their diligence." Mr. Levant walked around the green, a bounce in his step. "The strangest thing. A venerable institution like this, so established that it's invisible. Except to some new tax assessor with a mania for thoroughness."

Gore watched Mr. Levant gloat, the ball he'd driven into the weeds forgotten.

"Years of unpaid taxes," Mr. Levant said, "that coincide with the term of the previous assessor. Someone as established and invisible as Lost Lakes. Someone that only failing health could remove from office."

Mr. Levant squatted.

"I'm sure that the lapse in tax payments and the man's tenure were completely coincidental." Mr. Levant stood. "But someone forgot to pay off the new guy."

Mr. Levant struck his putt, but he'd miscalculated. It caught the edge of the cup and lipped out.

"God damn it!" Mr. Levant swung his putter over his head and drove it like an axe into the green.

It was the kind of behavior that would have gotten any golfer ejected from a course. But Arthur C. Levant owned an interest in this one and felt he could do as he wished. A blunder – his first, but not his last.

Oxenberg bristled beside me, and I chose not to trust his restraint. I grabbed his forearm, to hold him in place and to remind him of my presence. But something moved beneath my hand, beneath the fabric of his jacket. Something twisted and coiled, like it was preparing to erupt.

I released his arm as if I'd grabbed a handful of snakes. For all I knew, I had. Oxenberg stepped toward Mr. Levant, then stopped when Gore held up his hand.

I stared at Oxenberg and he stared back. Like a matchstick, I thought, trying to convince myself.

Mr. Levant, oblivious to it all, levered his putter out of the ground and stalked off, leaving a deep and ragged gouge in the otherwise perfect green. I bent to repair the damage, then froze as the gaping wound filled with a black and sticky pus.

I stood and caught up with Mr. Levant as quickly as I could. Did

I run? You bet your ass.

"We gotta get out of here," I said.

"Not until we're done."

"I don't like this place. Something's not right."

"You need to lay off the coke. It's ripping holes in more than your nose."

"I'm serious. There's something screwy about this place. And I really don't like those woods." They were all around us as we walked to the tee of the seventh hole.

He stopped and looked up at me, like my mother about to give me a tongue-lashing. Instead, he slapped me.

"Get your shit together. Look at what you're afraid of." He gestured at Gore and Oxenberg. "The Scarecrow and a fucking Munchkin. You're the Wicked Witch of whatever point of the compass you want. Start acting like it."

If I'd been smart, I would have left. Hiked back to the Lincoln and left him the number for Yellow Cab. But I didn't. Arthur C. Levant had made a difference in my life and allowed me to eat off a plate instead of out of a dumpster. I owed him a lot; I just wasn't sure how much.

Gore and Oxenberg joined us on the tee, and the four of us stared at the hole.

"Short par three to an island green. One hundred thirty-five yards." Gore's voice made my skin crawl.

It could have been a pretty hole, but it wasn't. The green looked like a lily pad floating in a frog pond, and was reached by a wooden bridge arched like the back of a cat. The forest had grown close here, so close that the lake surrounding the green was filled with the spindly remains of dead trees.

Oxenberg set Gore's clubs down and crossed his arms.

Mr. Levant noticed. "Care to show me the way?"

"I'm done for the day," Gore said. "But play if you like."

Mr. Levant shrugged. "Eight iron."

I handed him the club, then stepped back and positioned myself where I could watch his tee shot and our two friends.

"Why would you want Lost Lakes?" Gore asked. "A beautiful

course, but one with few development prospects."

"True." Mr. Levant swung his club like a clown in a fat suit. "It's about access."

"Access?" Gore looked truly puzzled. "Access to what?"

"To the electrical grid. The power company is planning a new transmission line. They'll pay handsomely for the right of way through this part of the state, especially if the route is over the mountain along a clear path."

"The only cleared paths are the fairways."

"Exactly." Mr. Levant smiled.

"Transmission lines?" Gore said, incredulous. "You wish to play in the marketplace of power?"

"I don't just wish. I will. With Lost Lakes as the key to my bid."

Eldritch Gore smiled then, in a way I didn't like. "Mr. Levant," he said, "you may have just inserted your 'key' into a receptacle of uncommon voltage."

Mr. Levant took what turned out to be the last shot of the day. Everything seemed to come together on that shot – the back swing, the shifting of his considerable weight, the moment of release as he drove through the ball. If he hadn't looked like a dumpling in plaid pants, it would have been visually poetic.

I could tell it was going to be a terrific shot. The ball started to the right but came back on a draw. Then it hung in the air for just a moment before it dropped. The ball hit the green about five feet beyond the flag, bounced, and backed toward the cup.

As I watched Mr. Levant's shot, I assessed its potential in much the same way I assessed the size, strength, and chutzpah of the men I'd bullied over the years. So I had this one pegged. The ball would stop within inches of the hole, leaving Mr. Levant with an easy tap in for birdie.

Except...

Something happened, something really weird. Something I could have chalked up to the afternoon light. Or a misfire in my retinas.

But this was Lost Lakes, where the sand traps raked themselves smooth and the water hazards harbored things with tentacles and you never, ever, went into the woods after your ball. Even though I told myself I couldn't believe it, I knew in my heart that I did.

The ball was losing momentum as it rolled backwards from its point of impact. It would stop beside the cup.

Except...

The hole suddenly stretched to the side, its edges sliding like a pat of butter on a hot griddle, oozing sideways until it slipped beneath the ball.

The ball dropped in.

And the hole snapped back into place.

"Oh, my God!" Mr. Levant screamed, and relief surged through me at the notion that he finally believed me, that this course was hinky, that we had to get the hell out of there. Then: "A hole in one!"

I turned in disbelief. His hands were raised like a referee signaling a field goal, his iron on the ground beside him. He danced, then pumped his arm like Tiger Woods.

The dipshit didn't have a clue.

I looked at Gore and got the grin, saw things crawling on those yellow teeth, things that pick clean the carcasses of the dead. I looked at Oxenberg, and he smiled, too.

They knew. And they knew I knew.

Mr. Levant walked down the fairway to the wooden bridge. I picked up his eight iron and followed quickly, to talk sense into him and to distance myself from the two ghouls.

"Did you see that?" I asked.

"Of course I did. I aced it!"

"With a little help from this screwy course!"

"A hole in one! My first!"

There was no bringing him around. As usual, he was oblivious.

I looked over my shoulder. Gore and Oxenberg remained on the tee, as if returned to the statuary stance in which I'd first seen them.

Mr. Levant strode to the green, his poise returned. I worked my way in front of him and kept a wary eye on the two men on the hill.

"After we get your ball, we're getting out of here."

"Don't be silly. I'm two under after seven!"

"I'm not kidding. We get your friggin' ball, and we head for the

Lincoln."

"Can't take a city boy into the woods, can we?"

When I stepped off the end of the bridge and onto the green, the green moved. Not a lot. Just enough to catch my attention. I froze, while Mr. Levant slipped past me to the hole.

Like a lily pad in a frog pond, I remembered thinking. Like something green floating on water, a blind for what swam beneath.

"Don't touch it!" I screamed.

"What?"

"Don't touch it!"

But it was too late. He'd already reached into the cup to grab his ball, the ball he'd mount on a plaque.

Something grabbed back.

His hand disappeared into the cup, and his eyes bugged out almost as far as Oxenberg's. He looked down in surprise, and then his eyes opened even wider.

He tugged. But whatever had him tugged harder. And pulled him down into the hole up to his elbow.

"Oh, Jesus!" he screamed, and looked at me with eyes that begged. Eyes like those of the clients I'd persuaded in my years working for him.

I ran to him, grabbed onto his arm and pulled.

A bad move, it turns out. The hand remained in the hole, but the meat of his arm – or what was left of it – lifted up as easily as the pant leg on a pair of trousers.

For all his screaming, I may have topped him on the decibel chart. I let go and backed away but couldn't stop watching as something jerked at him again and again, like a dog with a pull-toy, until his arm was into the hole up to his shoulder.

I banged into something, figured it for the railing on the bridge, then turned to find Gore breathing into my face.

"Don't stick your dick where it don't belong!"

My father's voice fell from those lips, as sure as I shit myself.

I backed away from him and turned, searching for a way out of there. Which is when I saw what has haunted my days and nights ever since.

It was by chance – or, if you believed my mother, the hand of the devil – that I started working for the guy. Arthur C. Levant changed my life. But my mother was wrong. I've seen the hand of the devil and just barely escaped its touch.

I don't remember much about running back to the Lincoln, although it must have made for quite a sight, a man the size of me screaming like a loon and dragging a load in the back of his britches. What I do remember is that the door to the Lincoln was open and the engine was running. But no one was around, no one to thank for the briefcase of cash that sat on the seat.

"A man of many interesting and useful talents," Eldritch Gore said the day we met.

He calls, every now and then, with little requests I always oblige. And every October, he invites me back to Lost Lakes. But there's so much going on that I always decline.

Golf, after all, never was my thing. Especially after seeing Mr. Levant pulled into that hole, screaming until his neck snapped, then slowly sucked out of sight like an overcooked piece of pasta.

Zombie Fishing Trip

Brian Rosenberger

No bites in the morning
save for bugs
drowning in ocular fluid
rubbing and rubbing
out plopped his eye
No bites in the afternoon
just a smell similar to raw fish
putting a stink in the air
a skunk would have been perfume
The water as quiet as a vacant casket
Just around midnight
a nibble
the remaining eye focused
on the rod tip
the line goes slack
slowly he reels
crank after agonizing crank
the hook empty
save for moss
the color of his smile
Barbs sink into soft flesh
a lily pad hue
He accidentally cast his thumb
slowly bobbing like a hitchhiker
needing a ride, before sinking from view
Another nibble transformed into a strike
The catfish cartwheels in the water

whiskers twitching like an exposed nerve
The line snaps
His forehead squirms in anger
No need to worry
still plenty of worms

The Bridge Chamber

Rayne Hall

November winds whipped along the cleft the railway track had carved into the mountainside. They pounded against the old bridge, rolled under its wide arch, and whistled through the openings that pierced its grey stonework.

Garnet rubbed her cheeks against the chill and stared at the vicious brambles which obscured the largest of these openings – thorny guards against entry that had grown since her last visit. But if she backed off now, the others would call her a coward again.

She anchored her hands on the cold sandstone ledge and hauled herself up. Thorns hooked into her sleeves, stung her arms and tore her skin, even through her thick denims. At last she managed to slide the branches aside and slip into the hollow.

"Hurry up," she yelled down to the two other children still scrambling up the embankment. "It's cosy in here, no wind at all. You're not frightened of brambles, are you? If you want to be explorers, you can't be afraid of scratches and blood."

To her chagrin, Nesta and Baldwin climbed up more quickly than she had. They were slimmer and more agile, even Nesta who was excused from school sports because she had something wrong with her heart.

"See?" Garnet gestured proudly. "It's different than on the other side of the bridge, just like I said."

The arching corridor in which they squatted almost mirrored the structure on the opposite end of the bridge. There, several tunnels opened on each side of the corridor. Here, most of them had been bricked up. Only two shafts were open. They gaped in dark silence, spewing out a dank, musty smell.

Baldwin simply crossed his legs and leant against the sandstone wall, contempt in his eyes. As usual, the laces of his trainers were undone, and he didn't bother to tie them. He seldom bothered with anything except what gave him pleasure, like piercing moths and kicking his old spaniel.

"Not that much different, Fattie." He curled his upper lip. "Hardly worth the build-up."

"These tunnels are different." Garnet pointed down into the darkness. "On the other side, they go down just a few yards and meet in a kind of chamber, right? Well, these lead much further into the embankment," she claimed. "A long way and really deep into the earth."

She hesitated before weaving a lie for them, but only for a moment. She had their attention now, and that was what mattered. "The chamber down there is really special, very different from the other one. It can be our secret place. Nobody's ever been there, except me."

That was a lie. Last year, she'd made several attempts to penetrate the dank depth, but failed. Although she ventured a foot or two further each time, the feeling of walls closing in always drove her back.

If Baldwin and his sister went all the way down one corridor, and came up the other, she wouldn't have to do it herself, and still be able to claim discovery. And maybe they would then stop bullying her.

"Nobody ever comes to this bridge anyway," Baldwin said, but the boredom in his face gave way to the attentive stare of a hawk.

At least his pale-faced sister showed open interest. She explored the sandstone and mortar with scrawny fingers.

Like an owner granting permission, Garnet said, "You can go down there if you like."

"You show us," Baldwin demanded.

Nesta nodded. "After you, Garnet."

"It's dangerous," Garnet hedged, rubbing warmth into her cold fingers. "It's quite, you know, slippery, and dark. Let's come back another time, when we have candles, so we can explore properly."

"I don't believe you've been in that chamber," Nesta said. "You wouldn't dare. You're such a coward, you haven't even been in the chamber on the other side."

Embarrassment drove heat into Garnet's cheeks. "Of course I've been."

Baldwin poked her in the chest. She backed away as far as she could, but he leant over her. "You haven't, Fattie. You're a tremblebird, a mommywhiner."

"I'm not!" she snapped. She might be frightened of dark spaces, but she never whined for her mommy. There was no point. Garnet's mum didn't care about her feelings, and probably wouldn't even miss her if she got lost.

Below, the rails sang, then a train rushed through.

For a long time, nobody talked. Baldwin pulled out a packet of cigarettes and lit one without offering the others a smoke. He leant back against the grey sandstone.

Silence prevailed. Few cars used this remote forest road. Even the wind's howls were blocked out. The scratches on Garnet's calves were beginning to sting, but she resisted rolling up her jeans to examine them.

At last, Baldwin tossed his cigarette on the cement floor and ground it with the heels of his cowboy boots. "Let's go. It'll be night soon, and Tremblebird here has nothing to show us."

Anger fermented in her stomach, fuelling her courage. She ducked into the darkness, crouched down and moved along. After all, what could befall her in this? It was just a corridor, that would lead to a chamber, and if she turned right she'd feel the parallel tunnel that would lead her out again. Besides, this was her part of the bridge; she felt she owned it, so in a strange way it was less frightening.

Thick darkness gaped before her. Light came from behind as she shuffled along, but then the other two bodies squeezed into the gap, shutting out what light there was.

Slowly, she slid along on her hands and knees, advancing inch by inch down the sloping corridor. The walls seemed to suck the air from the space.

Her mates were closing in behind her. "Hurry up, Fattie!"

She couldn't move faster. Not into the tightness that waited to digest her.

"We have to go slowly," she said. "It's dangerous."

"Bah!" Nesta chided. "What's dangerous? There's only one way, you can't get lost."

"There's." She tried to think of something. "Spiders. Huge spiders. And rats. I have to make sure we're not touching a rats' nest."

Did rats live in nests? Did they nest in tunnels? But rats were all she could think of. Rats with their furry bodies, fleet feet, and their long, vicious teeth.

"What?" Nesta asked from behind. "I can't hear."

Baldwin repeated for her. "Fattie says there are rats' nests in this tunnel, and big spiders."

"No!" Nesta screamed. "No rats! I hate rats! I'm not going to stay here if there are rats!"

The younger girl's outburst filled Garnet's lungs with a breath of courage. "You're not scared of rats, Nesta, are you? I'll warn you if I come across any."

Abruptly, the corridor's ceiling lowered. The wall texture changed from abrasive to slippery. The darkness became absolute.

"That's why I was so careful," Garnet improvised. "I knew there was a sudden drop in height somewhere around here. Mind your heads. We have to crawl now."

They crawled on their bellies like blindworms.

Cold sweat soaked her shirt and pants. Her body seemed to swell and fill the space.

Behind her, the boy was getting restless. "How long until we reach that chamber of yours? How far does this go on? I'm sure we're in the embankment by now."

"Not long now," she promised. But she was frightened. How much longer? How far into the belly of the earth had they built the bridge? It couldn't be much longer, surely not. "Almost there. But if you're frightened, we can turn back now."

"No, let's move on. How big is this chamber?"

"High enough to almost stand up in," she hoped.

The ground got slippery, icy cold, with rivulets of water running down the slope. Her exploring fingertips felt crusty lichen growth on the walls. The air smelled like flowers that had been in a vase for weeks until their stems went slimy.

"Please, let's go back," Nesta begged. "I want to get out."

Garnet wanted to go back, too. "Let's get back with Nesta, Baldwin. You and I can return and explore another time."

To her surprise, he agreed. "Yeah. Let's go home for the night, and bring torches tomorrow."

She drew a deep breath of relief. Soon she would taste fresh air again. She'd welcome the open space, the wind, even the thorny brambles.

Crawling back was far more difficult than forward. And it didn't happen fast enough. Her feet hit Baldwin's head.

"Take your dirty trotters out of my face, Fattie," he barked. "Don't hurry me, or you'll regret it!"

"I can't move." Nesta's voice was shaking with fear. "Help me. Help me!"

"You'll be ok," Baldwin soothed. "Just move backwards. We'll be out in a minute."

Then he spoilt it all by saying, "This comes from going with girls."

Nesta started crying.

Ahead fast feet rustled. Something skittered across Garnet's arm, light and quick. She screamed.

"A rat!"

Cold shudders shook her.

"I don't like this. Let's get out, quick," Baldwin commanded. After a while, he urged, "For heavens sake, Nesta, move! You don't want to be eaten by rats, do you?"

"Nesta?" But no reply came. "Nesta?" he shouted.

Garnet's heart contracted with fear. Her stomach iced over. "What's wrong? Is she still there? For gods sake, move, there are more of them, let's get out."

"I don't know," Baldwin said with a strangled voice. "She isn't moving. She's."

Garnet's mind rejected what he said. "Be sensible, Nesta!" she called. "Move, let's get back out there."

The boy's breath pushed loud, as if he was panting up a hill. "I think. I think she's fainted. Or dead. Her heart."

The blood in Garnet's veins chilled. Her pulse beat in her throat so violently that she thought she might choke on it. Then her bladder's hold broke. Warm piss ran down her thighs, and slid along her belly.

She fought down panic. "She can't be dead. Can't. Must have – fainted – just fainted. We must get her help."

"The exit's blocked. We have to go on to that chamber and out the other side."

"Right." She could barely force the word out of her constricted throat. She inched her way forward into the tightening space.

The tunnel squeezed her like guts pushing shit. She struggled for breath in the foetid air. "Baldwin, it's getting tighter. I can't get further."

"What do you mean, tighter?" His voice was sore with anger. "You've been here before, haven't you? Move on. Let's get to that chamber of yours. How far?"

"Baldwin." She spoke through clenched teeth. "There's no chamber. I lied."

"You bloody hell did what?" He yelled. "I don't believe it. I just don't believe it. Move on!"

"I can't! I'm stuck!" She screamed with all her might, but the stones swallowed the volume, returning only a muffled echo.

Now fear came into his voice. "There has to be a chamber, do you hear? There has to be. Find it. Move on."

"Wake Nesta! Or push her back out."

"Nesta? Nesta!" When she didn't respond, he whispered, "I can't shift her. I tried with my feet. No choice. Forward!"

"Slowly!" Garnet shrieked. "I'm trying. It's all wet here, a puddle, and so narrow. Keep your distance. I can't –"

"Get us out!" Baldwin yelled. "Out of here! I want to get oooooout!"

Would someone outside hear their screams? Not if they rushed by in a car or a train. What was the chance of a hiker crossing this remote bridge on a wind-whipped winter day? She swallowed. Her spittle tasted of metal and blood.

Her calves itched like mad, but the corridor was so tight she could not even move her arms to scratch.

"Baldwin – will your parents miss you soon? How many hours before they expect you home?"

"They're away for the weekend," he shouted, as if their absence was Garnet's fault. "They think we're staying with you. What about your mum?"

"She probably won't miss me," Garnet whispered. Her mother had been hitting the bottle again. How long before she woke from her stupor? Sometimes she didn't get out of bed for days. "And I haven't told her about the bridge. She doesn't know we're coming here to play."

"Oh God," he moaned. "Then we have to go on. Do you hear?"

She forced herself another inch forward. Her icy fingertips explored what lay ahead. They met stone.

"Dead end. We have to go back."

Baldwin gripped her ankles as if he was going to crush them. "Move! Go on! Forward!"

"Let me go, you idiot, get back!" She struggled and kicked to free her legs, and to stop him from crowding in on her limited space. "Shove Nesta out!"

"Move forward, you stupid bitch, get on, you bloody fat-arse."

"Push her out, damn it. Use your feet!"

His hands still clawed at her ankles. "Move on! You got us into this, now take us into that chamber! I want ooooout!"

"Let go!" she yelled, with a hard kick against his head.

A faint crack, a gulp, and the shouting stopped.

"Baldwin?"

Silence.

Lessons

Katherine A Patterson

The sun hung low in the sky above Boley Hill and still the dirt road lay empty. I chewed my lower lip and started another prayer in my head, desperate to see Talbert come riding up toward the house.

"Harlan, git from that window and come over here," Mama said.

I slid my prayer-folded hands off the window sill, I let them fall at my sides so Mama wouldn't know what I'd been up to. She didn't abide us praying anymore. Not since Papa turned bad.

I walked over to her and her rocker. Passing the eatin' table, my eyes wandered to the wood bowl of stew still sitting there, untouched.

When I got near enough, Mama snatched hold of my right ear. "Best abide what I say quick, boy, lest you end up getting a lesson like your brother's goin' get. You want that?"

"No, Mama. I'll be quick next time, I promise," I said.

She twisted me down to my place on the floor beside her rocker, then released my ear. Clovis scooted aside to make room – so I wouldn't get my fingers squished by her rocking chair. He blinked at me though the thick lenses of his spectacles, then went back to staring at the hearth-stones near his pudgy feet.

The floor was chilly since Mama let the fire burn out. After supper, she had me shovel the red embers into the tin bucket and had me dump them on the dirt-pile out back. I'd done what she said, and doused the coals black with a ladle of rain water from the barrel at the side of the house.

Ma didn't want no fire tonight. Not yet.

We waited while Mavis and Yancy finished up their chore at the

68

wash tub, scrubbing the supper bowls and Ma's cooking pot.

Mama rocked while she waited. Her rocker creaked, thunked, and kerthunked as she worked it back and forth.

The girls finished. Mama watched them fold their aprons, smooth out all the creases, then nodded as they placed them on the wood stool beside the ice box.

Talbert still hadn't galloped up as the girls joined me and Clovis on the floor by Mama's feet.

At supper, Mama told us Talbert had gone rotten like Papa. It explained why he'd been late for supper two nights already, and why he hadn't showed up for yet another. But rules was rules, as Mama said.

I felt sorry for Talbert. He'd always worked hard at pleasing Mama.

"Let us contemplate the meaning of trustworthiness," Mama said, while we sat at her feet. "How can one be loyal to family if they can't be trusted? If one can't be trusted to abide by rules, how can they be trusted to care about anything in this world?"

The four of us remained silent.

Mama rocked.

Creak, thunk, kerthunk.

With each creak of her rocker, my heart grew heavy. Who would get the touch? Who would she command to bring Talbert down to his knees?

I dreaded being picked for either job. In my mind, I prayed I wouldn't feel a callused hand upon my shoulder. I prayed I wouldn't hear my name whispered. Yet I knew if I were picked, I would rise and do what Mama willed. I also prayed Talbert had sense enough to keep on riding down Birch road, past the crooked fence post that marked the trail up to our house.

But I knew God wouldn't listen. He never heeded our prayers to save Papa.

Mama creaked back her rocker. The little rounded peg on one chair leg thunked back into its hole in the bowed rocker arm. Her wrinkled hands rest atop the black-leather cover of the Bible on her lap. The bible with the pages all glued together inside – all the pages 'cept for two middle ones of course.

She rocked forward. The little peg popped out of its socket, the defective chair kerthunked in protest.

Outside, the sky grew dark. I had to pee, but I kept my place and didn't move one hair.

Creak, thunk, kerthunk.

I nodded off, then woke hearing a horse snort outside.

Mama ceased her rocking and told us to hush.

She set her hand on Mavis' shoulder, and whispered, "Fetch my sewing kit."

Flipping open the Bible, she handed Clovis the white handkerchief with the tainted chicken claw in it.

Boots thudded across the front porch. The door latch clicked.

When Talbert stepped inside the darkened cabin Mama flicked a match alight. She tossed it in the readied hearth and the tiny flame caught on the oil-slick hickory sticks.

In the sudden fire-glow, shock and fear showed on Talbert's face.

"Mama? I – I got asked to stay late again at the saw mill. I'm… I'm sorry."

I nearly gasped at the lie. Mama had seen Talbert in town, when he was supposed to be working. She seen him smiling and talking to Missy Grace Summers, and saw him give her a pocket-pouch full of money.

"You missed supper," Mama said, giving Clovis the nod. "I left you some stew on the table."

Talbert gazed at the table.

Clovis scratched him right then with the chicken claw. Caught him on the forearm. Drew blood.

Talbert's eyes went wide. "No Mama! You…don't…understan–" His knees started to buckle as the claw-drug took effect and he struggled against it.

"Catch him," Mama said.

Yancy, Clovis, and I grabbed Talbert as he slid to the floor.

Kerthunk.

"Open up the cellar." Mama removed the key from the Bible.

Yancy and I moved the eatin' table. Then Clovis helped me pull back the wool rug. Mama fit the key into the lock of the trapdoor that lead to the root cellar below.

Mama dragged Talbert down the stairs. I kept his head from banging against the cellar steps.

Once we got him down to the cellar and the pull-string light was lit, Mama shooed three of us back upstairs. She let Mavis stay and help her work.

"Harlan, put a soup spoon in the hearth," Mama said. "Then throw down my cutting shears."

"Yes, Mama." Tears squeezed from my eyes.

⟡

When Talbert came to, he saw us all standing 'round him and he started to tremble. He couldn't blink or close his eyes. Mama had sewed his eyes open. Without a tongue he could only gurgle.

I held a damp towel to his lips, sopped up what blood I could. He spat a lot of it out, and swallowed just as much. Blood had puddled on the dirt floor, and a bunch of it glistened down Talbert's chest.

He struggled against his bindings, but Mama's rope-knots held him tight. Mavis and Yancy held his chair so he couldn't topple it.

I saw his eyes flash towards Papa's shriveled corpse in the corner, and hoped he knew Mama would never do him like that. Lying ain't as bad a sin as the one Papa committed. You can't commit adultery if you ain't married. Talbert was only fourteen.

"Fetch the spoon, Harlan."

I handed the blood-soaked towel to Clovis and went upstairs. I hated seeing my older brother sitting there naked and scared. In my mind I prayed. I asked God to kill me before letting me sit naked before Mama like that. I promised Him I'd be a good boy, that I'd abide by every rule there was for as long as I lived.

I fetched a work glove and used it to hold the handle of the hot spoon as I plucked it from the hearth-fire.

71

In the root cellar, I gave the second glove to Mama and she snatched the soup spoon from me.

Talbert started to squirm and howl.

"Let this be a lesson," Mama said. "Just like your lying tongue, your eyes won't ever let the sight of a woman keep you from abiding by the rules of family."

She pressed the hot metal spoon against each of Talbert's blue eyes.

⌾

While Talbert slumped unconscious in the chair, Mama used the shears to snip off his man sack. She had me reheat the spoon so she could cauterize parts of the wound so she could sew the remaining skin back together.

Talbert would be spared unlike Papa. Mama said Papa couldn't be cured. He had become an abomination. A thing Mama couldn't abide. She said lessons wouldn't have done him no good.

⌾

On Sunday, while Talbert remained drugged up in the root cellar, Missy Grace's daddy showed up on the porch. He said he had a gift for Mama on the back of his buckboard. Said it was a gift from Talbert – a surprise he bought with some of his work money.

Mr. Summers carried the gift in and set it down.

Mama cried. We all cried.

Mama sat down on her new rocker.

When Mr. Summers left, I snuck Clovis the chicken claw. I told him to go scratch Mama. We all knew she'd turned bad. She had become an abomination.

Popee

Justin Madison

Grandpa Hooper's unexpected death that warm August evening wasn't nearly as hard on his family as his coming back to life just moments later. Of course Grandpa's return surprised no one, considering the current state of emergency the world was in.

At dinner, Grandpa was busily eating his grilled cheese and tomato soup, when he stopped, placing his spoon next to his bowl. He lowered his hands to his lap, looked around the table at his family, and shouted, "Popcorn!" Smiling, he careened forward, falling head first into his bowl of soup, splattering the tablecloth and those sitting nearest to him with hot, red liquid.

Grandpa's odd and unforeseen death left the surviving Hoopers wearing matching expressions of surprise, and those sitting closest to him wiping soup from their persons. Utensils and sandwiches waited patiently, frozen between plates and mouths, as their brains processed the event.

Aunt Pauline broke the silence. "That was odd."

"Yep," Cousin Jeff responded. He dropped his half eaten sandwich onto his Styrofoam plate and pushed it toward the middle of the table.

"Is Popee dead, mommy?" little Georgina asked. Georgina had called Grandpa Hooper Popee ever since she'd been old enough to speak.

"I think so, honey," Shirley, the girl's mother, answered, cleaning her glasses with a napkin to clear them of the splattered soup.

The family stared at their oldest member's lifeless body, taking

73

in the scene like a dog lying in a nice sunny spot. Aunt Pauline sneezed and wiped her nose with her napkin. Cousin Jeff decided that maybe he could finish his sandwich after all and, retrieving his plate, began to eat again.

"Should we take his face out of that soup bowl?" Shirley asked to no one in particular.

"Yep," Jeff responded, chewing a big bite of turkey and Swiss. A fine rain of bread crumbs fell from his mouth and a little piece of cheese attached itself to his dimpled chin.

No one bothered to lift Grandpa's head. Instead his family continued to stare at him as if it were natural for him to be in face down in a bowl of tomato soup, something he did on a regular basis.

"What a shame," Pauline said. She looked at her sister, Shirley, and continued, "He was fine earlier. In good spirits too."

"Yeah, he was so energetic and happy. I thought this was going to be one of his good days. Then he goes and dies on us." Shirley pursed her lips and shook her head.

"Don't suppose it was the soup that killed 'im, do ya?" Jeff asked.

"I doubt it," Pauline answered.

"Good, 'cause I ate that soup too." Jeff tucked the last bite of his sandwich into his mouth.

Still no one attempted to remove Grandpa's head from the bowl.

"Do you think it hurt Popee?" Georgina inquired, looking into her own diminished bowl of soup, stirring it with disinterest.

"Think what hurt Popee, honey?" her mom asked.

Georgina looked up and clarified, "His dying like that."

"Probably not." Shirley shook her head for emphasis.

"But that soup was awful hot, mommy."

"Well, I'm sure he doesn't feel it, honey." She smiled, patting her daughter's blond head. "Now go on and finish your dinner."

Georgina began stirring again. She wasn't hungry.

Jeff took a large drink of Faygo cola. He burped loudly, setting the can back down on the ruined tablecloth. "That'll be a bitch of a stain to get out," he commented.

"I miss Popee, mommy."

"We all do, honey."

"Is he with Meemee now?" Georgina asked. Although she had died of throat cancer two years earlier, Grandma Hooper's influence on Georgina remained strong. Having been raised in southern Louisiana, Grandma loved the French terms for grandpa and grandma. She had taught all of her children and grandchildren the words Popee and Meemee, but only little Georgina ever used them.

"He might be." Shirley forced another smile. Even after all they had been through and seen during the past month, Shirley was still not comfortable with death. She reached across the table and took her daughter's hand in her own, giving it a good consoling squeeze.

"There any more Swiss cheese?" Jeff, who tended to drown his anxieties with food, asked.

Uncle Larry, silent until now, quipped, "No cheese, but you can have the rest of Granddad's soup if you're still hungry, Jeff. I'm sure he won't mind."

Jeff decided to pass; he wasn't that nervous.

"Was I hearing things, or did Grandpa say 'Popcorn' just before he died?" Shirley asked.

"Nope. Heard it too," Jeff nodded. "Funny though, can't remember 'im ever eatin' popcorn."

"Such a strange thing to say just before passing, don't you think?" Pauline queried, unconsciously massaging her plump left breast through her floral-printed blouse with her right hand.

"Who knows? Who cares? Can't say much for the way he died, but the old man lived a good, long life," Larry commented. "At eighty-two years, it was only a matter of time before he keeled over." Larry leaned across the table and poked Grandpa with his fork.

"Larry, please," Pauline slapped his shoulder with her left hand. "Show some respect."

"Just making sure, Pauline." Larry sat back down.

"Well, he's been like that for five minutes now. The surface of the tomato soup's even skinned up. How much more proof do you need?" Pauline rolled her eyes. "Of course he's dead," she finished.

Then Grandpa Hooper sat up. For a moment the blue plastic bowl stuck to his face. Then it slid off and clattered to the floor along with a shower of remaining tomato soup. A thin, red ring of congealed soup circled Grandpa's face like the ghost of a diver's mask; his eyes grey and glassy.

Everyone, excluding Larry, wore an expression of mild surprise.

"See. That's why I poked him," Larry said.

"Slurrrpppel," Grandpa vocalized. His head lolled limply from side to side as he looked around the table.

"Popee, you're alive!" Georgina squealed delightfully.

"That might need qualifying," Larry said. He leaned forward and poked Grandpa with his fork once again. Grandpa Hooper scowled and hissed, spraying a mist of pinkish spittle across the table. The white tablecloth was obviously ruined now; Shirley would never get that stain out.

"He doesn't like you doing that," Pauline said, trying to pull Larry back into his chair.

"Grrrunnnmph," Grandpa moaned. The front of his light green polo shirt was darkened with spilt soup and the thick strings of saliva that dripped from his mouth each time he opened it.

Larry took another jab at Grandpa with the fork. Grandpa Hooper's hands shot out. He grabbed Larry's right arm, pulling Larry toward him. Losing his balance, Larry fell onto the table, crushing what remained of his dinner. No longer interested in soup and sandwiches, Grandpa bit down on Larry's captured forearm.

"Oww!" Larry shrieked, jerking his arm away and breaking free of the old man's grip. Grandpa Hooper's false teeth slid out of his mouth with a wet slurp, continuing to bite Larry's arm. Then gravity took over and the dentures fell to the floor, each one breaking into three large pieces.

"You old bastard! That hurt." Larry swung at Grandpa. The fork he still held in his clenched right fist connected with the side of Grandpa's face just above his left cheek. The four pointy tines punctured Grandpa's leathery skin and sunk in about an eighth of an inch. When Larry let go and fell back into his chair, the fork continued to protrude from Grandpa Hooper's left cheek like a second nose.

"Mmmurrrpmm," Grandpa whimpered. He attempted to bat at the fork with a dead hand, but missed and succeeded only in smacking his nose.

Jeff watched with horror as Larry cradled his right arm. "Yer bit, Larry! Yer gonna become one of 'em things now!"

Larry shook his head. "You know damn well that's not so. It only goes that way when you're bit by real teeth, not dentures. Besides, he didn't even break the skin. See." He held up his arm to show that there were no puncture wounds, just a pale red imprint of teeth marks.

Surprisingly, through all that happened, everyone, including Grandpa, still remained seated around the table. Another minute passed in silence, until Grandpa Hooper slowly stood up, letting out a loud, stinky fart. Then with an agility that everyone found astonishing, Grandpa was up and across the table, tipping Aunt Pauline back in her chair and onto the floor in seconds.

"Gack!" Pauline cried. Her right arm, still fondling her left breast, was pinned between her and Grandpa. She beat at Grandpa with her meaty left arm, struggling to free the trapped arm and knock off her attacker, but Grandpa Hooper was stronger and kept her pinned to the ground. "Help! He's going to eat me! Somebody help me!"

"He can't eat you, Pauline," Larry said. "He doesn't have his teeth in."

"I don't care. Just get him off me!" Pauline thrashed under Grandpa's dead weight. "Get him off me!"

Leaving their seats, Uncle Larry and Cousin Jeff each grabbed one of Grandpa's shoulders and heaved him off of Pauline.

Grandpa lurched forward, and his weight shifted. Losing his hold on Grandpa Hooper, Jeff stumbled and fell to the floor. Free of Jeff, Grandpa turned on Larry. The dead man lunged forward, knocking Larry to the floor. Grandpa fell on top of Larry and attempted to eat Larry's nose.

"Oh, you sick, nasty old man!" Larry yelled while Grandpa gummed his nose. Frothy trails of slick saliva covered Larry's face as Grandpa continued to suck on his nose.

Back at the table, Georgina watched the events unfold with her mother like one of the WWF pay-per-view they used to enjoy in the living room when the cable still worked. "Why is Popee kissing Uncle Larry like that?" she asked.

"He's not kissing him, honey. He's trying to eat him," Shirley answered.

"Oh. Maybe he didn't like his soup," Georgina said.

Larry and Grandpa wrestled on the floor, knocking over the nearby chairs and breaking a cheap, imitation crystal vase. The old man was amazingly strong and Larry wondered if Grandpa had really needed all the help he claimed to need around the house when he was alive.

"Gaarrbllesflllub," Grandpa grunted.

"Right back at cha, ya old prick," Larry retorted. He grabbed the fork protruding from Grandpa's cheek, pulled it out, and then rammed it into Grandpa's right eye socket with all of his might. The fork disappeared into Grandpa's head, with only an inch jutting from the old man's ruined eye.

"Popcorn!" Grandpa shouted once more before going limp on top of Larry.

After a moment of struggling, Larry freed himself from under Grandpa Hooper. Panting, he got to his feet and shuffled over to the table, righting a chair and sitting in it with a relieved sigh.

Again everyone was silent. Uncle Larry caught his breath. Cousin Jeff picked up the knocked over chairs. Aunt Pauline stood, started to gather up the broken vase and then decided it could wait until later.

Little Georgina walked over to Grandpa Hooper and knelt

beside his corpse. He lay face down on the floor in a twisted lump. His right eye oozed a thin, watery puss. Georgina leaned over, gently kissing him on the top of his bald dome. She sighed, "Poor Popee."

Before You Say Anything

Amanda Lawrence Auverigne

Megan held Barry as the young man stood at her side. She looked at the faces of her parents as they sat on the couch in front of them.

They had chosen the time of their announcement well.

Before the evening news that held her elderly caretakers' attention each night.

Barry gave Megan's hand a squeeze as she repeated the announcement in a louder tone.

"Now I know what you are thinking. You think that we are too young to get married," Megan said.

Barry turned from the silent gawk of Megan's parents and pulled the weeping girl into his arms.

"But we love each other. And we want to get married right away," Megan said.

She pushed Barry away gently.

She looked at her parents' faces for a few moments.

She reached out and took Barry's hand in hers.

"We don't need your money 'cause I'm dropping out of school. There will be plenty of time for that later. Barry's gonna drive trucks on the weekends so that we can make ends meet. And I've already gotten a job at the post office that's during the day making good money so that we can be together at night," Megan said.

Megan stared into her Mother's wide eyes.

Megan turned to her Father as the old man let out a cough.

Megan stared at the floor before she looked up at her Mother.

She felt sad as she watched tears glisten in the old woman's eyes.

"I know this hurts you. And I know you wanted a different life for me. But you have to understand that this is my life. This is my choice. And I choose Barry. I love him. And he loves me," Megan said.

"So. Before you say anything. You need to know that we are getting married. Tonight. And there is nothing you can do about it," Megan said.

Megan turned from her parents and flung herself into Barry's arms.

Barry held her close to him and edged her gently in the direction of the door.

Megan stared at the wide splashes of blood that covered the walls, floor and furniture in the room.

Barry grinned at Megan as the axe he held in his right hand fell to the carpet.

Megan turned to stare at her parents.

Their bodies sat on the blood-smeared couch in pieces.

Their heads had been placed neatly atop the rear portion of the couch.

Thick tendrils of blood dripped from their ragged necks and their glassy eyes were fixed on the large projection screen television in front of them.

Barry wiped his hands on his shirt and wrapped his arms around Megan.

Megan stared at the blood soaked couch in front of them.

Megan shuddered as she watched a single tear fall from her Mother's right eye.

Barry glanced at his watch and let out a sigh.

He stared at Megan and pulled her close to him before he placed a kiss on her cheek.

"I think they took it pretty well," he said.

The Bride wore Black

Brian Rosenberger

Not so much a shotgun wedding
as a shovel and suture ceremony
The groom immaculate,
save for the lab coat
bloodstained sleeves clotted with his life's work.
The garment his father's
an inherited fashion sense
along with a morbid fascination for biology
a passion for puzzles
of the mind and body
the central nervous system his specialty
but skin and tissue his favorite.
The blushing bride, not from embarrassment
but from renewed circulation
her lips as red as her wounds,
so recently cross stitched
her gown fresh as a graveside bouquet,
a cemetery smile hidden behind her veil.
Betrayed and buried,
she was axed by her ex
his fists as striking as the resemblance
to her current resurrecter and future spouse.
Their love affair tragic as it was brief.
The doctor didn't survive the honeymoon
over come with emotion and lack of breath
brought on by applied pressure to the trachea.
The strength in such small hands,

both formerly owned by a masseuse.
The widow persevered
living well so to speak
thanks to her husband's living will
and her own successful career
Modeling for anatomical drawing classes.
Student and teacher alike vying for her attention
But it's still Ms. Frankenstein to you.

The Sutherland King

David Hutchison

"I'm gonna bake my baby,
An apple pie this evening,"
sang Kennac, as she unrolled the pastry lid over the cinnamon drenched apples.

"Cooker turned on low,

My heart is like butter melting."

Kennac waltzed over to the oven door.

"My head feels just like dough."

Kennac slid the pie onto the top shelf, shut the oven and checked the kitchen clock.

"Should be ready at twenty two," she thought, as she brushed her hands against her apron.

She wrung a damp cloth under the kitchen tap and was just about to wipe down the table when the phone rang.

❦

"Well, Kennac. Are you all set for Friday?" cackled her sister-in-law.

"I don't know why I bother, Flora. You always win anyway," said Kennac.

"Och, that's not true, Bella won the Cup, when was it now?" gloated Flora.

"You know fine, twelve years ago, and you've won it ever since," retorted Kennac.

"Oh well, I've just baked some scones. Come over," said Flora.

"OK," replied Kennac and rang off.

She scuttled off through to the kitchen and finished wiping

down the table. She took off her apron, pulled on her favourite mohair cardigan and went off out, down the garden path, in her mules. The sweetly coconut smell of the yellow gorse mingled with the stench of the drain as she ambled towards her front gate.

"I hope that plumber turns up tomorrow," she thought.

Kennac crossed the road, and opened the back gate to Briar Cottage. Like everything else that Flora did, the garden was perfect. Regimented rows of white alyssum and blue lobelia flanked the flagstone path towards the back door. Floribunda and tea roses framed the kitchen window.

"Cooeee, it's me," called Kennac as she opened the door to the smell of freshly baked scones.

"Come in," fussed Flora, as she swirled hot water around a teapot, "go ben the house, the fire's on."

"You wouldn't think it was summer with this chill," agreed Kennac, keeping her cardigan on.

She trundled through to the immaculate sittingroom and sat down in the armchair next to the television. The fire was fairly banked up. A coal fell onto the hearth. She bent down and scooped it up with her calloused hands and deftly threw it to the back of the fire.

Kennac leaned back. Woodchip walls plastered with nostalgia. There, above the television set, next to George's casket, was that faded photograph of the day they all went fishing at Loch Fionn. George and Jim, proudly holding up their catches of brown trout. Flora sitting on the tartan rug in the background, pouring coffee from a flask. Kennac remembered taking that photo as if it was yesterday. They all looked so young. She leaned forward and peered at the neat writing underneath: "June 1973". Kaleidoscopic memories of Jim flooded her mind. She never kept any photos whereas Flora had a gallery dedicated to the dead.

"What're you entering into the competition?" Flora called from the kitchen.

"One for apple pie that Johanne gave me," replied Kennac.

"Oh, not Johanne MacLeod for heaven's sake!" gasped Flora as she came through with the tea tray, "I'll never forget 1978. The cat hairs in the Victoria sponge."

"Och no, not her. Johanne Graham, the doctor's daughter," laughed Kennac. "She cut it out of The People's Friend."

Flora placed the tray down on a small side table and poured the tea into china cups. She passed one over to Kennac.

"Oh thanks dear," smiled Kennac taking the cup into her wrinkled hands.

Served on a d'oily, the spread of hot scones topped with strawberry jam looked scrumptious. She picked one up and greedily bit into it.

"Oh, they're wonderful. Why don't you enter them for the Sutherland King?"

Flora leaned back with a knowing smile. "I don't care what anyone says. A scone should be eaten within an hour of baking. The baking has to be entered the Friday morning, then it's lying there the whole afternoon before the judges come round. A scone has never, ever won the Sutherland King."

Flora's eyes went up to the especially made shelf above the mantelpiece. There, basked the Sutherland King; an ugly monstrosity of a cup in silver plate.

Kennac delicately pushed a rogue crumb into her mouth. "I wish you'd give me the proper shortbread recipe."

"Now Kennac, I've given you it several times," sighed Flora.

"Well, it must be your oven, or some method in the mixing. Couldn't I watch you making it?" asked Kennac, hopefully.

As Flora was about to answer, Hamish, Flora's gigantic black tomcat jumped up onto her tweed skirt, knocking over her plate.

"Hamish! For goodness sake, get off me!" scolded Flora as the cat ran off round the armchair.

"You should have had him done years ago. What a difference it made to Aggie's tom," admonished Kennac.

Flora ignored the comment. She got up, wiped the crumbs onto the hearth and brought down the Sutherland King Cup from its shelf. She sat down and lovingly cradled it in her hands.

"Look at that. Mrs F. Wilson 1974. Mrs F. Wilson 1975. Mrs F. Wilson 1976. Mrs F. Wilson 1977. Mrs F...," she sighed, turning the cup around slowly, the flames of the fire dancing in the silver.

She gently handed the Sutherland King across to Kennac.

Kennac lifted her glasses from the chain around her neck and gave the lenses a good clean with the tail of her blouse. She propped them on her nose. She traced her finger across the crossed rolling pins emblem engraved above the words, "For Excellence in Baking", and in smaller words beneath, "In memory of Eleanor Sutherland King". The cup was crowded with engraved names and dates. A wooden base with an empty silver plaque had been added.

Flora took the cup from Kennac, pointed at the empty plaque and said, "The final winner's name will go here. The committee have decided that there is no room left and are getting a new cup. Whoever wins it this year gets to keep it forever."

She placed the cup firmly back onto the shelf.

"Oh well, I'd better be getting back. The pie's due out of the oven," said Kennac, glancing at the clock.

"Yes, and I'll have to start on the shortbread," replied Flora getting up stiffly and bustling Kennac out.

"Well, thanks for the scones and tea, then," sighed Kennac as she waved from the path.

Hamish wandered from behind a bush and rubbed against Kennac's leg.

"OK, you can come and get some milk," relented Kennac. Hamish followed her across the road to her front gate. The mingling smells of the septic tank and gorse seemed to be worse as she walked up the path. "When was Murdo going to come round and fix it?"

"What was that other smell though?" Kennac thought as she went to the kitchen. She rushed to the oven and opened the door. Choking smoke belched out. She used the edge of her cardigan to pull the tray out. A smoking pile of carbonised pie was plonked onto the sink drainer.

She thought, "It looked quite pretty in an ugly sort of way. Maybe she could peel the top off and varnish it. Make a clock like those toast clocks she'd seen on some television programme one time."

Kennac opened the window. She noticed that Flora hadn't drawn her curtains as usual.

"I wonder if she's making the shortbread?" thought Kennac.

She went through the house and up the steep wooden stairs then along the short corridor, lined with stuffed animals. Taxidermy had been Jim's hobby. She opened the warped damp door of "the workshop".

The room was stacked with cases of dead animals, in various stages of stuffing. On the window ledge, next to some artificial eyes and plastic ear liners, was Jim's binoculars. Kennac pushed past a group of stuffed pinemartins and moved some gamehead mannikins out of the way.

She looked out the window.

"Yes, the curtains were still open," she thought. She opened the window and let some fresh air in. Kennac sat on two cases of trout castings and picked up the binoculars. She leant her elbows on the sill, crunched up her eyes and focused on Flora's kitchen window.

Yes, up here she could see over the gorse and get a good clear view.

There was Flora, in the kitchen. The ingredients were neatly stacked at one end of the table. She was measuring some sugar out onto her big old-fashioned scales; she'd been given them when she left her job as the school cook.

Next, she cut up some butter into small chunks into her stoneware mustard-coloured bowl.

Flora lifted the edge of the bowl and started beating the sugar and butter together with a wooden spoon. After a while she stopped.

"That didn't seem long enough," thought Kennac.

Flora put the spoon down and went to the sink.

"She's going to shut the curtains!" thought Kennac.

Flora poured out a glass of water from the kitchen tap, went back to the table, tilted the bowl and started beating the mixture again.

A few minutes later Flora put down the spoon. She turned her back to Kennac and fumbled in a drawer. She turned round with a sieve which she laid over the mixing bowl. She shook some plain flour onto the scales. She added just a pinch of salt. She tipped the dry ingredients into the sieve and shook it over the mixture. Flora picked up the spoon and worked the flour into the mixture.

"No sign of farola, semolina or even rice flour on the table," thought Kennac.

Flora walked out of the kitchen into the sittingroom. Kennac adjusted her position and saw Flora beside the television.

Kennac thought, "Oh no, she's going to sit down and watch television. I'll have to wait here for ages."

Flora didn't sit down. She picked something off the television and went back to the kitchen.

Kennac adjusted her position again and looked though the kitchen window.

Flora was holding George's casket.

Flora put the casket down on the table and pulled off the lid. She scooped around the casket and put a spoonful of the powder into the sieve.

Kennac felt her heart jump. "My god, George's ashes were the secret ingredient. Oh goodness me!"

Flora lifted up the casket and looked into it. She frowned as she turned the casket upside down and patted its base. She put down the casket and went to the cupboard.

Kennac thought of all the times she had eaten that melt-in-the-mouth shortbread. Slivers of golden biscuitness, edges shaped with the back of a spoon, evenly pricked and dusted in sugar.

Kennac got up stiffly and placed the binoculars back on the sill. She wove her way through the dead zoo. As Kennac slowly went down the stairs a thought struck her. "Jim's ashes were in her china cabinet. Maybe? Well Jim wouldn't mind!"

Kennac went into her kitchen and started to make the shortbread.

2 ounces of farola, 4 ounces of cornflour, 8 ounces of plain flour, 8 ounces of butter, 4 ounces of icing sugar, just a pinch of salt. She went to the china cabinet and took out Jim's casket…

An hour later Kennac was sitting watching television having a cup of tea. The shortbread was cooling on a wire tray.

Kennac heard a whining noise and got up. It sounded as if it was coming from upstairs. Kennac went to the stairs. Hamish looked down at her from between the bannisters.

"Oh Hamish, here, puss puss!" coaxed Kennac.

Hamish looked down then started to groom himself.

Kennac slowly climbed the stairs. When she was on the last few steps she reached out to pick up Hamish.

"Come on Hamish, we'll get you that milk now," she whispered.

She lifted up Hamish. Hamish squirmed and she lost her balance. Hamish went flying out of her arms.

"Hamish!" she screamed.

She grasped for the banister but grabbed air. Everything seemed to go in slow motion as Kennac tumbled. Memories of Jim fishing, stuffed animals, eating shortbread, Flora, the Sutherland King Cup, sieving flour, cracking an egg…

One week later there is a plate of shortbread sitting on Kennac's coffin, in Flora's sittingroom. The wake is in full swing.

"More tea anyone?" Ina, Bella's sister, popped her head round the crowded kitchen door.

"Oh yes Ina," answered Bella.

"I'll just let it brew a min," said Ina, and fought her way back into the kitchen.

Bella turned to Flora. "Sorry, who found her?"

Flora looked at the coffin and said, "Murdo the plumber found her. I told her it was dangerous climbing these stairs at her age."

"It would have been over quickly. She wouldn't have suffered," said Bella, munching away on a piece of shortbread.

"Yes, the poor soul," Johanne sobbed in an armchair.

"Mmmh, this shortbread is excellent," said Bella.

She sipped some tea and then carefully chose another piece, from the plate displayed on the coffin.

"I love the texture. It's no wonder that it won the Sutherland King," said Bella.

Flora looked up at the empty shelf and said, "Well, wherever she is now, I hope she's laughing. I saw her shortbread lying on the table. Must have been the last thing that she did, poor thing. So I just stuck it into the competition for her and it won. It was really even better than mine. I can't figure out what she put in it."

"Rice flour perhaps?" suggested Bella.

"No, there was only farola in the cupboard, and I looked in the bin too," answered Flora, puzzled.

"So where is the Sutherland King?" asked Bella, looking at the shelf.

Flora replied, "Off getting Kennac's name engraved on it. Then it will go back up on that shelf. I'm seeing about getting a top made for it to contain Kennac's ashes."

"Yes, I think she'd like that!" said Johanne, as she broke into a smile.

"Comin' through!" declared Ina, with a scalding pot of tea.

Bella banged against the television as she let Ina past the coffin. George's casket went flying onto the hearth and spilled open. Everyone went quiet and looked at Flora and then at the ashes spread over the hearth.

"Oh, Flora I'm so sorry," gasped Ina, horrified.

"It was my fault," Bella blurted.

"Don't worry about it," laughed Flora as she bent down to the hearth, picked the brush from the fire set and started sweeping the ashes into a pile.

"It's just cornflour. Storing it in the casket beside the fire keeps it dry. I scattered George's ashes in the garden among the tea roses. He was so fond of them," said Flora as she swept the cornflour onto the shovel then into the fire.

Payday

Bryce Stevens

It was Thursday so Fritch had every reason to feel scared. The heat from the concrete penetrated the cardboard that he used as soles for his taped-up shoes. His throat was scorched dry and the brutal heat from the summer burned urban dog waste to powder. With a face wrinkled from too many days in the salt air and a forehead like unbeaten copper, Fritch shuffled along the street towards the Sacred Heart Mission. His erratic steps betrayed the onset of Korsakoff Syndrome. He grinned as if with some secret thought. The beard, stained with nicotine, twitched, seeming to slide a little across his face. Head down and back arched to the skin-shrinking heat, Fritch scuffed his way towards the Church mission for his midday meal. Even through his fear he knew that if he didn't eat he would not be able to face the night ahead.

He seemed to sense when there was someone nearby that he knew and occasionally lifted his head to nod to another street-walker. At the mission several stragglers hurried their pace to wander down the side of the church to stand in a line amid the flutter and cooing of the scavenger pigeons. Here was the smell of rollup tobacco, urine and the diseased coughing from a life of indulgence. Men of all ages and women with small children milled around and chatted with streetwalkers and assorted denizens of halfway houses. They were society's outcasts. Some were doomed to live short lives amid the squalor of rooming houses run by greedy proprietors, while others were the voluntary homeless, too tired to reach up for a better life.

Fritch moved forward to keep up with the shortening lunch

line. His stomach told him that he would survive another ten minutes. Here scuffles occasionally broke out, but mostly the hungry were here to whisper their deals of drugs or to make promises of repaying a 'fiver' to their peers when pension day came. Fritch waited with a resignation borne from years on the streets. No bed for him in a doss-house or a charity bed; he was of the streets and his home was the urban sprawl, wherever he happened to be when sleep dogged him. He counted his steps to when he approached the food counter.

The chatter and mumble of many dialects and bright colours from the opportunity-shop clothing bins filled the spacious mission hall. Music from a radio station that no one would voluntarily switch to was piped over the racket in an effort to make the midday meal event run smoothly. No one ate in too much of a hurry, nor did people protect their food from the person next to them. Here there was dignity away from the prying eyes of society; here none judged on the way a fork was held or on the manner which one picked up a slice of bread. Pride it seemed could not be taken from those who had nothing of the finer things. Fritch sat alone at the end of a long table, not noticing or caring the urine-sticky trousers crinkling around his testicles. He smelled no better or worse than some of those around him.

His pension day was a few days off and he had enough pavement butts to keep him in tobacco for a while. His stomach was being fed and he'd managed to sell some second-hand paperback books to supply him with a half-measure bottle of vodka. In days past these simple needs would have caused him to think he was doing all right. Now, ever since he had met those others, things were different. Today he was frightened.

Leaving the mission he wandered down past the shops to his favourite tree in the park bordering the bay. Pigeons and sparrows and sea gulls surrounded him in the hope that he would fling them a morsel. Their eyes watched from their cocked heads for any movement or sound that would betray the presence of food. Street wise and impatient, these birds soon knew nothing was forthcoming and they peeped and screeched before seeking easier pickings.

He stayed under his tree for the remainder of the afternoon and with nothing better to do he dozed fitfully until by the dipping sun he saw it was time for him to move. Stomach ulcers slicked with gastric juices and growing dread knotted his insides as he stood. He licked his parched lips and swallowed bile. His hand fluttered, trembling and strayed inside his soiled jacket. He patted the billfold that lay there, snug, full of twenty-dollar bills. Looking around at the reddening summer sun he knew that he should be making his way to the tram stop. A piece of the sticky tape he had used to keep his shoe together had curled under the sun and it made a crackling sound on the pavement as he walked. His stomach tightened as he resigned himself to what lay ahead and realised the futility of forestalling the inevitable.

The tram clattered and shuddered on its tracks, like a drunkard reeling down a darkening street. Dusk was moments away and the fierce heat from the summer drought buffeted the outside of the streetcar. Commuters inside squirmed as if trapped, rubbing against each other with no room to move, looking everywhere but at each other. The air was thick from stale breath, increasing the irritability of the passengers; metal wheels squawked on the hot rails, setting teeth on edge. The unbroken heat wave caused many to sag with exhaustion, while a few sat desultorily on the sweaty seats.

The tram jerked, braked and stopped. Doors slid open allowing the cruel heat to penetrate the interior. The blast of dry air brought with it two lean men. Looks of hunger and urgency and scalps abristle like new-freed felons set them apart. The commuters inside the vehicle were too weary and full of thoughts of air-conditioned houses to notice restrained violence rubbing shoulders with them. Doors rattled shut. The tram jerked forward. The two men glanced from face to face, looking for something to hold their keen interest.

Towards the rear of the streetcar Fritch sat unmoving. The seats closest to him were empty and the people nearest huddled more tightly, upper bodies leaning away from the cloying stink of urine. Anger went unspoken and no one looked at the man.

Passengers left the tram and the remainder gave silent thanks and spread out the length of the stuffy vehicle. Night closed in. Three stops from the end of the route the tram was nearly empty. Fritch pulled out a greasy billfold, opened it with a sticky sound, like a wet leather mouth smacking its lips. Two stops from the end of the route all but the tramp and the two furtive men had left the vehicle. He poked a soiled finger into the billfold and began counting the twenty-dollar bills. The two bristle-scalped men stood, muscled frames moving lithely under tight shirts. One reached to pull the exit cord. Then they saw the old man and their eyes betrayed the hunger.

Fritch looked up, startled, a hunted look filming his gaze. He blinked, smiled faintly, nervously, quickly replacing his billfold into the inner pocket of his grass-stained jacket. The two lean men exchanged glances then ignored him as they moved to the exit. The tram stopped, screeching as if in protest. Heat enveloped the men as they stepped down into the night.

Glancing out the window Fritch saw that the men were not watching him. He sat staring ahead, his hands trembling. The tram rattled on. A moment later the tramp stood, his shaking fingers gripping the bell cord and he pulled down hard. Up front the driver checked his mirrors to see why the cord had been pulled for the final stop of the route. He sensed being watched and glanced forward grinning sheepishly. The tram stopped, the doors sliding on their rubber tracks. Gripping the handrail he stepped slowly with arthritic limbs down onto the grassy verge and looked up towards a side street. The hungry men glared at the retreating back, their hooded eyes sparkling with a need. They walked slowly forward ignoring all but the tramp hurrying ahead of them.

Quickening his pace to a stumbling run, he clutched at his bill-fold tucked snugly inside his stinking coat. He breathed heavily, each exhalation whistling through his clenched teeth. A gurgling rattled in his strong chest, long used to fight the onset of emphysema. Reaching the side street, he wheezed as he glanced back, his eyes shining wide and moist beneath an unbroken street lamp.

The young men strode swiftly on, passing the streetlight,

allowing them to see their fleeing quarry turn in between two fences on the other side of the street. They began running. A little way along the alley between the two sagging fences they stopped, realising that they faced a dead-end. The stink of piss was strong and they could hear the wheezing of someone just in front of them. They stepped forward into the gloom, around old cartons and tyres. They stopped as the one they pursued came forward out of the darkness to meet them. Exchanging glances they did not notice several shadows detach themselves from the empty crates lining the fences behind them.

Fritch smiled, his teeth shining whitely. Cocking his head at the approaching steps the old man's smile widened. His pursuers became aware of movement and turned in sudden alarm. Curved talons caught the rays of the street lamp glowing dimly lighting the mouth of the alley. Gasping with the onrush of panic the two pursuers blinked with fright. They saw only the street lamp and the silhouettes of four big figures.

Gurgling and wheezing with laughter whistling from between his teeth Fritch looked over the men's shoulders. The two trapped men could not look that way from the clicking talons of the four silhouettes. The black shapes moved stealthily forward, no sound coming from underfoot. An acrid smell filled the hot night air, pungent, suggesting clay pits and leaking gas. In dreadful silence talons lifted fully into the light. Fritch backed further into the shadow and squatted painfully down into the dry, crackling grass. He put his hands over his ears to shut out the sounds of tearing and splintering.

Fritch crouched when he felt the silhouette rise, come lithely, leisurely toward him. The figure was silent and from it came a smell of leaking gas and wet clay. Fritch cringed and pushed himself further back against the drooping boards of the old fence at the end of the alley. Terrified, he did not know what these things were, did not wish to know. They had come to him out of the night and always slid back between the cracks of splintered darkness.

The silhouette leaned forward, limbs reaching – unfamiliar with the surroundings.

Fritch rubbed his stinging eyes. Trembling, he placed his greasy billfold onto the spade-sized palm. He screwed his eyes shut, waiting breathlessly, chest tight. The smell sickened him. He swallowed copious saliva. Bile was disgorged up the esophagus, to swill at the back of his throat. He swallowed the stinging fluid. He concentrated hard on telling the things not to touch him. He was nothing. He felt something fall into the grass at his feet. He half opened his eyes and waited. He heard his own breathing

Squinting down amid the gloom, Fritch scrabbled around in front of him, finally feeling the billfold under his hand. Picking up leather he opened the damp lips and felt inside—more twenties. They had rewarded him. He stood shakily, stumbling forward, not looking directly at the light opposite the alley. Two dark shapes crumpled like stuffed bags of laundry lay at his feet. He stepped around the would-be predators. Daring one timid glance behind, he stepped on trembling legs out from between the fences. With his scalp momentarily tightening he shuffled off towards the suburban bottle shop. He'd done his duty for this week. He'd cleaned the streets…and it was payday.

The Little Girl Who Lives
in the Woods

Ralph Robert Moore

Morton Street travels long and flat into Hargrove County, past tilted mailboxes, the straightness of the street ending fourteen miles in, at an isolated cul-de-sac.

One-story houses, built eighty years ago, sit around the cul-de-sac, five of them, far back from the circle of black pavement.

Beyond the cul-de-sac, nothing but woods, deep and dense, full of fallen trees, brown puddles, bird cries.

Within those woods, lives a little girl in a long, white dress.

The parents and children on the cul-de-sac have seen the little girl in the distant criss-cross of branches.

Police have been called out, more than once. The officers return from the woods with muddy shoes, mosquito bites, but no little girl in a long white dress.

The story about the little girl is she once lived in one of the five houses around the cul-de-sac, although no one is sure which house, since ownership changes almost yearly, and while she lived in that house, one night her father stood in her doorway for a long, long time, then went inside her bedroom, pulled down her pink sheets, and raped her.

The story is she became pregnant by that rape, and her father kept her out of school once she started showing.

The story is her baby was taken from her as soon as it was born in a back bedroom, and she fled to the woods, in grief.

The story is she was nine years old when she was raped.

The story is she wanders through the woods, and has for several years, in the long white dress she was wearing when she fled, and that as she wanders, she holds up in her small right hand a white rock she took from a garden she and her father planted, thinking the rock is her baby's head.

The story is she no longer speaks English, but instead talks in a guttural language, of her own invention.

No one knows if any of this story is true. All anyone knows is she's a little girl, and instead of living in a house, like the rest of us, she lives in the woods.

Cory lived in the cul-de-sac. He shared a one-story white house with his mother. Each week day the mustard school bus dropped him off, half a mile from his home, the last stop for the school bus on Morton Street before it backed up at a slant, rear tires running off the edge of the pavement, crushing the green grass, usually in the same brown ruts, rolled forward, backed-up again, then drove back down that long, straight stretch.

Cory would walk the last half mile looking down at the black pavement, school books dangling from a red rubber strap around his right wrist. Sometimes, before his mother came home, Cory would go out the back screen door, down the gray wooden steps, wander into the woods. A few times he saw the little girl in the long white dress, standing by herself in the safety of distance. One time, he waved at her. Another, he shouted, "Hello!"

It must be lonely to live in the woods, to not have anyone to hold onto, especially if you were a kid. His mother always gave him a big hug as soon as she got home, after she brushed her teeth. He loved his mother. Once, on a field trip, he sacrificed his lunch to buy her a big bottle of green perfume.

Each time, the little girl stood her ground, a hundred yards away, not waving, not shouting back.

Cory was tall for his age.

In gym, he'd strut through the gray tunnels of the boys' locker room in his red bathing trunks and bright blond hair, wetting his white towel under one of the silver shower heads, holding the dark towel away from his hip, twirling it into a rat's tail, whipping the heavy, wet tip of the towel against the naked boys' legs.

He was feared. Each day in school, each boy kept track of where Cory was.

Cory ruled the kids on the cul-de-sac. The parents knew nothing. Each night after dinner the kids had to meet in the circular pavement at the center of the cul-de-sac, then Cory would bring them into the woods, but not too far, pull out a pack of matches, or squeeze a halved green lime over his fingers, make each boy sniff, then have the boys pull their pants down, even their underpants, and lie on top of each other, like cordwood.

One Saturday, Cory had all the neighborhood kids hike half a mile down Morton Street to a deep pond behind the Rutherford's place.

Every boy had to strip naked, then get out into the middle of the brown pond, dog-paddling. One kid, Hollis, refused to jump off the dead tree fallen like a pier halfway across the pond.

Cory, out in the middle of the pond, dog-paddling, raised his voice in fury. "Come on!"

Hollis tightroped out to the rotted end of the trunk, bending his knees. "I can't, Cory!"

Cory dog-paddled his chest all the way out of the water, to his hips. "Do it! Jump!"

Hollis waved his hands by his shoulders, jumped.

His feet landed in the center of the pond, where the brown water was over a kid's head.

Hollis went under, cheeks bulging, popping his dirty head up. Big fish eyes. "I can't swim!"

Cory paddled next to him in the deep brown water, poking his shoulder. "Just swim."

Hollis grabbed onto Cory's forearm, vomiting pond water. He grabbed Cory around the ribs from behind, his weight dunking Cory's head underwater.

Cory struggled to the surface, spewing water, Hollis' orange fingers around his nose and forehead.

Cory punched him in the face, punched him again. "Get your hands off me, pervert!"

Hollis' muddy face trickled red blood.

"Swim! What's the big fucking deal?"

Hollis' head dipped underwater, elbows, splashing hands.

His head bobbed back to the surface only once, eyes squinting.

Cory swam to shallow water, standing up.

Hollis' knobbed spine broke the brown surface, amid tiny rings of larvae, legs and head still submerged.

By the time he was fished out, by Cory and some of the other neighborhood kids, Hollis was dead.

Gray face, big teeth.

The police came out. Blue and red cop car lights rotated in the dusk around the green tree tops by the muddy pond. Hollis' drowning was ruled an accident.

The neighborhood parents decided they didn't want their children playing anymore with Cory.

At school, all the kids went to the opposite side of the hall whenever he walked down. If he said Hi to any of them, they just stared.

Cory spent more time in the woods, by himself, waiting for his mother to come home.

One time, deep within the bird cries, he spotted, off in the distance, the little girl.

Like he would with a rabbit, he tried taking one step forward, then another, another, stopping each time; under his sneakers, a branch broke.

Over the course of an hour, he got to within fifty yards of her. He gave her a shy smile. "Hi."

She stood even more erect in her long white dress, right hand holding her white rock, eyes watching him.

He sensed she was trying to decide if she could trust him.

He moved forward a few more yards. "Hi."

She raised her head. "Gar." Her voice sounded hoarse.

And she melted away in the convergence of branches.

The next evening, Cory brought some bread slices with him, half a head of iceberg lettuce.

She was where he had seen her standing the previous day.

She watched him, eyes alert, as he moved closer, until he was only twenty yards from her. He raised both his hands, her shoulders rising in alarm, showing her the bread slices and lettuce.

He put the food on the ground, waited to see if she would come forward. When she didn't, he backed off a dozen yards.

Carefully, slowly, she made her way through the brush and fallen limbs, until she reached the spot. As he watched, she got down on her haunches, put the white rock down, picking up the bread slices in both hands, pushing them into her mouth, dirty face glancing up constantly to check he was still far enough away.

After that, each night he'd bring her food, finally, after a week, being able to sit on a log only a few yards away from her as she squatted down in her white dress, eating the slices with both hands, like scooping up water.

"Is there anything special you'd like me to bring you?"

She pushed her long, middle-parted hair away from her face. "Gartcha cartlin."

Cory looked down at the ground. "Isn't it lonely living out here?"

She watched him with her blue eyes, said nothing.

The next evening, sitting on the same log, he watched her wolf down the food he had brought, then he pulled something from behind his back, holding it up so she could see it.

· A naked doll.

She looked up from her gobbling, eyes widening, sad mouth sickled down.

"What's this? Is this a baby? How are you, baby? Are you okay? Oh, I'm so lonely, I want my mother to hold me. I'm so cold. Why won't my mother hold me?"

The little girl in the long white dress keened to herself, staring at the doll.

"Do you want this baby? This baby is a lot more real than that white rock you carry around. But if you want this baby, if you want to take care of it, you have to show me something."

Her dirty face twisted to one side, dumb eyes teared-up. She came even closer, reaching out with both hands. "Gartcha cark!"

Cory shook his head. "No, no. You have to show me something first." He looked into her stupid eyes. "Show me." He twirled his hands around his shirt buttons. "Show me, then you get your baby."

She stood up, pushing her long hair from her face, motioning for him to follow her, deeper into the woods.

After a hundred yards of tramping, she turned around, gesturing with both small hands at a tree trunk, pitiful eyes glued to the doll in his hands. "Garchoo charit!"

Cory looked over at the tree trunk.

"Gart! Gart."

A large, eight-legged spider, black and brown, slow-crawled head first down the rough bark, to a green niche at the base of the trunk, where in a spread of gray roots, a tablespoon of rainwater lay.

As Cory watched, the spider hung its front end over the tiny pool of rainwater, stretching its horizontal maw to the pool's surface, pulling up water.

"Gart!" She stood up, confident, demanding with her hands the doll.

"No, that's not what I meant."

Cory held the doll out to her.

As she reached for it, all caution gone, he slapped a handcuff around her right wrist, slapped the other steel circle around the base of a strong sapling.

"Cark!"

He pushed her on her back, hands finally able to touch her body.

"Cark!"

She yanked on the metal tether of the handcuff, but couldn't get loose.

Cory threw the front of her long, white dress up over her face, exposing her bare legs, blonde pubic hair.

Held her down with a forearm across her throat. As she dumbly screamed to the sunlit treetops, he raped her.

Afterwards, he rose off her, wiping the length of his cock with two tissues.

He left her handcuffed to the sapling, the naked doll, abandoned, just out of her reach, her stretching fingertips, for hours after dark, trying to touch the hard beige plastic of the doll's left fingers, but there was always that last inch of space between real and plastic beyond the most desperate stretch.

꩜

The next morning, Cory got dressed as he always did, walked out to the kitchen, blinking to hide his nervousness, but there was his mother as always, on the phone.

School went as it always did. No police car out front, no teacher came to his classroom during the day, asking him to go to the principal. At night, when he arrived home, there were no police cars out front. His mother was on the phone. Gave him a wink.

Weeks went by. Cory stayed out of the woods, just in case.

Sometimes, at dinner, if his mother served something good that was easily carried, like a beef patty, he fantasized about dropping it in a towel in his lap when his mother's back was turned, then bringing the beef patty to the little girl after dinner. He was sure she'd like it. But he knew he'd never do it, because criminals always return to the scene of their crime.

A month after he had last seen the little girl, he got tired of watching TV one Tuesday night, it was just stupid repeats, so he decided to go to bed.

He stopped at the hall bathroom to pee, brush his teeth. Looking in the medicine cabinet mirror as he brushed, he realized he was close to crying. He flipped up the light by his bedroom door, eyes hot.

His bedroom was bigger than his mother's, although it didn't have as much furniture.

Staring in through his bedroom window was the little girl.

Her long, middle-parted hair, her sad, sickled mouth.

"I can't help you any more. I'm sorry." He pulled the shade

down. Plodded over to his bed, face crumpling, got in fully-dressed, pulled the sheets over his head.

❦

The next evening, after dinner, at about the same time as the previous night, he went to his room, to see if the little girl was outside again. His window was open.

"Ma, did you open my window?"

His mom, still in the kitchen, leaned her upper body out into the hallway, talking on the phone, holding a drink. "It's my son. No, hon."

Cory stood in the center of his room, turning around, looking at the blank walls, the magazines and clothes on the floor.

If she were in his room, the only places she could be hiding would be in his closet, or under his bed.

His closet door was ajar. Had it been before?

Open window, open closet door.

Frightened, acting quickly, before he had time to think, he pushed the door closed, leaned his palm against the door until he heard it click.

He backed away from the closed door, wondering if he had her trapped inside.

Would he hear the doorknob turning, while he had his back to the closet, to look under the bed?

He wasn't sure.

He walked over to his bed.

Got down on his hands and knees, lowered his head, keeping his eyes on the closed closet door, then quickly switched his head to glance under the bed. She was lying there on her stomach, in her long white dress, staring back at him. She reached a small hand out towards him.

Cory plowed across the carpet away from the bed, getting to his feet, running bent forward down the hallway.

His mom was still on the phone. "Ma! Ma. There's something under my bed."

"Hang on. What?"

He stood in front of her, hands clenched. "There's something under my bed."

"Can you hold on? I'm sorry. My son thinks there's a monster under his bed."

She walked down the hallway with him, Cory getting behind her dress as they entered his room.

She walked over to his bed. "Is it an animal?"

"No."

"What is it?"

His heart sank. What if he were wrong? What if he imagined it? "I don't know."

She gave him a look, went down on her knees.

Cory, standing behind her, watched her kneeling figure as she reached her right hand out, lifted the bedspread, looked under. "Honey, there's nothing here."

He got down on his knees, looked himself. Nothing.

"Maybe it's in the closet."

"What is it we're looking for?"

"I don't know."

She walked over to the closet door, opened it. Turned around to face him while her hand reached behind her, in the interior darkness, waving for the light chain.

"Did you have a nightmare?"

"No."

She pulled the chain down.

The interior of the closet jumped into light. Lots of hangers, some clothes, a few pairs of shoes on the floor, the swinging light chain.

"Go to sleep, hon. I have a lot of phone calls tonight."

After his mom left, Cory walked back over to his bed, got down on his knees, looked underneath. Nothing.

He changed into his pajamas, got into bed.

He woke after midnight. Peered from his sheets at the still-open closet door. But in the late gloom, couldn't make anything out. Realized there were small arms holding him from behind, around his ribs, hands clasped in front.

He rotated his head around on his neck, saw her face on top of his left shoulder.

He let out a scream, scrabbling across the mattress, slowed down by the weight of the little girl clinging to him from behind. Fell off the edge of the bed, the little girl on his back. Screamed, screamed for his mother.

The light went on.

"What is it?"

Cory crawled across the carpet, sobbing.

"What is it?"

"She was in bed with me! She was hugging me!"

His mother looked angry. "Cory…What are you talking about?" Behind her, the phone started ringing.

He tried explaining, spittle and babble, finally slowed down, took a deep breath. "It's the little girl from the woods. She was in bed with me."

His mother gave him an exasperated look. "Honey, that's impossible. That little girl is dead."

"No! She–"

"Honey? I have to get back on the phone. The little girl who hung out in the woods is dead. The police found her body a couple of weeks ago. Somebody handcuffed her to a tree, and she starved to death. They buried her in the paupers cemetery."

Cory gulped down his sobs. "It was her."

"It couldn't have been. She's dead. You just had a nightmare."

He seemed reluctant to give up the idea. "It was really creepy. Like that time my dad visited, and had to sleep in the same bed with me?"

The phone stopped ringing. His mother looked angry again. "That wasn't your dad. Look, I have to get back to the phone. You had a nightmare. Be a big boy and get back in bed. You're not still a baby, are you? I have diapers in my closet. Do you want to wear a diaper to school tomorrow?"

He lay in bed the rest of the night fully-dressed with the lights on, not sleeping, blue sheets down around his shoes.

Cory went to school the next day even though he had gotten very little sleep. He didn't want to be in the house.

He fell asleep during Ethics class. When he woke up, with a start, the teacher was shaking his shoulder. "So what would you do, Cory? Would you keep driving at full speed to avoid a certain death, or would you slam on the brakes to avoid hitting the baby?"

"What?"

He heard sniggers. Looking around, he saw the other seated boys in the rows and aisles, even the weakest ones, staring at him, for the first time ever daring to laugh at him.

The mustard yellow school bus dropped him off half a mile from his home.

He walked the last half mile looking down at the black pavement, school books dangling from a red rubber strap around his right wrist.

His mother was already home.

She was seated at the kitchen table, a big, dark-haired man drinking a beer from the bottle.

"Hi, honey!"

Cory looked at the man, who was watching Cory over the upraised bottom of his beer bottle.

She didn't get up to hug him. "Hi, ma."

"This is Brad."

"Hey, Cory!"

"Hi."

"Brad's gonna be spending the night."

"Yeah?"

"I told Brad about the nightmares you've been having? So he's volunteered to sleep with you tonight, just like your dad would if he were still around, to make sure you get a good night's sleep."

Brad put his empty beer bottle down on the kitchen table.

"That's okay."

Brad pushed his chair back. Stood up. He was a lot taller than Cory. "No problem, chief. Want a drink?"

Cory looked at his mother. "I was gonna go out for a little while."

Brad pinched the bridge of his nose. "I'll bet you're a scotch man. You like scotch, Cory?"

"Ma, I was thinking maybe I'd go outside, just for a little while. It's still light out."

Brad turned around from the kitchen counter with both big feet planted solidly, wide apart, on the vinyl floor. He had a bottle of scotch in one hand, an empty glass in the other. "Hey! I'm offering you a drink."

"No thanks."

"I'm treating you like a man. Have a drink."

"I'm not thirsty."

Brad shrugged his big shoulders. "Maybe you're not grown up enough to drink. You want some milk, Cory? I could put it in a baby's bottle for you, warm it up on the stove."

"I'm not a baby."

"I didn't think so. You're tall for your age." Brad poured scotch into the glass, both of them watching it rise until it was six inches tall. Held it out to Cory. "Don't be a fucking sissy. Have a drink with us."

Cory accepted the drink, put off by the fact he could feel the warmness of Brad's hand on the glass.

"Brad here bought me a beautiful new dress, Cory. It's tourquoise. It goes with my hair."

"Yeah?"

"C'mon, chief! Bottoms up."

Cory looked at his mother. "Is it okay for me to drink this?"

His mother put her hand behind her back. "Of course it's okay! C'mon, drink it up. Most boys your age, they'd be honored to be served scotch in their own home, with their mother watching."

Cory closed his eyes, gulped some of the drink. He gagged at its heat.

Brad reached over, gave a light punch to Cory's shoulder. "There's my man!"

Cory put the half-empty glass down on the kitchen table. "I can sleep by myself. That was just a nightmare I had. I'm okay now."

Brad stood in front of him, watching him. "That a fact?"

"Yeah."

"Nothing wrong with being scared at night. A lot of weird things happen at night."

"What?" Cory raised his right hand to his eyes, flexing his fingers.

"You okay, chief?"

Cory rubbed his hand across his forehead.

Brad cracked his knuckles under the overhead light, really loud. "You look tired, partner."

Cory staggered in a small, backwards circle.

Cory's mother stood up from her chair, putting Cory's right arm over her shoulder, leading him down the hallway. "Just sleep, honey. You don't have to be worried. Just sleep through it, and that way, it never happened."

Cory felt himself being laid down on his bed by his mother, his shoes lifted up onto the mattress, his sheets pulled up around him, a kiss placed on his forehead.

He scooted over on the mattress so he was as far away from the side of the bed Brad would sleep on as possible. His scrunched body only occupied about a fifth of the mattress surface.

He started praying, fumbling the words.

He looked groggily over his shoulder. Brad was standing in the doorway. He stood there for a long, long time.

Morton Street travels long and flat into Hargrove County, past tilted mailboxes, the straightness of the street ending fourteen miles in, at an isolated cul-de-sac.

One-story houses, built eighty years ago, sit around the cul-de-sac, five of them, far back from the circle of black pavement.

Beyond the cul-de-sac, nothing but woods, deep and dense, full of fallen trees, brown puddles, bird cries.

Within those woods, lives a little boy.

The parents and children on the cul-de-sac have seen the little boy in the distant criss-cross of branches.

Police have been called out, more than once. The officers return from the woods with muddy shoes, mosquito bites, but no little boy.

The story about the little boy is he once lived in one of the five houses around the cul-de-sac, although no one is sure which house, since ownership changes almost yearly, and while he lived in that house, one night his father stood in his doorway for a long, long time, then went inside his bedroom, pulled down his blue sheets, and raped him.

The story is he fled to the woods, in grief.

The story is he was nine years old when he was raped.

The story is he wanders through the woods, and has for several years, and that as he wanders, he holds up in his small right hand a bottle of green perfume.

The story is he no longer speaks English, but instead talks in a guttural language, of his own invention.

No one knows if any of this story is true. All anyone knows is he's a little boy, and instead of living in a house, like the rest of us, he lives in the woods.

The Kylesku Trow

Stefan Pearson

How long Morgan had been unconscious was difficult to say. Long enough to be dragged into the tunnel, and definitely long enough for the wound on the side of his head to have thickened into a matted blood clot. In the darkness it was impossible to estimate time in anything but abstract terms. He could feel and smell excreta caked onto his naked legs but it was perfectly possible he'd fouled himself when he'd been knocked out and didn't prove how long he'd been hanging there. Perhaps he'd been awake before? ... a shuffling in the darkness ... a clang ... but there was no way of telling whether the noises were real or just hallucinations excavated from the bedrock of his concussion. He measured time in hurt alone.

There'd been a cyclist. On Kylesku bridge. In the middle of the road, crumpled over his bike, panniers strewn across the tarmac. Morgan was driving home from a lodge meeting and had dropped John-Angus off in Badchal minutes before when his headlights picked out the prostrate figure by the roadside. He'd pulled up and stepped quickly from his car. The rest was hazy, but somehow, as he'd bent over, there was a sudden flurry of limbs, a fire in the side of his head, and an explosion of white light. For some reason, as he'd lost consciousness, he'd smelt stovies. Then there was darkness.

A camping light, on the floor, in the middle of the corridor. He blinked. A jumble of shapes lay scattered across the concrete and piled up against the walls...shelves, a row of car seats, plastic ice boxes, the canopy of a tent forming a makeshift partition and, dominating a space in the centre of the concrete floor, a camp stove and gas bottle, pots and pans: camping gear mainly. Hanging from the wall on an iron hook was a twisted mountain bike.

"Hello?"

What the fuck was going on? Who'd done this to him? What did they want? He shivered, teeth rattling in his skull. "'Hello!" He tugged at his chains but they were buried deep in the wall.

A thud resonated along the length of the corridor sending a shock-wave of tiny vibrations probing along the concrete walls and burrowing into his back. Morgan's heart kicked, guts coiling with fear.

Shuffling footsteps, from further up the corridor. Ten…fifteen …twenty steps…thirty…fifty or more, Morgan soon lost count. Wherever the door was, it wasn't close. A shape lumbered out of the darkness. A man, quite short, wiry, dressed in jeans and a checked shirt. A baseball cap. Dirty boots. The cyclist from the bridge? Morgan couldn't be sure. The man hadn't noticed Morgan was awake. From nowhere the rectangular flare of a TV leapt out of the darkness and filled the corridor with sound, music and voices. The man was sat on a large car back-seat, facing away from him and watching a portable television. Morgan almost laughed at the soft, embryonic voices echoing around the tunnel's walls. It sounded like a holiday programme… "Wish you were here?"

"Are you hungry?" A local accent. Definitely Sutherland.

"… Whu…what?" Bang. Awake. The stench of stovies, B.O. and a stale washing smell that reminded him of the folk his daughter shared a flat with at Uni. Morgan was ravenous. He felt like he hadn't eaten in days. Fear could wait. He was so parched it was a struggle to muscle his tongue to speech. "Must be. Do you want water? Nod."

"Yuh." He nodded, trying to stifle violent shakes. Could humans smell fear, the way dogs are supposed to? The man produced a bottle of mineral water. Morgan drank, swallowing hard.

"I have biscuits, tinned soup. Some beer?"

"Who the fuck are you?" he spat. "Just tell me what you want." A stalactite of watery drool hung from Morgan's bottom lip.

The man sighed, lowering his head, his face obscured by his cap. The peak was stained with finger grease. Bang, a punch to the stomach, hard enough to drive the wind from him and leave him doubled up gasping for breath. The man waited until he'd stopped gagging. Morgan's guts felt as if they'd been ruptured – his stomach ulcer flaring agonisingly.

"It's very simple. You don't speak unless I ask you to. Ever. Understand?"

Morgan nodded, stunned.

"Good. Now. Again. Are you hungry?"

"Yes!" The man came back with biscuits. Some cooked meat. Fruit. Morgan ate, and as he was being fed he took the opportunity to study his captor's face. Impassive was the only way he could describe it...bored almost. Small beady eyes, a slight kink in the left so that Morgan wasn't quite sure if he was looking straight at him or just beyond. Stubble – several days' growth – obscured what looked like a hair lip, but it was difficult to tell. Bad teeth, too...with breath to match. Was there really any need for Morgan to be naked? It was fucking cold in the tunnel. He resisted the temptation to ask for his clothes back. Better to wait, suss the situation out a bit. Get his bearings and try and find out what the fuck was going on.

A day or two had passed since the man first spoke: Morgan tried his best to judge time by the occasional snippet of television he was able to catch. He'd risked pleading with his captor only a few hours before and could now barely see through his right eye, which was swollen shut, the flesh around the socket distended and bruised. When he pushed at one of his bottom incisors it rocked. Still, the temptation to try and reason with the man was severe. He struggled to suppress the urge. What the fuck did this madman want with him? When Morgan wasn't woken by intermittent roars from above, or the fitful rumble that seemed to permeate the concrete for hours on end, rats nibbled at his toes and ankles. One had already paid with a broken back and lay in the darkness on the other side of the tunnel where he'd punted it.

"I have a riddle for you."

Morgan could smell his own shit wafting from the floor between his legs. The man took no notice, which, in some absurd way, he found comforting.

"A riddle?"

"Yes, a riddle."

"What kind of riddle?"

"A special kind of riddle. One that, if you guess correctly, will keep you alive. If you answer three riddles in a row, I'll probably let you go." Morgan's heart pounded. Even though it was absurd, that in all likelihood he'd die hanging here at this psycho's mercy, that there might even be a chance of reprieve overwhelmed him. He tried his best to suppress the gut feeling that the man had spoken the words before.

"And what if I get one wrong?"

The man smiled. "This is your first one. You've got till I come back to tell me the answer:

It starts bright and small, and is oft seen to fall;
it gets shorter and flatter and broader and fatter.
When it's narrow, it's swift as an arrow;
but when it's slow, it's bent like a bow. What is it?"

He repeated it once more and then he was gone. On his way beyond the lamplight and down the corridor, Morgan saw him lift the mountain bike from the wall.

When Morgan heard the metallic thud of the distant door a few hours later he already knew the answer. A river. It was a river. He shouted out into the darkness, but the words caught in his throat when he realised that the man was carrying something – a person, slumped across his shoulders. A thickly set middle-aged woman, the brown trunks of her stockinged legs poking out from beneath a valance of tweed skirt. What new horror was this?

The weeping didn't seem to bother their captor – he just turned the TV up, but it was driving Morgan mad. He'd caught her name in the beginning…Flora, or Fiona maybe…but before she'd even been pinioned to the wall the man had kicked her in the stomach for what must have been nearly a minute. After that she'd gone quiet. She whimpered as he heaved her into her chains a few meters away from Morgan on the opposite side of the tunnel. He'd never even noticed the other set of fetters before.

She wouldn't listen to him. She'd screamed at first, just like he had, begged, messed herself. And every time, the man would walk calmly over and punch her until she passed out. Morgan could barely remember what she'd looked like the day that he'd brought her in – her bloodied face was a lumpy homogenous wound. If only she'd listen she might survive.

On one occasion, when their captor had disappeared for a couple of hours, Flora had come to. She told Morgan she was a district nurse and lived near Scourie. She'd been on her way to make a house call at Drumbeg when she'd seen a cyclist lying in the road half way across the bridge. Morgan found her hard to understand. Her face was a carbuncle of swollen flesh and scar tissue, and her words were badly garbled, interspersed with sobbing and whimpering. He tried to comfort her: told her about the riddles, and that she shouldn't talk unless the man told her to. She nodded, wept, and asked Morgan to turn his head away when she pissed. He knew she'd die before he did.

"In a marble hall, white as milk,
lined with skin as soft as silk.

116

Within a pool crystal-clear,
a golden apple doth appear.
No doors there are to this stronghold,
yet thieves break in to steal its gold. What is it?

"Breathe a single word to her and I'll slice off one of your balls."
He turned to face her: "You've got until this film's finished." He
nodded towards the TV. The sound was too low for Morgan to
make out what it was. Just for good measure, the man pulled one
of Morgan's teeth out with a pair of pliers.

By the time the credits began to roll, Morgan knew the answer;
for the entire length of the movie he'd been lost in thought, his
mind blitzkrieging from one tangent to another, tongue probing
the bloodied socket in his gums. The pain helped him focus. He'd
always been quite good at lateral thinking, usually had a stab at The
Scotsman's cryptic crossword. It was a question of discipline. As
soon as he'd realised the answer, he tried to whisper it across the
tunnel to Flora, but either she hadn't heard him or she wasn't even
conscious. It was impossible to tell. Morgan didn't dare whisper
any louder – at one point the man got up out of his seat and stared
at him, the blade of a knife flickering in the light from the TV. A
trickle of urine seeped down Morgan's leg, his balls clawing back
up into his trunk. The answer was an egg. Morgan was certain Flora
wouldn't know the answer.

She didn't. Each bite of the cleaver sent sanity scurrying from
Morgan's brain. He screwed up his eyes, but could still hear...still
smell! He'd run out of tears long ago and burning bile stuck in his
throat.

The psycho disembowelled Flora. He'd dispatched her with a
blow to the forehead. Before Morgan could even scream, the
woman was dead, her body juddering like some spastic marionette
against her chains. Morgan retched and sagged.

It took the man almost an hour to completely render Flora
down, methodically gutting, skinning and stripping the flesh from
her bones. When he'd finished he walked casually past Morgan and
smiled at him, carrying the black-red bulk of Flora's limbless trunk

in his arms. A white offal-filled polythene bag yawed obscenely in her empty stomach cavity. Morgan retched again, his mind spiralling into oblivion. When his captor returned a few minutes later he was empty handed.

Days…for the past three days or so – it was impossible to tell – Morgan hadn't eaten. Almost a week had passed since Flora had been dismembered and only the telltale stains marring the wall were a testament to her presence. But Morgan knew in his bones that the mealy smell that emanated from the man's cooking was more than just stock. He'd refused his stew every time it was offered.

"Look pal, you won't get any food or water again if you don't take some stew. It's good for you!"

A grimy spoon was held beneath Morgan's face. The smell set his stomach to a primitive grinding. He refused again and received a kick in the balls. Twice this week his shit had been black, and lumps of coagulated tissue had spat from his cock when he pissed. Morgan wondered how much longer he could go on like this? Which would take him first: hunger, insanity, despair, or bloody murder? Anything was preferable to this. He already felt as if his skin was hanging off, flesh giving ground to his bones.

Morgan agreed to eat some stew for another riddle. But the truth was he was hungry, so incredibly hungry that when the man offered to exchange another riddle for some stew, Morgan's desperation was apparent. Minutes later of course, he was copiously sick. He knew he'd just eaten Flora.

"Okay then, here comes your next riddle. Excited? I can tell you are." Morgan worked his lips unconsciously – he'd ceased to notice how bad he smelled. He felt like he had an abscess where the tooth had been pulled. "Here goes:

I sow seed that cannot grow,
in furrows where none may go;
My crop is used to season
though I oft plant it without good reason;
Without a keel but with a prow of steel,
I navigate through the water;
In my wake, your journey will be shorter.
What am I?"

He gave Morgan until the second German biker was finished to answer. Morgan hadn't even noticed if the tourists had got theirs right, so intent was he on his own. He'd even stopped wondering why his captor allowed him such a long time in which to figure his riddles out, when the two holidaymakers had been dispatched the same evening they'd appeared. Morgan was gumming a particularly tough piece of meat – he had only a scattering of teeth left – when the answer hit him. For some reason he was reminiscing about the journey back from his daughter's halls of residence when he'd driven down to Dundee to pick her up for the Christmas holidays. They'd been stuck behind a gritter for nearly three hours. Morgan almost wept when it dawned on him. His whooping roused the man from his chair.

"A snowplough! It's a snowplough! One more, one more. Give it to me, please. I'm ready."

"Not yet. Soon, but not yet. Are you hungry?" The man smiled. Morgan nodded. He was regaining a little weight, but his arms were still matchstick-like and the wounds on his wrists were slowly working their way up towards the base of his thumbs.

Morgan was no longer sure what the outside world looked like, and found the rectangular flare of the television more and more disorientating and unreal. These days, if he stared at it for too long he began to feel sick and afraid. Night and day were been replaced by roaring-time and silence-time, both of which seemed about the same. And Morgan waited. Waited for the final riddle. The riddle that would open the door. Eventually his patience was rewarded.

"Ready for your last riddle, Morgan?" It was the first time the man had called him Morgan, and he was momentarily taken aback. "Morgan". It sounded absurd. The word buzzed mantra-like inside his skull, rattling there, repeating itself over and over. He could see his captor's mouth moving in front of him, speaking, forming words, but was incapable of distinguishing them anymore. Perhaps he was finally insane? The man's words washed over him, each syllable an ablution, cleansing him, freeing him. Was this the final riddle?

A sudden explosion of white-hot pain. Morgan's claws gouged into his captor's face, fingers finding soft tissue – an eye maybe. His thumb hung simian-like where he'd wrenched it from its bindings. He yanked free his other hand feeling bones pop and grind. It too found the flesh of his tormentor's face. The man staggered back, blinded and screaming. Morgan heard him crash heavily to the floor, tripping on something.

Within seconds he'd wrenched his foot free from its metal cuff. The pain was excruciating but liberating too. Torn skin flapped at his ankle. Releasing the other foot brought a zodiac of tiny white flares behind his eyes, delicate bones concertinaing under the pressure. Morgan dragged himself away, out of the radius of the Tilly-lamp, into the dark and whatever lay beyond. He tried to stand but his legs buckled under him. As he entered the shadows, he suddenly remembered how he'd always scoff at hapless murder victims on TV shows, or the teen meatloafs that would end up diced and despatched like so much kindling in the dumb horror movies his youngest daughter would rent from the video store in the village. He was determined not to become one of them. The more distance he put between himself and the howling madman the better. There were no other considerations.

The screams receded. Surely the corridor wasn't much longer?

"Bastard...Bas...tard! I'll sl-uh-ice your fucking face off when I catch you!" A silhouette. Ten, maybe fifteen yards away. "You'll eat your own face! Do you hear me!" A long hard shadow hung in the murderer's grip. Torchlight swept the floor nearby. "Where are you? You can't escape from me here. Why do you think I didn't kill you before now, eh?"

Morgan's heart was close to bursting, adrenaline shunting him forward.

"Why do you think I didn't kill you?" The figure seemed to be limping slightly, dragging one of his feet. "You're like me... Don't you see? You're like me Morgan!"

But Morgan scrambled on, like some prehistoric fish questing forward from one pool of darkness to the next. The torchlight swept the concrete ahead of him. His captor screamed obscenities limping close behind.

The corridor went on forever. Morgan felt the last of his energy bleed away. It was a matter of seconds now. The torchlight played closer and closer with every sweep. Morgan's hand touched something soft in front of him. Something cold and pliable. Like flesh.

"Thought you could hide did you Morgan?" his tormentor said as the light came to rest on Morgan's shoulders. Morgan turned and saw him step deliberately towards him, a matter of feet away. Morgan didn't bother to turn over. Let him do it here, face to the ground. He had no desire to see the man gloat. At that moment the beam swept over the object Morgan had found himself pressed up against. A body...lots of bodies, it was impossible to estimate from the jumble of rotting limbs, heads and trunks that lay heaped on the ground around him. Morgan was amazed he hadn't noticed the stench.

"Come on then you...sick fucker! Finish me! At least you won't have to carry me here to dump me!"

"You could have joined me Morgan. You don't realise how close you were. A few more weeks. A couple more killings. You didn't even hear the riddle did you Morgan?"

Bizarrely Morgan felt that somehow this meant something, something vital. He heard the man step closer, planting one foot on either side of him. It was at that moment that Morgan spun, and with every last ounce of his strength, brought the severed arm up and round in a powerful arc until the point of the jagged wrist bone embedded itself to the elbow in his captor's belly.

How long Morgan had been unconscious he didn't know. But when he woke again the blood that had gathered in a black pool around the stuck body was thick and congealed. Morgan pulled out the dead man's wallet and an enormous bundle of keys. John Marcus MacKay. He'd worked for the council maintenance depot.

Morgan picked the torch from the ground and wiped the blood from the lens. A few yards away an aluminium ladder led upwards towards a manhole in the ceiling of the tunnel.

The climb to the surface was torturous, the pain searing from his dislocated thumbs and broken foot threatening to topple him back to the ground time and again. But Morgan persisted, resting after each step, clinging to the ladder like some pupating larva. Patience was something he'd learnt. Morgan found the right key, pushed open the manhole and clambered out.

The wind was deafening and the lashing rain threatened to flay the loose skin from his bones. Morgan staggered to his feet, raising his face to the storm. It was night on the bridge and pale moonlight shone on the water far below from between ruptured clouds. He was at once exhilarated and terrified. Reborn.

Two searing pinpoints of white light sped towards the bridge. There was nowhere for Morgan to run. Nowhere to hide. Terror seized him. He was blinded by it.

Charlie Dunkeld was probably driving a little faster than he should have been, but for some reason a storm always made him drive that wee bit harder than normal. It was a bad habit, reckless even, but satisfying all the same. He only just slammed on his brakes in time when he saw the creature curled in a foetal ball in the middle of the road. His bumper stopped inches from it, so close in fact that he couldn't even see it properly until he got out of his car. Charlie's legs gave a little twinge as he stepped into the squall.

It was a man. If you could call it that. What the fuck had he been through! Where? Charlie gave a little boke, spitting a trickle of sick from his mouth. He set to heaving the figure into the passenger seat of his car. He wound his window quickly down inside. The man stunk. He moaned, a pathetic whimpering, like some mal-treated collie, but offered no resistance. Charlie put the car in gear when the creature looked up at him from beneath a raft of matted, stinking hair:

"Weight in my belly,
trees on my back.
Nails in my ribs,
feet do I lack… What am I?"

The Bloom Of Decay

Patricia MacCormack

Persephone (persefene); In Greek mythology, the daughter of Zeus and Demeter, Goddess of agriculture and fertility. Abducted to the Underworld by Pluto, allowed to return to the Earth for part of each year, identified with the Roman Proserpine.

Eloise froze, a combination of breathlessness and repulsion. The man, if indeed that's what he was beneath the filth, had just wrenched the ear from a nurse and held it high as a victorious prize. When she'd arrived at the casualty ward all had been silent, as if in sleep the tenants of the southern memorial had ceased to be alive. Eloise had spent three quarters of an hour alone and fearful, concentrating on breathing. She had assumed asthma attacks constituted some kind of understated emergency, but until the man had appeared no-one was visible, in or out of the offices and makeshift casualty rooms. Now, however, it was a different visage entirely. Two nurses, one almost pubescent in her youth, were desperately (and hopelessly) attempting to contain the maniac flailing of the half hobo, half clown which assailed them. The side of the young nurse's face ran rivers of sticky blood, but she seemed not to notice the pain, more intent on retrieving the coveted ear. Suddenly the large overhead fluorescents flickered and then died, the death inspiring the demise of the commotion. Eloise had all but forgotten about her lack of breathing, as the two nurses, almost in slow motion, flew through the corridor, slamming, one against the vast whitewashed wall, the other into an enormous steel door. Eloise immediately wondered how she had seen all this beneath extinguished fluorescents. She gradually lifted her eyes to where the man stood. He was a towering titan, almost filling the entire tunnel of the corridor, and, most extraordinarily, gave off, from every pore of his partly exposed flesh, an ethereal, phosphorescent light. It ran over his skin like glowing slugs and licked his nostrils and mouth in smoking wisps. His massive, sunken eyes were glazed over, like a drugged rodent, so when he lowered his gaze to where Eloise cowered, he seemed not to register her, simply to know she was there. When she could finally tear her eyes from his, Eloise saw something far more frightening. The man's intestines hung in oily coils from a wide opening in his lower abdomen, and surgical clamps grasped them in two places. A clear rubber glove poked out from beneath a fold of multi-layered skin. Various thick, small tubes protruded here and there, in opaque blues and reds. These were not the only colours which assaulted Eloise's eyes. She had never realised how incredibly colourful the internal body was. Deep, wet cobalts contradicted offensively bright yellows, buried beneath slippery crimsons. Suddenly the brightness of the entrails was assaulted by a massive cascade of dark, dry red and brown flowers which emerged from the abdominal orifice. They made a crisp cavalcade as they spewed out onto the grimy tiled floor. Eloise could not fathom that from the writhing life of this man's insides had come the incarnation of the death of spring's bounty. Looking up, the pasty white of the man's face seemed necrophic in comparison with the kaleidoscope of images Eloise had just witnessed. It seemed also closer. He stood now over her like a suffocating predator, but instead of devouring her he took her hand, opened it and placed the stolen ear in her shivering palm. "Persephone," he whispered.

Eloise was a sensible woman. Indeed she had just metamorphosed from child to adult. She had no fear, no paranoia. She fervently consumed all forms of horror, film, literature. Thus she was armoured against and fully prepared for any unexpected occurrence. Which of course was hardly necessary considering the control she had over her life, being such a sensible woman. This is why her dreams troubled her now so very much. She was plagued, these last few nights, with visions of a clown faced man methodically turning himself inside out. She knew that in his visceral per-formance he was attempting to communicate with her, make her explicitly aware of something. And she wanted desperately to trans-late this surreal message, because occurring simultaneously with these dreams was a viral infection of growing, inexplicable horror. Eloise had sat in bed the night before last in a cold fever, scared to move in case they saw her, or heard her, or smelt her. Who or what "they" were she had no idea, but the previous evening had seen her plead to stay with her sister, and though the dream remained, the cold fear which sunk in her abdomen vanished. Until today when she returned home. And now she sat huddled on her couch, clutching hot, sweet tea, wishing the fat cushions would grow over her and swallow her in their protective padding. She sighed angrily and chastised herself vehemently for allowing such a non-entity as fear (fear of something which she could not name and therefore did not exist) to paralyse her. She would go to bed, and would make as much movement and noise as she desired.

Eloise clasped her book and held her breath, and listened. She had been sitting in bed in exactly this pose for eighteen minutes. The same line of her novel had been perused forty-six times, yet she couldn't remember what it said. All she could think about is what she was, or wasn't hearing coming from the roof. Something was between the roof tiles and the beams. Actually she figured there was more than one of them. But they were slight. They moved lightly, which is why she had to strain to hear them. She pic-tured them in her mind as emaciated, monkey-like creatures with the pointed ears and viciously sharp faces of Boschian demons. She knew that they made just enough noise to torment her peace of mind, but not enough to entirely convince her that she wasn't being paranoid, and slowly going mad. The noises didn't really tell her much though. All good and well if they actually were up there, but what were they doing? "Enough of this crap," thought Eloise. She got back to the re-read line, and convinced herself for all of five minutes that there were no noises to be heard. When her frayed nerves finally bound themselves up and she fell asleep, her dreams offered many horrific suggestions as to what the creatures were doing, up there, in the vast chasm of her roof.

Eloise walked to the railway station the next morning wrapped in a blanket of raw exhaustion. She assumed the reason that her vision seemed so uncertain was due to this exhaustion. The trees which lined her street seemed to wither, consumed by decay, whenever she looked straight at them. Yet when she turned her gaze away, the corner of her eye registered the leaves and buds re-blooming, as if they died in fear of her eyes seeing their abundance of fertility. This hallucination seemed particularly poignant when Eloise visited her doctor the next week. The inability to sleep, the extreme paranoia and what Eloise considered aural hallucinations had inspired Cal at work to bug her relentlessly to see someone, so she had made an appointment with her doctor. Eloise reluctantly went for tests, lots of tests, and today was the day of revelation. Some revelation. Dr. Hullser could give her no information on what she wanted to know, but plenty on what she didn't. "I hadn't seen you since last Christmas, Eloise," Dr. Hullser explained in the voice doctors always use just before they tell you the results of tests you never gave permission for. "So I took the liberty of taking a few extra swabs with your Pap smear." "Charming," thought Eloise. She could feel, low in the pit of her belly, that the doctor was going to tell her something which she didn't want to hear. "I know you're very young, and the gravity of the matter may not hit you for quite a few years, but...well, there is no subtle way to say this, Eloise, you're infertile." Eloise went numb. Not for any of the reasons she should have gone numb for. She didn't think about the baby she would never bear, or feel incomplete in her femininity. She felt as if she had lost all protection against the creatures in the roof, and all defense against the visitations from the clown-faced man. He would feel the true impact of this. He would rejoice. It was like her infertility had paved the way for all these horrific inex-plicable forces to penetrate and devour her entirely. But perhaps this revelation would destroy her inability to divine the meaning behind the dreams? A thousand conceptions bore fruit in her mind, and none of them had anything to do with the fact that she would never be a mother. "Strange I know, considering your mother's almost excessive fertility." Eloise could vaguely hear Dr. Hullser. She could, however, hear the tauntings of a myriad of nightmarish, charnel creatures, eager in expectant anticipation. All gathering around the fugue of her house. All gathering around the fugue of her head. Eloise fought to contain the fear-inspired pressure which forced the contents of her stomach up her throat. She was not, however, successful in this. Strangely, Eloise felt exceptionally alone in her antediluvian predicament; she loathed any outside interference or penetration. As she sat in nauseous fear in her bed that night, she was almost ashamed of what was happening to her. Her telephone hung from the receiver, and she wholly despised the concept of a caller at the door. What could she say to any such caller? That she couldn't talk at the moment because the creatures in her roof may or may not be making noises which she was trying to hear? Oh yes, that would sound just fine. And the brief relief of reality that company would provide would make the sounds seem all the more insane when she returned to bed. So, through self-imposed exile from reality, Eloise sat preserved in an environment which, at best, could be called unsane anxiety. What could she hear now? The regular, amorphic rumblings had seemingly moved across the roof-beams to directly above her bed. Her bowels became loaded with terror. "All in my mind, all in my mind, all..." An enormous, heavy tumbling travelled down the through space between the plasterboard dividing wall next to her. Eloise felt the acidic gall hurl up her gullet. It was a pig. They had thrown a pig down the wall. A sow to be exact. A suckling sow. Eloise couldn't see the sow but she knew innately that that's what it was. It was between her walls, its teats ripe and burdened with milk. It was, by the sounds of it, snuffling about among the cobwebs, stuffing and debris, probably crunching on a spider or six-legged beast. She felt sorry for the poor, cramped creature. She knew the creatures were squatting above her, in the roof, waiting for some reaction from her. Eloise wondered whether she should be afraid of the pig, as she was of the creatures. Was it just an ordinary pig? Or had they done something to it, to make it like them? A moist stain appeared next to her on the wall. It seeped larger and larger. It was coming from the pig. Eloise bent over from her bed and wiped her finger along it. She put her finger first to her nose and then to her tongue. It was milk. Something was suckling the sow. The silence in the room was thick as treacle as Eloise strained to hear what it was that suckled the pig. The shock came when a piercing, curdled squeal shattered the emptiness. The milk stain seeped dark crimson. It stained the wall, flowering like a morbid Rorschach down the inches to the carpet. Eloise jumped out of bed, and urgently pushed the frame away from the wall, suddenly possessed by the desire to preserve the bed from the taint of the pig's blood. Eloise slept on the couch that night. She did not dream.

Eloise began to shed her skin three days later. It started on her palms, the soles of her feet and inside her mouth. Where she peeled the skin, the fresh layer beneath was white as clay. She felt repulsed looking into her mouth and seeing a white, parchment-dry cavern. Eventually even the rims of her eyes peeled to white, and the only colour which remained on her face was the moist green of her irises. She laughed at the irony of having eyes the colour of fertility and life, as she began to look less alive. She had to wear copious amounts of cosmetics to work, and only the most reticent of her co-workers did not comment on the fact that she looked like a drag queen or hideously over-painted china doll. If she wanted to wear a skirt Eloise had to first flail all the shedding sheaves of skin and then dust her legs with dark face powder. The easiest solution was to simply not go out, unless to work. But being at home made Eloise sick with anxiety, which in turn made her shed more. She could not help but laugh at her ridiculously surreal situation. "I feel like a snake," she thought. As she started to shed, so the dreams returned in glaring technicolour. Never before had the fire slash mouth of the clown-faced man stood before her so vividly. Never before had she felt so akin to this bizarre looking entity in her excessive pallor, almost desiring the crimson slash, almost allowing herself to be devoured by the dry white worm of a tongue and serrated rapier teeth. Eloise knew that the more she resembled the clown-faced man the more she would embrace him, and he her. And hopefully the less the creatures in the roof would torment her. Perhaps they would even reveal themselves to ease her wracked and flayed nerves. But perhaps not. Yes, definitely not. From her experience of them Eloise did not ever want to risk having to confront them. After the unknown (but obviously grim) fate of the sow, Eloise innately knew that the love of the creatures could easily be infinitely worse than their wrath. Still, essentially she desired neither. Eloise felt constantly nauseous with the expectation of their new games. Her revulsion towards the creatures lacked any thrill or unconscious yearning. She did not find them strangely exciting or their comings an indication of her unique value. She found them horrifying, and their being in her roof caused terminal aversion towards even being in her own home. Her bed was a pit which closed in around her each night and caressed her with tendrils of dread. The nine feet between the bed and ceiling stagnated thick with the promise of some unnameable atrocity, waiting to fall down and smother her. Eloise's ordinarily quite unremarkable imagination wandered through labyrinths of potential tortures and fleshly phantasms. What alarmed her most was the idea that these creatures did not fulfil her visual expectation of them, that they were not demonic satyrs, but that they, like the clown-faced man, resembled her, in her new, unreal incarnation. For to be consumed by these monsters was a horror surpassed only by the thought that she was consuming them, absorbing them through wall and ceiling. The vulnerability of mind and nerve-endings at that time seemed a particularly ripe condition for embracing demonic influence. Perhaps the archaic notion of forced abduction by fantastic entities had been superseded by the transformation of the desired into the enemy. Seemed neat.

Eloise consumed these ideas endlessly as she haunted new environments. She found herself compelled towards places which previously had never even entered her realms of thought. The decayed country cemeteries drew her hypnotically. Here the dead may never have lived; even their vast generations had gone the same way. The rotted vegetation and tiny rodent corpses which littered these places intrigued her as much as the almost pagan slabs, bearing names so out of fashion they were now considered alchemic. The vast, unfurled roots of the Olympian trees whipped momentarily out of the dust and curled deep back in as if they found something warm and delighting beneath the earth. The skeletal teeth and claws of hares and foxes chewed and scraped the dry soil, hanging on with longing to their precious makeshift graves. When she dozed against a tree here, Eloise dreamed nightmares which failed to scare her. Rather she felt like a matriarch of power in the phantasmagorical landscapes which assaulted her closed eyes. Similar reactions occurred when she visited the closed markets and wallowed bacchant in the rotted fruits and vegetables. She would loiter like a thief behind the great wooden gates until the excess produce was discarded, and proceed to writhe in and consume the worm-riddled pears, black tomatoes and every other form of repellent vegetation. Their colour and stench made Eloise feel more alive and sensory than she looked. Afterwards she would sneak home consumed with a similar guilt she used to feel after sex in her teenage years. Then Eloise was convinced that she deserved to be tormented by the creatures, and expelled her guilt in the evening with fear. The clown-faced man seemed excited by her newly awakening urges, he encouraged her in her dreams to be respondent to all which lived and grew only in anticipation of its death and subsequent corruption. He loved her love of the rotting and deceased, even though she found it repugnant. Eloise more and more grew uncomfortable being around the fruitful, robustly healthy, or growing. When Cal practically begged her to escort him to the bi-annual office party, a formally dressed but rather lively, often embarrassingly wild affair, she agreed but regretted it immediately. It was obvious the invitation was offered out of pity and concern rather than affection. She took over two hours in her dimly lit bathroom attempting to paint some life onto her now quite surreal complexion, but she ended up painfully aware of how strange she appeared. Though it was a cocktail party Eloise was forced to wear a man's suit, with high collar and gloves, to conceal the remainder of her shedding skin. She looked like a nightmarish ventriloquist's dummy. She could hardly blame Cal for the look of disgust his face failed to conceal when she greeted him at her door.

She knew she had made a big error of judgment in conceding to go. This conclusion was cemented when she arrived.

Though the guests were decorated exquisitely with baubles and paint, all Eloise could think about was the corruptive demise which awaited each person in the room, and how exquisite they would look then. She was shocked at these, her own thoughts, and attempted to involve herself in banal conversation in an attempt to exorcise them. It didn't work. Each time a flushed, luscious reveller spoke to her, Eloise became obsessed with the idea of his or her death. Somewhere in the back of her consciousness Eloise believed that this person's death would bring them into the possession of the realm of the clown-faced man, the creatures... and herself. To own, embrace and be lord over this person when they lived forever aroused in her a fervour she had only slightly grazed in her most memorable moments of passion. Sex was so transient, it relied on life to perform. Life itself was suspiciously unreliable. But there existed another world, where just to be animate was an almost unbearable climax. It was when these philosophies metamorphosed from thought to word that Cal suggested to Eloise it was time to go home. He declined coffee. The experience of the party convinced Eloise that she was rapidly losing her natural place in functional society. She almost began to crave the night terrors of the roof creatures. At least in their simple world of torture and torment she figured as a real entity. The more she went out now the less alive she felt. The remaining thread of belonging which tentatively held her to others was dwindling. It didn't have much life left in it. Neither did she by the way she was looking. Extraordinarily, however, she felt almost too alive. Every movement she made, from pouring her morning coffee to pulling the coverlet protectively around her at night seemed like a highly arousing physical accomplishment. These small satisfactions were made more acute in the darkness, she discovered, and consequently the blinds and curtains were nailed to the window frames. Eloise didn't know whether to scream joyously with revelation or sign her own committal papers. There was still enough normal humanity left in her to make her painfully aware of how unnatural her identity was becoming, and, worse still, how amazing it made her feel. Where the hell did this go? Was she to become a hermit? Well she wouldn't starve to death, seeing as the only food she could stomach now was mouldy, rotted fruit. She could just stock up, and continue eating the fetid food for years.

She could no longer stomach meat. Each time she saw a slab of animal flesh she was assaulted with images of its owner wandering aimlessly and eternally along the river Styx waiting for its leg or wing. She hoped the pig in her wall (which was, at this point in time, stinking up the entire house) had not been mutilated or de-limbed in any manner. Eloise was finally given an answer to her hermit dilemma when all the water in her house began to flow upside down. Her baths and showers ceased as a result of not being able to contain any of the water. It simply flowed from the faucet up to the ceiling and absorbed in there. It did not drip. Luckily all her sweat glands had dried when she began to shed her skin, so she didn't have to smell like the food she ate. She did, however, experience spells of dizzy disorientation, naturally enough, when she watched the water fly up to splash into the ceiling plaster, pool, and eventually disappear into some phantom drain. Eloise was now forced to recognise that she was a player in some bizarre conspiracy, or else she would have to believe herself entirely insane. The fact that she was still amazed at the goings-on gave her comfort. A mad person would probably not register sur-prise. As the gravity pull of liquids altered in her house, so too did the dwelling of the roof-creatures. They had migrated into her walls. This made Eloise frightened to leave the exact centre of any room. She became so paranoid, in fact, that she threw tape meas-ures across the floors of each room, diagonally from the centre, to ascertain precisely where she would be safest. But the mysterious thumping of the creatures altered with their change of environ-ment. Cooing and snickers had become audible through the thin plasterboards. Eloise couldn't decide whether this was a more or less benevolent portent. So she took no chances and ignored the noises as best she could. The creatures became increasingly diffi-cult to ignore. Since she chose to no longer leave her house, they chose to no longer leave her in peace. She found that they knew her name, but often chose to call her another strange, longer name. She couldn't remember ever hearing it before, but it didn't sound entirely alien. The voice they used when citing this alternate name was seductive and inviting, but her own was expressed with harsh malice and disdain. One morning, when she woke in her makeshift bed, in the middle of the lounge room floor, Eloise became aware of a number of dried flowers and grains, shafts of parched wheat and such, surrounding her. They had, it seemed by their deliberate arrangement, been left as some kind of bounty or offering. "Well, this is nicer than a slaughtered pig, I guess," thought Eloise. Each morning from then on a mass of new offerings appeared. Eloise began having to put them in the study to accommodate their vast quantity. The potent smell stifled her, and her head swam constantly with the perfume. Her malodorous fruits became welcome relief from the heady flowers. She could not throw them away, however. They belonged to her, and to treat them as expendable seemed as taboo as treating one's children or pets as such. So, despite their overwhelming mass and odour, Eloise lovingly found a new corner for each bundle and posy. Her house looked like some kind of wiccan temple.

Eloise awakened to a house shrouded in a winding sheet of lack. Three months had passed since any phenomenon, welcome or unwelcome, had insinuated itself in the dwelling. She had become used to the insane routine of her evolved world, and relished the questionable grasp she had on daily occurrences. The whispers, oblations, her new appetite, all comforted her. More than she realised. Because when they weren't there this one morning, Eloise came as close to madness as she was ever likely to go. She searched for the new flowers and seeds. She knew each bundle, its time of offering, its kindred sheaves. Though the fresh ones were always left by her bed, she thought (hoped) that perhaps the site had been altered. It had not. They were not there. She howled in rage and desolation. Her appetite came to her after five hours of squatting upon her mattress with glazed eyes. When she entered the kitchen, however, the glaze was rudely peeled from her pupils. There on the bench was a bounty of fresh, young fruit. She had no idea where the vines began, but it must have been somewhere ridiculously fertile, for the tendrils of green writhed like live electric cables, spewing out round, ruddy fruit of all description, many of which Eloise had never seen before, and certainly could not name. One species of vine alone was giving birth to this myriad of abundance. It did not impress Eloise.

She turned her gaze away and promptly retched an enormous amount of what could only be described as filthy river water. It amazed Eloise to see all this liquid coming from her body. It was the first indication of moisture her flesh had given in months. She could not return her eyes to the triffid vine. She was inspired to do something which, one day ago, would have been absolutely unmentionable. Eloise ran to the nearest wall, and thumped and pleaded for the creatures to respond to her. As her riot went unanswered, or unheard, she became unnaturally distressed. For the first time in an eternity she was alone. Hearing true silence. Her bowels had not moved in fifty-four days. They gave way. She fell to the carpet in fear and anger. Eloise woke some days later. Still alone. She had dreamt real dreams. Hollow, banal dreams, of longing for the world which first embraced her and had now forsaken her. She couldn't weep, for she had no means to produce tears. Her body just jerked spasmodically in hysteria. She felt such hunger for rot. The smell of the still-growing fruit vine was driving her mad. She had to have decay. Even if she created it herself. That was when the idea of the baby hit her.

Eloise returned home in darkness, clutching a bundle wrapped in brown paper. It had taken some serious deceptions and stealth, but she had received what she coveted. Thankfully, human infants didn't express fear and arouse pity as most mammal infants did. If this baby wasn't happy it just screamed, and that was enough to make you want to kill it anyway. Eloise took it into the study, placed it upon a bed of wheat ears, and left it. For fourteen days. It was dead when she fetched it, just as she had hoped. She had not killed it. Killing was against nature. It had simply died. She didn't know what exactly had finished it but, then, she didn't really care. It was dead now, and she could watch it corrupt, embrace it, possess it. It was a euphoric release from the repulsive fertility of that horrific vine. Each day the tiny corpse shrivelled and dried. Eloise left the heating on to emphasise the disintegration. The smell was like opium. She languished in it. Within weeks there were little of the features left. Just mysterious chunks of bursting flesh. The baby looked riper in decay than it ever did in life. The simple, passive experience of watching nearly overwhelmed Eloise. She had managed to create a tiny slice of the realm which had left her. She yearned for it even more strongly as she observed the infant. This yearning did not go unheard. The baby was soon finished and that is when he came.

Eloise woke in a fright from a deep, hibernative sleep. She had felt something cloying the room. She had felt suffocated. Her hair miraculously transformed, through fear, from black to flawless white as she opened her eyes and saw what stood before her. It was the clown-faced man. He towered, eight feet above her, and only when her eyes traced down his vast length did Eloise realize he stood in a long wooden boat. In a canal. Upon whose bank she lay. His eyes were glazed, black rat eyes, with a smoke of red fire beneath their glossy surface. He looked down towards her, but did not seem to be looking at her. The overcoloured slash of a mouth curled out, expelling thick, putrid breath. A serpent tongue emerged, tiny flies dancing upon its surface. She could hear the emphysaemic breathing of the man as he inhaled deeply, and hissed at her. "Persephone," he rasped. "I have come for you, Persephone." Eloise's face drained of blood. She gasped in horror. She was to escort this old god, this ferrier of the dead, to her new home. A very old home for many. An eternal home. He extended a hand towards her. Tiny fly larvae writhed in and out of suppurating breaks in the skin. The darkness caressed her lovingly. The realm had returned thousand-fold. Her clown-faced man was her new subject. One of many million. They would love her as only the dead could love. A frighteningly infinite love. Her eyes clouded over as she entered the boat. She felt a thousand hot, fetid breaths on the back of her throat. As the clown-faced man began to sluggishly manoeuvre the barge with his long pole of bone Eloise heard him whisper, "Persephone is dead. Long live Persephone."

Final Girl

Joe L Murr

The morning Krystal told me she was pregnant, one of the others killed Rod. Again. I forget exactly how. I wasn't downstairs with them. If I could ask them, I doubt they'd remember either. It'd be like asking you what you had for lunch four months ago.

Maybe one of them lopped off Rod's head with an ax. Maybe it was full bodily dismemberment with a chainsaw. Or maybe it was the time Corey found a novel use for the wood chipper, which I regret not having witnessed – the aftermath was spectacular. No, I'm quite sure that wasn't it. I'd remember it if that was the case. After all, that was the morning I found out I was going to be a father. It must've been some method we'd used hundreds of times by then: axe, chainsaw, rifle, pitchfork. It had all become much of a muchness, all that business of killing.

That morning, I woke up to see Krystal next to me in our bed. She was looking at me intently with those azure eyes of hers that were like shards of the sky. It was the look she often had when she wanted a seeing to in the morning.

"Mmm," I said, rolling over to her. "You randy little vixen."

"Stop it," she said and extricated my hands from her perfect breasts. "Not, like, in the mood, Gary."

"Oh. How about a Jerry Hall, then?"

"Not now. I've got something to tell you."

Then she told it to me.

I sat up. I stared at her. I muttered something inane.

"And, yeah," she said, "I'm sure."

That's when we heard the noise of the killing – a rifle blast, maybe, or a chainsaw revving up.

Neither of us paid it much attention.

"You're sure?" I said. "You're…"

"Yeah."

"Oh God, not now, not here."

"We've gotta find a way to get out of here soon," she whispered. "For the sake of the baby."

I groaned and flopped down onto the bed. "We've tried. We've tried everything already."

"I want our baby to grow up right."

Our baby. My baby. Fear pooled like cold oil in my guts.

"There's gotta be a way," she said, and capped it off with one of her beloved platitudes: "If you love me, you'll find a way."

Love her. No, I didn't love her.

I could barely stand her. All that she had in her favor was her body. The rest of her was simply not there. This was a trait she shared with the others, the vacuous others.

On that morning, the morning of the baby news, the impending bundle of joy morning, there were six of us in that house in the woods. Follow Krystal and me downstairs to meet the others. Down the creaky stairs, watched over by the black glass eyes of stuffed deer heads, and into the living room littered with the sentimental detritus of the house's former owners.

Here, meet the vacant others: Rugged Corey and muscular Brad and elfin Cherry with the sexy wide mouth and rocket-tits Tina. They were wearing tattered jeans or shorts and shirts spotted brown by bloodstains that hadn't come out in the wash. That's pretty much what all of us wore all the time. But they looked great in their rags. Say what I will about them, these jocks, these cheerleaders – these perfect youth always looked perfect.

I asked them what had happened and one of them pointed, grinning, at the door. Rod had come, with his machete in his gloved fist, and Rod had been killed. Again. I peered out at the body on the porch.

I sighed.

Then we did what we usually did. We dragged Rod into the pit in the backyard and set fire to him. Krystal nuzzled in close to me and muttered one of her clichés. I thought of how unfit she was to be a mother, of how terrified I was of the idea of being a father. We watched Rod's body burn for a while. His white mask bubbled on his deformed face. The pink tip of a tongue stuck out from between blackened teeth. The smell of his charring flesh mingled with that of burning plastic. It was like a barbeque in the shadow of a chemicals plant.

We turned away and returned to the house. We weren't jubilant. This was no victory. Rod would return, several days later, with his machete and his blank mask, to kill or be killed. Burning the body only gave us a longer reprieve. Without that extra effort, he would've risen in a matter of hours.

I think you're probably wondering why we didn't use that reprieve wisely and bugger off. Well, I'd best tell you how I got there. And that'll explain why we couldn't leave.

All I did was take a wrong turn.

I was en route from Orlando Airport to San Nascimento in a rented car. I was a traveling man, representing an Australian mining equipment company. So there I was, driving down unfamiliar roads, fuzzed out by jetlag and too many in-flight drinks and mulling over the almighty row I'd had with my wife just before my departure from Sydney. She wanted kids. I didn't. Somewhere between my resigned resolution to just give in to her demands, and my decision, some sixty miles later, to dump the cow, I'd turned off the main road. I backtracked. No worries. Thirty odd miles later, I'd concluded that maybe the best thing to do would be to start taking male contraceptives and plead infertility. And that's when I finally realized I was utterly lost. I'd ended somewhere off the map, deep in the woods, at that two-storey house overgrown with creepers. I remember pulling up in the yard: I saw the solitary tyre hanging off an elm on a frayed rope. I saw the dirty windows. I saw a beautiful face behind the panes: Krystal.

I got out, thinking she'd be able to direct me back onto the main road.

The front door opened. She stepped out and shouted, "Behind you!"

"What?" I said, leaning over the roof of the rented Ford.

Brad appeared next to her, a hunting rifle in his hand. He lifted it to his shoulder. I stood there, frozen.

"Duck!" she screamed.

I shouted, "Hey, I'll just leave, then, all right?"

"Duck, man!" Brad shouted. "Get the fuck down!"

It finally clicked: something bad was coming up at me from behind. I turned. I had a glimpse of a man dressed in fouled denim overalls and a blank white mask. He held a machete aloft. He was less than ten yards away, trundling towards me at a deliberate rate. I reeled back into the car and locked the door behind me. The rifle went boom and I peered over my shoulder, seeing nothing out there anymore, and then scrambled out of the passenger's side door.

"Stay there!" Brad shouted as he ran towards the car.

He disappeared from my view and I heard another shot.

I went around the car to where he stood.

"Dead again," Brad said, glancing at me, then at the corpse on the grass.

"This," I said, "has nothing to do with me. I'll just be leaving now."

"Sure, dude."

"Take me with you," Krystal said.

I took in her face and shapely body. "Certainly. Right, love, get in the car."

"See ya," Brad said.

We got in. I steered us down the dirt road through the forest. The way back seemed unfamiliar – endless – nothing but trees and shadows. The road just went on. And on. And on. I kept asking

Krystal questions but she just stared mutely ahead until, finally, she whispered, "He's not going to let us leave."

"Who?"

"Rod. The guy with the machete."

I stopped the car.

"He's like, undead, or something." She paused. "He just keeps coming back."

"Right."

It was getting darker already. Impossible. It was only four pm by my watch.

"Take us back to the house," she said.

"No."

"Turn around – then you'll see. How long have we been driving?"

"Too long."

"It'll take us maybe two minutes to return."

"Bull."

"Turn around," she said, staring out blankly. "You'll see."

A faint mist was rising. Faint tendrils wove between the trunks, phosphorescent in the murk.

"There's others," she whispered, "but they stay in the woods. They never come to the house."

"Others?"

"Things. In the woods." She gripped my lapels. "I'm serious. Take us back to the house now."

"Forget it." I shifted into first and turned the headlights on.

"Come on, please." She put her hand on my thigh. Her face was pale, sweaty. She smiled, lips clowngirl wide and trembling. "If you take us back, I'll, like, blow you, okay?"

"As much as I'd love to take you up on that, I have a very important business meeting tomorrow morning."

Her fingers found my zipper.

"Hey, stop that."

"I'm really good."

"I'm sure you are. But, the fact of the matter is, I –"

Something appeared in the headlights. Something squat and

powerful, like a bulldog running upright. It loped towards the car. I hit the brakes. Krystal squealed. Her fingers tightened on my crotch. I squealed. The bulldog thing bounded onto the hood of the car. For a second I stared into its face, all its pale flesh and serrated teeth. It raised one of its arms. I shifted into reverse. A clawed paw hammered into the windshield. Glass spiderwebbed and sagged. I hit the gas. The car surged backwards. The bulldog thing tumbled away. I spun the wheel – I figured there was enough space for a three-point turn. The car veered. I didn't brake soon enough – the rear bumper crunched into a tree. I shifted into first and gunned the accelerator. We bounced forwards. In the rearview mirror, I saw the bulldog thing getting up. In the woods, other creatures like it came into view.

I drove as fast as I could.

I kept glancing back, certain that the bulldog things would pursue us. I didn't see any of them, but I knew they were there, flanking us, waiting for their opportunity.

A minute or two later, just like Krystal had said, we were back at the house. The soft glow of oil lamps pooled on the downstairs windows.

"We're safe now," she whispered. "For now. They don't come to the house. Only Rod does."

They were waiting for us in the living room, the vacuous others. Introductions were made. Muscular Corey and rugged Brad and perky-tits Cherry and luscious Tina – photogenic and disheveled in their ripped clothing, quivering with young sex. I stared at them all and thought, Whatever hell this is, it isn't my hell.

"Explanations, please," I said. "What are those things?"

"Monster dogs, dude," Brad said. "They're Rod's pets."

"And, pray tell, who is Rod?"

"He's a local legend," Corey said. "We used to tell stories about him around the campfire."

I thought, Oh for fuck's sakes. I may have said it too.

Corey leaned in, eyes gleaming: "He was born before the First World War, nobody knows exactly when. Thing was, he was deformed."

"How deformed?"

"Like, totally. The lumpiest potato in the world. Could crack any mirror he looked into. His parents were religious freaks and believed he was an abomination and kept him chained in the basement. Right here, in this house. He had an older sister, Ruth, and she fucked him because she was kind of messed up too."

"Right," I said. "Sure."

"When he was sixteen, he escaped. The first thing he did, he killed Ruth. Then he flipped out and killed thirteen other kids around here before he was shot by a posse. They buried him in the woods close to the house. Now he's back. That's the story."

"Ah," I said. "So, he killed fourteen kids, and now he's back for more? And why is he back?"

"Oh," Brad said, "Andy and Jennufa – they're dead now – went out into the woods and, like, had sex right over his grave. That raised him from the dead."

"That's certainly very enlightening. It makes a lot of sense. Anyone else have anything illuminating to tell me?"

We were all silent for a minute or so, until, in tones of great concern, Tina asked: "Are you hungry?"

"No," I said, "but thanks."

"You change your mind, help yourself to the stuff in the kitchen." She pointed. The kitchen entrance was located to the rear of the living room, directly opposite the front door. I could see open cupboards, a grimy dripping faucet, and the back door.

"Hope you don't mind spam," Brad said, "because that's all we've got."

"The basement's full of spam cans," Tina added.

"There was creamed corn at some point, too," Cherry said, "but that got eaten real quick."

"How long," I muttered, "have you been here?"

Krystal said, "Seven months."

"Seven months. How do I get out of here?"

"You don't," Corey said.

"I don't intend to remain trapped here, thank-you-ever-so-much."

"The only way out," Corey said, "is to die."

"So!" Tina chirped, clapping her hands. "Anyone for Twister?"

"Actually," I said, "Krystal, perhaps you could show me where I can sleep. Things have suddenly become seriously absurd, but maybe in the morning…"

Corey opened his mouth but Brad cut him off by saying, "Dude, don't."

Krystal looked at me with sympathy. "Okay. Do you have luggage?"

"Yeah."

"The boys can get it. Better not leave your stuff in the car. It might be gone in the morning."

(In fact, the whole car disappeared overnight.)

"Sure. Leave the bags downstairs." I tossed the car keys to Brad. Krystal took an oil lamp and led me to one of the upstairs rooms. A mattress lay on the floor.

"This used to be Heather and John's room, but you can have it now."

"Heather and John?"

"They're gone now. Rod got them."

I had to ask: "How many of you were there, when you came here?"

"Thirteen."

"Jesus." I closed the door. "Let's think of something else. I need to think of something else."

She was luminous in the oil-light glow. I felt a stir. Basic principles reasserted themselves. Under the circumstances, why not?

I murmured: "I brought you back. Remember your promise?"

"Sure."

"Okay then. I'll take you up on it."

She put the oil lamp on the floor and kneeled.

And that's how I ended up at the house in the woods and how my thing with Krystal started.

Four months had passed since the announcement of the blue or pink new arrival and I hadn't come up with an escape plan.

Everything had been tried already. Everything. It was obvious that as long as Rod was alive – or undead, as the case may be – there was no way out.

Basically, we were fucked.

That's what I was mulling over – uselessly – as I sat in the dark living room, the rifle in my lap. It was my turn to be on watch. We did four-hour shifts. Being on watch was always bad. It made you stay alert. It kept you thinking about things.

I listened to the drip-drip of the leaky kitchen faucet, each drop pinging loudly in the steel sink, and thought of plans and questions and answers and the baby.

The porch creaked.

I pricked up my ears.

There was the sound of boots on wood – solid clunking thumps. He was never one for stealth, our Rod. I rose to my feet slowly. I aimed the rifle at the front door and clicked off the safety. I listened to the boots. The door handle moved, ever so slightly.

I held my fire. That was sure to be a trick. Rod had wised up at some point. What would he try this time?

I waited.

Slowly I began to become aware of a change in the sounds around me. I focused, listening carefully. Then it hit me: the droplets dripping from the faucet no longer pinged when they hit the sink. The sound was softer, muted. I turned on my heels. The kitchen entrance was almost completely filled by a hulking figure that held a flashing machete. He'd come in through the back door.

I fired. The bullet caught him in the head. He dropped. I relaxed my grip on the rifle. That was that. He was dead again. A bullet to the brain always did the trick.

Behind me, the crack of wood and a sudden slam. I saw a blur of motion go past me. A snarling ball of muscle and sharp fangs and claws landed on top of Rod's body and went tumbling into the kitchen. I pulled back the bolt of the rifle, slammed another bullet into the chamber. The bulldog thing was getting up. I fired. Its back blossomed with blood. I reloaded, fired again, got it in the head.

I turned and tried to close the front door, but the bulldog thing had bust the lock and the bolt. I jammed it shut with a chair under the handle and then went into the kitchen to inspect the remains.

Rod was barefoot. The bulldog thing was wearing his boots on its hind legs.

Someone clomped down the stairs.

"Dude, you all right?"

"Yeah."

Brad, an axe in his hand, peered at the bulldog thing and the boots. "That's new."

"Yeah."

He nodded. "How come that thing came to the house? They've never come to the house before. Thought they weren't, like, allowed or something."

"And why's that, you think?"

"Dunno. It's a rule."

"No, I reckon it's just that he wanted the pleasure of killing us himself."

"So what's changed?"

"I think," I said, pointing at Rod, "that he's getting impatient. The rules have changed."

"Why?"

"Yes, that's the question, isn't it?" I pulled Rod's body up by the shoulders and propped him against the wall. I peeled his mask off. Looked, once again, at his deformed features. He, too, was a teenager. A huge, butt-ugly, homicidal teenager. I stared into his dull eyes. "That's the question."

Brad shrugged. "Hey, we better wait until morning to clear up. Might be more of them circling the house."

"Right," I said and settled into a chair to keep watch over the bodies.

And I returned to the question. The why of it.

In the morning, as we burnt Rod and the bulldog thing in the pit, we became aware that we were being watched. There were bulldog things in the shadows at the edge of the forest, dozens of them, all frozen as if waiting for a signal to attack.

We hurried back inside.

"This is bad. This is so bad." Krystal sat against the wall, cradling her knees. She rocked back and forth. "Have you found a way out?"

I lay back on the mattress. "No."

"Think of the baby."

"Believe me, I'm thinking. I'm thinking."

She crawled over to me. I smelled her. Her scent had changed. Now I sometimes found her vaguely repellent. She pawed my chest and looked into my eyes.

"I love you so much."

"Me too," I lied.

She lay down on top of me. Her belly bulged. The baby was already kicking inside. She kissed my neck, but I turned my head away. She ran her fingers through my hair. I took hold of her wrist and said, "Stop it."

"What's wrong, Gary?"

"We only have a few days at most," I said, "before Rod rises again. And this time, he'll bring his pets with him."

"What are we gonna do?"

"Find an answer to a question. And the question is: 'Why?'"

We gathered in the living room.

"We're so dead," Corey said. He took the rifle and calmly opened the front door. He walked out. We filed out onto the porch. Corey kept walking.

"Dude, where you going?"

"Into the woods." Corey turned around.

"You can't take the rifle," I said.

"Make me give it back." Corey backed away, pointing the rifle at us, and then sprinted into the woods. None of us said anything. A few minutes later, we heard shots, then a scream, then silence.

"Retard," Cherry said.

"He totally lost it," Brad said.

"And we," I said, "lost our rifle."

I returned into the living room, seething. Then I picked up the poker from the fireplace, twirled it in my hands, and batted the stuffed armadillo that perched on the mantle. It went flying and thudded against the wall. That felt good, so I took aim at a porcelain Jesus. It shattered. I kept going, flailing and thrusting in an idiot frenzy, until I speared a photo of Rod's mother. Got her right in the chest. That stopped me.

Breathing heavily, I stared at her inbred face and thought of motherhood. Then I realized what had changed. Krystal, the poor cow, I thought, they can smell her pregnancy. Her scent was making Rod and his pets impatient. I imagined them at the edge of the forest, snouts in the air, intoxicated by the smell of fresh meat.

"Fourteen," I whispered.

"Dude?" Brad said.

"Nothing," I said, and dropped the photo.

That night, I couldn't sleep. I kept thinking of the monstrous plan that was emerging in my head. In the past, Rod had killed fourteen. Maybe by killing the same number now, no more and no less, he'd be able to end his cycle of violence and rest again. That was the way it worked in fairytales. It seemed intuitive. It felt right. And to get out, I'd have to bet on that.

Krystal woke up sometime in the middle of the night.

"Honey," she whispered, "what's wrong?"

"Nothing." I patted her bulging belly. "Go back to sleep."

I thought of her. I thought of the baby. And I thought of escape. And the plan, it would not be denied.

The next night, it was my watch.

I stepped out onto the porch. I saw Rod standing, immobile, at the edge of the woods. The machete gleamed in his hands. He saluted me with the naked blade.

I returned into the house. I kissed the sleeping Krystal on her forehead and then, as silently as I could, I gathered up most of the weapons – except the axe Brad always kept by his side – and hid them in the basement. Then I went out into the darkness before dawn with my suitcase. I walked up to Rod. This was it. Either this worked, or I'd be dead. I stared into the dark holes of his mask. An infinite sadness radiated from them.

"All yours," I whispered. "Thirteen teenagers. And the baby makes it fourteen."

He nodded. The deal, it was done. I'd live.

"Rest in peace," I said.

I didn't turn to watch him march to the house. Bulldog things emerged from the woods. They streamed past me, wreathing me in the smell of carrion. When I heard the screams, I covered my ears.

It didn't take long.

Finally, I turned to look. Rod came out onto the porch. He was fading. The bloody machete dropped from his translucent hand, and then he was gone back to whatever hell he called home. I didn't go up to the house again. What was done was done, and I didn't need to see the aftermath. I started trudging away down the dirt road, thinking, How much can a man make himself forget? I still don't know. An hour later, I'd reached a blacktop road, and a guy in a pickup truck stopped to give me a lift.

"If you don't mind me saying so," he said, "you're looking plenty rough. What happened?"

"I drove off the road."

"Damn."

"Yeah," I said. "Damn."

Eine Kleine Nachtmusik (1943)

Lavie Tidhar

The drugs uncle Ludovicus gave Alicia were beginning to peak. She wandered through the hotel's empty corridors, feeling them take hold of her soul.

First the mushrooms: the moonlight streaming in turns the window into a vast, multifaceted mirror, through which uncle Ludovicus stares and leers and cries in a hundred different expressions, a hundred different shards. The mushrooms are white and pasty and look a little like grubs, and their tea, when Alicia drinks it, tastes faintly of cum the way mushrooms do.

"Now are you ready?" he asks. Alicia helps herself to a handful of red pills on the dresser and glares at him. The old man sits in a wide leather armchair, his naked skin glistening in the heated room. He is intensely beautiful to her of a sudden, the pale fat and sweat transformed into a white flower, ringed by dew.

She stands there staring at him, transfixed.

"You want more money?" uncle Ludovicus pulls out a large wad of notes and waves it in Alicia's face. His features contort and warp. She blinks, but he continues to change, as if viewed through a distorting lens.

"Stay there," she says. "Must get some fresh air."

She takes a deep hit on the hookah by uncle Ludovicus' feet, exhales and passes it to him. "Just keep calm."

An idea hits her and she begins to giggle uncontrollably. "Keep calm," she repeats. She holds the hookah's pipe to uncle Ludovicus' mouth, which is expanding and contracting like a blowfish, and clamps his nose, hard, watching in fascination as the smoke pours into his mouth. After a couple of minutes of this game uncle Ludovicus' body is still.

"Stay here," Alicia says again, and pats him on the head. "Be right back."

She takes a swig from a bottle of dark, red wine that is sitting half-empty on the floor, and walks out into the corridor.

The Wonderland Hotel, Berlin, 1943: a night like a postcard written but never sent, a fairytale with the names distorted and changed. Outside are war and marches and crowds, but at the Wonderland all is quiet, subdued, a run-down luxury that appeals to the gentlemen who come to stay there, the foreign merchants and bankers, the smugglers who traffic in people and the renegade spies. There is a giant sunflower lying on top of the stairs outside of room 205.

Alicia bends down to examine it. Around her, the old corridors are constricting like snakes. The doors ooze and peel to the floor. Moonlight commits acts of unspeakable violence from the visual abyss of mirrors.

"Late, so late..." a white armadillo ambles past her, its armoured shell blazing.

"Where are you going?" Alicia shouts after it. The armadillo ignores her.

"I'm late..." it murmurs as it disappears behind the corner. "You're late..."

The hotel brakes and re-forms around her. Alicia feels weightless. Her hair flows away from her shoulders and up, until it is nearly vertical. The sunflower winks at her, becomes a bright yellow eye that begins to burn in an intense fire. Alicia covers her eyes, her arm fighting the thick, dream-like quality of the air.

"There is nobody home." There is a young girl standing outside room 207. Her white dress hangs in tatters and her eyes are closed.

"Are you real?" Alicia asks.

Real. Real. The words echo and fracture around her. There is no answer from the blonde girl.

Alicia keeps walking. 207, 209, she wanders past doors made of polished wood, the discreet numbers fading and glaring in painful strobes of light.

Drugs taking hold; consciousness expanding. Partial paralysis takes place.

Alicia's movements become those of an automaton, mechanical and jerky. She stops, breathes once, and falls to the floor.

The red carpet engulfs her and she lies motionless.

The Wonderland shrinks behind as Alicia's mind batters against her skull and is out, flying. She looks down on the ageing hotel, on uncle Ludovicus lying comatose in his leather armchair, his belly hanging and his mind full of impossible dreams; on the mannequin shaped like a girl in the corridor. And higher. Over Germany, rendered like a dark, impossibly dark board upon which lights are being extinguished. She can feel each light, each life as it is snuffed out, and she soars even higher, looking for a tear in the world, a gash into wonder.

And there it is, back where her body lies prone on blood-red carpets, a hole growing in the substance of space, and Alicia is falling, falling in a maelstrom of wind, falling with the white armadillo and the sunflower and the mannequin girl, falling into a wonderland, a real wonderland, falling through the rent in the world.

On the red carpet Alicia shudders once and is still.

Evangeline

Andrew J Wilson

P astor Virgil Weems was a man sustained by his faith: he
believed in God, of course; but most of all, he believed in
himself.

Weems relaxed his bulky frame on the rippling waterbed and lit
a bootleg Havana cigar. He might only have been the tenth-ranked
televangelist in the Bible Belt, but he was installed in the deluxe
suite of Tennessee's number one brothel. A fifth of sour-mash
whiskey was decanted on the table beside him and the TV was
tuned to a hardcore cable channel.

These days, Weems needed visual aids like this to stimulate his
middle-aged libido before dessert. His first hooker of the night had
taken a great deal out of him, but still, he had taken even more out
of her. The preacher rubbed his bruised knuckles gently.

The girl had been too good at her game, and once again, he'd
lost control. She'd been dressed as a nun but made up as a slut,
and Weems had debased her in his usual manner, with his usual
relish. But then, at the end, the girl had mumbled, "Holy Mary,
Mother of God," through clenched teeth, and a tear had escaped
her eyelids.

By the time the cathouse bouncers arrived, he'd broken three of
the hooker's ribs and half throttled her with her own rosary. It was
small consolation that he hadn't permanently scarred the girl – or
worse – and that the management was willing to accept his apolo-
gies and a generous tip for the privilege of physical abuse. Weems
knew full well that it was only his long-term patronage of the estab-
lishment that had saved him from a crippling beating.

The movie ground on, the light from the TV screen playing

across the flock wallpaper of the windowless room and turning the space into a tiny universe of its own. Only the simpering clown in the lurid oil-on-velvet painting on the wall shared the moment with him.

Weems' mind slid back to his original sin; his fall from grace, as it were. Twenty years before, he'd been on his first big revival tour when the woman had approached him after a show. Outside the billowing tent, she'd asked him to perform the laying on of hands for an affliction he could no longer remember. He led her towards the shelter of the woods.

It was during the ritual that Weems had finally submitted to his baser urges. The little woman was attractive – perhaps all the more so in her woeful distress – and his hands began to rove over her face, her breasts and then beyond. She submitted silently, out there among the trees beyond the lights. He took her twice, expending his years of repression, and in a red haze of lust, he had a vision.

Weems saw clearly for the first time that Woman was the corrupting vessel used by the Devil to distract Men's minds from higher things. He saw that he had fallen too. Nevertheless, he also knew that, despite what others might say, nothing one did with – or to – Woman could be wrong, if one remembered what the Lord had shown him, that She was the enemy. It was no sin to punish those who were already damned.

When he was done, the preacher smashed her head in with a rock.

Lying in the plush cathouse suite all these years later, waiting for his second girl of the night, Weems found himself unable to explain why these thoughts should return to him. He hadn't become a butcher. Only two more women had died at his hands; on both occasions, it was to stop their tittle-tattle revealing his proclivities to the baleful eyes of the media. In many ways, he regarded himself as a model of moderation and abstinence.

The preacher dismissed the irrelevant memories as a little someone tapped meekly on the door. He called her in as he wallowed on the waterbed, surrounding himself with mysterious plumes of cigar smoke. His meaty hand reflexively tapped his trouser pocket. It contained the switchblade – the razor edge of his wrath – that now stood him in good stead when he was called upon to act as the last of God's Angry Men. The eyes of the clown on the wall seemed to follow his every move.

The leather-padded door swung open and the new girl was ushered in by a pair of bouncers who slipped away immediately. She was a slender creature with skin pale enough to show the blue map of her veins. An ash-blonde cascade of hair showered over her shoulders and covered all of her face until slim fingers swept it away to reveal her blood-red lips and deep-set grey eyes. The girl wore an outsized white T-shirt that reached the top of her knees and was clasped round her waist with a thick, black-leather belt.

She looks like an angel, Weems thought, but she is the spawn of Eve, first Woman, first Corrupter.

"Angel in Eve…"

The preacher heard the phrase quite clearly, but the girl hadn't opened her rich, full-blooded mouth yet.

Don't think such thoughts, he told himself. Woman must be made to suffer, she has to be punished for carrying the fruit of the bad seed.

"An evil gene…"

Weems shook his whiskey-fuddled head, ground out his cigar and broke the restless silence.

"The name's Virgil. What's yours, sweetheart?"

"Evangeline…" she whispered in reply.

His back shivered with excitement. That was a terribly Holy name for hooker. It would be the first black mark against her, he decided.

"You look awful young, darlin'," the preacher teased. "You sure you know what you're doin'?"

"Oh, you don't need to fear none on that account, sir. I can read you like a book." She paused, her mouth open in a petulant pout and added, deadpan, "Like the Good Book, even."

Weems ground his teeth together. That little joke would be the second blasphemy to count against her. Now adrenaline was coursing through his blood, and his pants were tight against his crotch. He had to hand it to her, she'd granted him the kind of thrill that the dirty movies couldn't give him anymore. He would relish putting her through her penance even more than he'd enjoyed beating up on the nun. This would be worth a lot of money in damages.

The preacher tried a crooked smile, "Come to Daddy…"

Then she scowled and spat in his florid, sweating face.

"No – you go to Hell!"

In disbelief, he felt his apoplectic fit turn into twisted pleasure as he thrashed helplessly on the surging waterbed. Weems gasped in tortured ecstasy and then the lights went out. He trembled feebly in the darkness, then something smashed between his legs and he blacked out too.

When the preacher came to, Evangeline was standing by the light switch and all the chichi lamps were on again. Despite the excruciating red waves of pain pulsing from his bruised groin, Weems could also see that she had bolted the door. Not only that, but she had taken his switchblade from his soaking trouser pocket with the wad of Kleenex in her hand.

He writhed on the bed in a futile attempt to ease the agony.

"What do you want?" he hissed.

She smiled at him.

"I want you to atone for your sins, Virgil Weems. To atone for all the women you've raped, beaten and killed."

"And just how do you expect me to do that?"

"How do you think, missionary man?"

Although Weems worshipped a brutal, misogynist and vengeful version of God that was all his own, he was devout and absolutely faithful – so he began to laugh at this personification of the Absolutely Evil Woman.

"God is with me, you bitch. Maybe you can make me atone for the Justice you call Sin, but I will always stand vindicated in the eyes of the Lord."

"Will you now?"

Weems watched the girl who called herself Evangeline wipe the last of his juice from the switchblade. She folded it shut and threw the sticky tissues aside. Then she dropped the knife down the neck of her T-shirt and let it slide between her breasts.

Evangeline stretched out her arms and cocked her head to one side in a parody of the crucifixion.

"All right, preacher – your universe against mine. Catch me if you can. Take your blade back and make me suffer for my sins..."

Weems gauged the pain in his tortured groin and decided to go for it. She wouldn't be able to reach the knife in time. He would overpower her and then –

He rolled off the waterbed and lunged for Evangeline. His arms flailed and he gasped as the room seemed to part like the Red Sea. He struggled for purchase on the floor and kicked himself into space. Everything elongated and Evangeline slipped away from him although she held her cross-shaped stance against the wall.

Weems tried one last effort and felt himself sinking into the writhing, warping carpet that now stretched itself out to fit a tunnel rather than a room. For a moment, he was sure the painted clown laughed out loud.

"Which universe, Virgil Weems?" Evangeline called from half a mile away.

The preacher staggered to his feet, confused by the tortured perspectives. Then the twisted, elastic tunnel snapped back on itself and Evangeline was in front of him.

She punched his baffled skull with her small but bony hand, knocking him flat on his back on the bed again.

Grey fields of oblivion blotted out his vision and he dearly wanted to black out once more, but it was not to be. The girl walked up to the waterbed and looked down on him, her long blonde hair tumbling around her face and hiding her features. This faceless, faithless nemesis sniggered at what she saw.

How could the Lord suffer such a creature as this to exist? It was an abomination. This Woman-thing was too terrible to be allowed to exist, but how could the She-devil be stopped?

"In God's name, who or what are you, bitch?"

Evangeline smiled the Gioconda smile.

"I'm your daughter, Daddy…"

"I have no children!" Weems screamed.

"Oh, but you have – I'm just the most mature of them."

"Lies, all lies!"

"Listen, Father, do you remember my mother, your first murder?"

Weems gaped like a fish on the line and the blood drained from his face.

"What are you talking about? I smashed her skull in!"

"Of course you did, you murdering bastard – but something was conceived that night two decades ago. Do you remember what she asked you to do? Do you know why she wanted to be healed?"

Weems shook his head and moaned, closing his eyes to hide from the truth.

"She had cancer! A tumour was eating her from the inside out – so she came to you to ask the Lord to take it away. And what did you do, Daddy? You betrayed her trust – you pounded her till she bled and then you killed her!"

Weems began to sob.

"Yes," Evangeline hissed. "But something was conceived in those woods, and each year, as you committed your filthy crimes and told your filthy lies, you nurtured me, you made me grow all the more real…"

"No, no, this can't be! For God's sake–"

"Your god, if He ever existed, is dead. You have only your children to succour you now…"

"No!" screamed Weems, "I deny you!"

"And if thine eye offend thee," she whispered in his ear, "pluck it out…"

Weems gasped for a moment longer then forced his thumbs and forefingers into his sockets. The jelly of his eyeballs gave way and he tore them free.

He fell back groaning on the bed, and Evangeline plucked the bloody lumps from his fingers and gave him back the switchblade.

Weems heard a voice say softly, "They say the eyes are windows of the soul..."

When the bouncers finally broke down the heavy door, they found the preacher in a pool of bloody water. He'd slashed the waterbed apart while he tried to carve the Number of the Beast across his chest with the knife.

Even this would not have been enough to turn the guts of the hardened rednecks, but they could no longer control their mutinous stomachs when the pathetic, bleeding creature began to urinate and raised his face towards them.

Virgil Weems' raw, gouged sockets gaped as he screamed, over and over again, "For Christ's sake, I can still see her!"

And the helium-filled blow-up doll they'd given Weems to satisfy his lust floated angelically above them all. The surprised "O" of its mouthpiece had gone, though – the plastic lips were closed forever in a satisfied smile.

For a Steal

Stephanie Bedwell-Grime

Somewhere close by in the darkness I hear the shifting of a heavy body followed by a wet grunt.

I turn toward the outline I can only vaguely make out in the gloom. "I know you're there. I can hear you breathing."

Something sniffs at my ankle. I kick out and hear it land somewhere off in the blackness.

"Not talking?" I ask my reticent companion. And receive only another choked moan in reply.

So, how did I get here, you're wondering now. Well, I'll tell you...

I had a pretty good career in the business. I'd hit most of the estates on the winding hill that comprises our pathetic little town's version of an upscale neighborhood. I was having a good summer. Still, one house eluded me. One potential place of employment, so to speak. And summer was nearly over. Rich people returned from their vacation homes. Cool weather drove them inside. Now or next summer, I thought. And decided to give it a try.

To call the massive old estate spooky would be an understatement. A huge rambling place, it had a haphazard look to it, as if each generation had built their own wing. A crumbling rock fence ringed the property, easy enough to scale. And still all my colleagues left it alone. Creepy, they called it.

Well, creepy didn't bother me.

The remains of a rose garden crunched underfoot as I climbed over the top of the fence. I hung there for a moment, waiting for a

160

guard dog, some unexpected barbed wire, a hidden alarm system or something. But I found nothing, except the stagnant air of a hot afternoon.

I made my way across the brittle lawn and knocked on the door. I'd brought my usual bag of take-out Chinese. If I got caught, it would be my alibi, if not, lunch.

No one answered the door. I tried the handle and found it locked. Tell you the truth, open would have scared me. People usually only leave their doors open when they're home. The lock looked as old as the crumbling estate. It would probably give if I gave the door a good kick. But that would make noise, something I fervently wished to avoid.

I circled the house, looking for a more secluded entry; somewhere sheltered enough that I could spend some time there engaging in my craft without being discovered. A grotto of overgrown bushes offered me just such a chance.

Branches clawed at me as I crept beneath them. A window beckoned just above my head. I stretched up and glanced inside.

The curtains were open, revealing a well-furnished living room. A huge chandelier hung over a table at one end. In the china cabinet beside it, I caught the dull gleam of unpolished silver. Closer to my perch on the window, I saw dusty end tables and a couch covered in a white sheet. But the fireplace held a fine collection of silver candlesticks. Deciding the room held the promise of a good score, I tested the window.

Wood had swollen with the dampness in the air, but the window opened with a scraping sound. I crouched beneath the window, waiting for someone to come investigate. Minutes ticked by, but all I heard was screech of a far off crow. I braced my leg against one of the bushes and heaved myself over the windowsill.

Conveniently enough, there was a set of bookshelves beneath the window that decreased in size like a set of stairs. Laughing, I stepped down from the window.

But I stopped laughing when I turned around.

The shelves formed an intriguing design, yet they sat completely empty. No books, no knick-knacks, no photos of the family, just empty shelves of dark wood, set in decreasing height below the window. Easy to dust, I thought with a shrug, but it did kind of give me the creeps.

Still, there was nothing wrong with the silver. I scooped as much as I could carry into my knapsack and went in search of something better.

For some reason people keep most of their valuables in their bedrooms, for reasons I could never fathom. Jewelry, stock certificates, watches, any of it would bring me a good price. And better still, it was easy to carry.

As I left the living room, I noticed the walls. What I'd taken at first for embossed wallpaper, turned out to be thick padding. It hung in sheets, a more decorative form of the stuff they line freight elevators with.

Padding. Okay, I admit it, now I was getting spooked.

But I had the silver and I wanted some gold before I called it a day. I had a living to make after all.

I hung back from the door, listening to the silence of the house. From somewhere down the hall, I heard scrabbling, like rats in the walls. That a house this old might be infested seemed entirely probable. Hearing no footsteps, I ventured into the hallway.

There was no one in the kitchen. The faded blinds were drawn tight against the daylight. A rickety table and a pair of chairs with torn vinyl seats sat in the corner. Ordinary enough, except for a thick chain that trailed across the stained linoleum. If a dog lived in the house, I wanted to know about it. But no dog collar lay at the end of the chain. Instead, I found the jagged teeth of a rusty bear trap. Dried blood tipped the edges, matching the brown streaks someone had hastily mopped up on the floor. I almost bolted then. But I'd never abandoned a job before, not even a difficult one.

Backing silently out of the kitchen, I turned to head up the stairs and stopped.

A huge steel door barred what could only be a stairway to the basement. It was bolted shut from the outside and further secured with a rusted padlock. Below, I heard that shuffling sound again.

I am so out of here, I thought. Whatever was down there

sounded far too big to be rats. A dog, maybe. That might be bad if it started to bark.

But I heard no human footsteps, and the door was securely bolted. One quick look upstairs and I'd be gone, gold or not, I promised myself.

I put my foot on the stairs. Wood creaked beneath my boots, loud in the silence. The shuffling beneath stopped. I held my breath. Silence. I started up the stairs.

Eyes looked out at me from ageing oil paintings as long-dead ancestors followed my progress up the stairs. They're only paintings I told myself, but still they gave me the creeps. I reached the landing and continued up the last flight of stairs.

Four very solid closed doors greeted me. Who leaves their doors closed in the day, I wondered. But really, who cares? My mission was to find out if anything of value lay behind those doors and steal it.

My fingers closed around the doorknob of the nearest door. I yanked my hand back in surprise. Instead of cool metal, the doorknob was warm, as if someone had had their hand on it for a very long time.

I glanced behind me, but nothing moved in the hallway. No sound came from behind any of the closed doors or from the barricaded door below the kitchen.

Nerves, I decided. All thieves get them. Some get addicted to the adrenaline rush. Deciding it was just the old house getting to me, I swallowed my fear and turned the knob.

My fears were groundless because all that stood in the room was a bunch of old furniture covered in white sheets. Still, it gave me the impression of a bunch of sleeping ghosts.

I found the door to the next room slightly ajar even though I was sure it had been locked when I reached the top of the stairs. But I hadn't heard anyone moving around, so I must have been mistaken.

Jackpot! The room held more furniture covered in sheets, but the uncovered bureau held a stained glass jewelry box that gleamed with gold even in the dim light.

Now who would go away and leave all their jewelry on their

dresser, wondered a little voice in the back of my mind? And why wouldn't they at least throw another sheet over the dresser? But the prospect of a score was too great and I silenced it.

Sapphires and diamonds sparkled in a nest of gold. Rings, watches, chains lay entangled in a hopeless knot. Too bad, I thought with a wry grin. I'll just have to take it all. I reached my hand into the mass of treasure.

Something sliced into my finger. With a curse, I yanked my hand back.

Blood dripped from my fingertips, splashing down on the carpet. Damn. It wasn't good form to leave DNA evidence at the site. I swore and peered into the jewelry box. I suspected an open pin, the sharp edge of a broach. Instead, I found the edge of a rusty razor blade nestled in amongst the diamonds and gold.

Someone's idea of a booby-trap. I should have left then. I know I should have. But being a practical kind of guy, I figured I'd just find a better way to transport my booty and be done with it.

Grasping the jewelry box by the edges, I upended it into my knapsack. Rings rolled across the carpet, a bracelet bounced under the sheet-covered bed. But by then I was getting more than a little spooked, so I left those trinkets, and headed for the stairs.

A sliver of light cutting across the floor stopped me. There hadn't been any lights on when I came upstairs. That much I was sure of. And I hadn't heard anyone come in. Could be a light set on a timer. I don't know why people think those stupid little tricks will fool us. All the better to see the treasure with, my dear. Just saves me from having to turn one on.

And if there was a light on in that room that probably meant there was something in there worth acquiring.

I crossed the hall and flattened myself against the wall. Peering around the doorframe, I cast a glance inside. A dim lamp did indeed shine across the vacant room. Two wing-backed chairs faced a fireplace. Behind them stood a shelf of books and a couch. Unlike the other rooms, no white sheets covered the furniture. This room had been lived in, until quite recently.

Oh, I know. I should have left. Fine for you to say. And I might have left that instant, if I hadn't noticed the golden statue on the mantle.

Even in the dim light the figurine had the kind of gleam only true gold has. One last trophy and I'd be gone. The to-die-for score. I crossed the room, reached for my prize.

Only to find myself stuck to the floor, the statue just out of reach. I glanced down to find a pool of glue around my feet. Struggling, I tried to lift one of my shoes. Strings of glue came up with my foot, only to suck it back down. I tried the other foot and found it already adhered to the hardwood.

"Ah, greed," said a voice. "It seems no one can resist that particular piece." I twisted at the knees and looked behind me.

A gray-haired old man perched in the corner of one of the wing-backed chairs. Dwarfed by it would be a better description. Frail and thin, I had no doubt I could take him. Assuming I could unglue myself, it would have been a piece of cake.

He stood, circled me, taking care to avoid the glue. "Tut, tut," he said as I struggled. "It's industrial strength. Quite effective, as I'm sure you've realized." He pulled a nasty little gun from his suit jacket.

I dropped my knapsack and raised my hands. The knapsack fell with a wet impact and stuck in the glue. "Just let me go," I heard myself pleading in the most humiliating voice.

"Can't do that," the old man said. "What's the point? You'll just be back." He sighed, gestured with the gun. "There was a time when I might have, you know. A time when I thought the locks and burglar alarms would protect me. But my house is isolated up here on the hill. It takes even the police some time to arrive. And you and your colleagues merely scoffed at my alarms. Ripped the sirens off the walls, smashed the windows instead of bothering with the locks. Eventually, even my insurance company wouldn't cover me any more. So I was forced to take other measures."

Things were about to get ugly. Didn't have to be Einstein to figure that out.

These days I never come to a job without...resources. And my hands were free. I reached behind me, yanked free the knife I keep in a custom holster. And lunged.

The gun went off. A bullet cut the air close to my head. The old man darted out of my way. I overbalanced, tumbled forward on my knees.

And found my shins, knees, hands and my knife buried in the glue.

Until then, I had debated taking off my clothes, leaving my jeans and my running shoes in the puddle of glue. Stupid, stupid, stupid, I should never have gone for the knife. But the old guy would probably have shot me in the back as I raced half-naked across his lawn. And damned if I was going to go out like that. Not that spending my last moments on earth caught like a fly in a giant spider web would play any better with the boys.

A pair of highly polished shoes appeared in my limited field of vision. I looked up. The old man shook his head. "I could call the police. Except that they've been here so many times, they no longer come when I call. And what good would it do to add another lost soul to our already overflowing prisons?" He studied me for a moment, then said, "You understand now, why I've had to find my own solutions."

That said, he wandered off, out of my line of sight. From behind me, I heard the door slam shut. "Wait," I screamed. I had visions of being left there to rot.

Which would have been so much more humane.

"You can't leave me here!"

A hissing sound answered me.

Craning my neck, I looked up to find a fine spray raining from the ceiling. The bastard was going to gas me to death.

I struggled like my life depended on it, succeeding only in coating more of myself with glue. Fog encroached on all sides of my vision, until it seemed like I looked down a long tunnel. The tunnel shrank in diameter, until it became a single point of light.

Then darkness.

I awake to the dank smell of basement. From all around me comes the sound of shuffling feet. That same sound I heard coming from beneath the kitchen. I lift an arm, try to wipe my face, only to find my wrists ringed with heavy manacles, attached to heavier chains, attached to the cement wall. In the dimness, I can make out the darker shadows of bars fencing me in on all sides. Shuffling feet stop on the far side of the bars. Another cell. I look up at the shadow hovering above me.

"So," I ask. "What are you here for? What did you do?"

Again, I'm answered by silence.

"Don't feel like talking, huh?"

The shadow shakes his head.

Light cuts across the floor, to splash on the bedraggled creature in the next cell. I see the old man silhouetted in the doorway.

The guy in the next cell utters a wet sound of terror. Haloed in the light, he opens his mouth. It takes a moment in the pale light to figure out what I'm seeing.

A bloody mouth, devoid of teeth. Or tongue.

The old man takes a step in my direction, fumbles with the lock on my cell. My own knife tumbles from his hands to lie just out of my reach beyond the bars. "Tut, tut," he says again. "We can't have you making noise down here, disturbing the neighbors. This is a nice neighborhood, after all."

I scream then. The last sound I will ever make.

Frankie

Matt Wedge

rankie had always worried that he would die in his sleep. He was not afraid of "the Boogeyman" or some other imaginary enemy. Just death. This was an enemy that was all too real, even to someone as young as Frankie. It was this one all-consuming thought that stayed with him in his bed, night after night, as he struggled to stay awake. This night was no different.

He had heard older people, namely friends of his grandparents, talking almost blissfully of a silent death during their nightly slumber. This always seemed foolish and frightening to Frankie. If you were asleep when death arrived for you, you would have no opportunity to ask forgiveness of Jesus for all your sins. If you were unable to do that, it was like getting a one-way ticket to hell. Even if you asked forgiveness before you went to sleep, you could have a sinful dream. Then what could you do? This was Frankie's reasoning, and it made perfect sense to him. Frankie had heard enough about the differences between Heaven and Hell to know which destination was more desirable to him.

So here he lay, exhausted, but fighting sleep with every fiber of his being. He mumbled the Lord's Prayer over and over. He wished he were Catholic, so he would have some of those cool beads to handle while he prayed. His friend Anthony was Catholic, and those beads always seemed so important to his mother. His eyes slowly closed.

Frankie snapped awake, angry with himself for falling so easily into his body's trap. He looked at his digital clock, glowing red (as Satan's eyes, Frankie often imagined). He had only slept for twelve minutes. He could hear moans and thumps coming from his parent's room. Even at only seven, Frankie knew they were having sex. He felt uncomfortable with this knowledge, since he was sure that it was a sin to know such things. Against his will, his eyes closed shut. He dreamed of the bus ride home when Anthony had explained to him (and several other boys) how sex worked. Since Anthony was a grade ahead of them, they listened with rapt attention.

"You see, first the Mom and Dad get naked."

There was a sharp intake of breath as the boys immediately tried to drive the image of their naked mothers from their imaginations.

"Then they wrestle on the bed for a while, before the Dad pees on the Mom."

Frankie could not control his disgust.

"Gross! You're lying!"

Frankie looked around at the other boys. Their faces were pale, reflecting the disgust that Frankie had vocalized. Even though they had said nothing, Frankie was confident that he had spoken for all of them.

"I'm not lying! That's what I saw my Mom and Dad do!"

This time, there was no recoil, as the boys lingered on the vision of Anthony's naked mother in their heads. Even Frankie admitted to himself that the thought still invaded his mind.

Frankie woke with a start. Bright sunlight was spilling in through his window. He muttered a quick prayer of thanks for surviving through the night. He stared at his clock. It read 10:37. Frankie climbed out of bed, confused as to why his mother had not roused him for school. He walked to the window, expecting to see snow on the ground. It was the only possible explanation for her decision to let him sleep in. There was no snow, just the brown grass and muddy fields that came with winter in the Missouri countryside. He left his room, to find out why his mother had failed to wake him.

Frankie stared at his parents' bedroom door with dread. He knew what they had been doing the previous night and was worried that they might not be finished. Frankie knew, however, that he was supposed to be in school, and he needed his mother to get him there. This understanding in his mind, Frankie pulled up his courage and opened the door.

His first thought was that the red was the exact same color as the numbers on his alarm clock. It was everywhere. It covered the walls in streaks, obscuring most of the floral wallpaper that his father hated. It was even on the ceiling, as though it had been splashed with paint. He watched a drop of it lose grip of the ceiling. It fell into his mother's open eye.

His mother. He hadn't noticed her until that very moment. She looked like she was screaming. Her eyes were as wide open as her mouth, but no sound came from her throat. Frankie initially thought that she had been painted red, as well. He soon realized, that the red had come from her. Frankie could not help but flash to his mind's vision of her naked.

But she was beyond naked, and Frankie knew this. He was seeing his mother, not only without her clothes, but without her skin. Large pieces of flesh, that Frankie could only assume belonged inside her, were spilled out on the bed and the floor.

He was still staring in frozen silence at her bloodied corpse when the phone rang. It sounded unusually loud inside the quiet room, and returned Frankie to a functioning state of mind. He began backing out of the room as quickly as he could. He stopped when the phone ceased its racket on the second ring.

"Hello?"

It was his father's voice.

"Oh yes. I'm sorry I didn't call earlier. Frankie woke up with a cold today. We're going to keep him at home over the weekend."

His voice was calm. No trace of panic betrayed his act as a reasonable man.

"I apologize again, but I appreciate you checking up. Goodbye."

Frankie heard the phone settle in its cradle.

"I forgot to call your school."

Frankie's father sat up in bed. His naked torso was stained pink. Little pieces of skin and muscle were trapped in his chest hair. He had been under the covers, lying next to his wife's body.

"You want some waffles?"

Frankie's mind nearly snapped at this last statement. The invitation of a normal breakfast was too absurd to comprehend. His father did not wait for a response.

"Well I do. Get dressed and come down to the kitchen."

Frankie walked back to his room. He knew of nothing else to do.

Frankie found his father in the kitchen. He had dressed in a white T-shirt that was rapidly staining a pink color. Frankie was so focused on what had caused the stain that he was startled when the waffles popped from the toaster. His father matter of factly buttered the waffles and poured some syrup on them. He placed them on the table.

"Hurry up, before they get cold."

Frankie sat down in front of the plate. His father placed two more waffles in the toaster.

"Remember our talk about the boogeyman?"

Frankie heard this question, but did not respond. He was seeing, in his mind's eye, the single drop of red stream from his Mother's eye and down her face.

"Frankie?"

Frankie looked at his father. The kind face staring back at him brought a sense of normalcy.

"What happened to Mom?"

"The Devil got her, Frankie."

Frankie closed his eyes tight at this revelation. It made perfect sense. Frankie began muttering to himself.

"The Lord is my shepherd; I shall not want. He maketh me to lie down in green pastures: he leadeth me beside the still waters."

"Frankie."

Frankie stopped, and looked down, unable to face his father.

"It's too late for that now."

"I know."

He looked up at his father.

"Why did the Devil want her?"

He knew that he had to ask the question, but feared he already knew the answer.

"Because she did very bad things, Frankie. You're mother did evil things. And when you do evil things, the Devil makes you pay."

"She was a sinner?"

"She was a sinner."

Frankie relaxed slightly. Given the news, Frankie understood it was a strange reaction. But he was unable to help himself. Even though it was a confirmation of his deepest fear, it made him feel better to know that he hadn't been keeping himself from sleeping for nothing.

Armed with the knowledge of his mother's transgressions against God, Frankie even set about enjoying his days away from school. He spent all day eating candy and watching television. Every day, his father phoned the school to give an excuse, and every day Frankie lounged around the house. But by the sixth day, unnerved by the continuing presence of his mother's body in the house, Frankie began to have misgivings about how his father was handling the situation.

"Shouldn't we tell somebody?"

His father sat him on the floor outside of his parents' bedroom, staring off into space. The stench creeping out of the room had become increasingly worse since that first morning. It now bordered on the unbearable. Frankie tried his best to hold his breath. His father slowly focused his eyes on Frankie.

"Who do you think we should tell?"

An instinct in the back of Frankie's mind told him to keep quiet. But, after a moment's thought, he ignored the warning.

"Don't you call the police for something like this?"

His father responded in an uncharacteristically loud voice.

"Frankie, what happened to your mother is between her and God. She sinned against you, against me and against God. The Devil punished her for it. The police have no business interfering in God's work."

"But what do we say if people are looking for her?"

"We tell them she's not here, because she's not. I told you, the Devil took her. That body in there is not your mother. It's just a shell that has been left behind."

Frankie processed this information while he lay on the couch, watching cartoons. While he believed his father, the thought of his mother's body rotting in the upstairs bedroom still nagged at him.

He found his father stuffing towels at the base of the bedroom door.

"I still think we should tell the police."

His father stopped his work and stared at him.

"I know that it's none of their business, but if we don't tell, we're lying."

His father said nothing. Frankie considered this an invitation to continue his thought.

"And lying is a sin. That means the Devil can get us too."

His father's eyes watered slightly. Frankie just assumed that it was the smell.

"I suppose you're right, Frankie. We'll go into town tomorrow and tell the sheriff."

Satisfied that he had done the right thing, Frankie returned to the couch. He watched television until he fell asleep as the day gave way to night. His father picked him up and carried him to his bed. Once he had put him under the covers, he shook Frankie's shoulder.

"Wake up, Frankie."

Frankie rolled over and blinked awake. He looked at his father in confusion.

"Did I fall asleep? I didn't mean to."

"Yeah. I figured you'd want to say your prayers, so I woke you up."

Frankie smiled.

"Thanks."

Frankie closed his eyes and muttered quietly to himself. His father moved to a chair in the corner of the room. He sat down and held tightly to a pillow on his lap. Frankie finished and opened his eyes.

"Did you say all of your prayers?"

Frankie nodded in the affirmative.

"Did you ask Jesus to forgive you for all your sins?"

Frankie nodded again.

"Okay, why don't you go back to sleep. I'm just gonna sit here for a while."

Frankie's heavy eyelids fell shut.

Stuck

Samuel Minier

"Goddam mice."

"I'm sorry," she said absently, thinking he'd said "mess". She swept at the clean table top around their dinner dishes.

"Just look at this."

He pointed inside the kitchen cabinet with a jutting finger. They seemed too big to share his palm with each other, his fingers. Every line and whorl permanently stained by decades of oil and other machine fluids, ugly black ridges –

"Nora. Earth to space cadet, come in?"

She had to cross the room before she could see the grainy nuggets scattered around the coffee filters. Hard little pellets that could almost be mistaken for coffee grounds, except that Jerry would never leave a mess like that. Who would have suspected a life-long bachelor, someone with such discolored hands, would be so orderly? Nora had looked forward to the role of housekeeper and gentle nagger. Instead she was the one who needed reminding to pick up the towels, put away her shoes.

Jerry lifted the bag of sugar before seeing the gnawed-open corner. A comet-tail spilled from the cabinet to the counter to the floor, immediately turned to paste in the damp sink.

"Goddamnit, that's it!"

Nora stood with her hands holding each other at her belt buckle while he stamped into the garage. Jerry would probably want the sugar thrown out. Weren't mice filthy, the bearers of the Plague?

She tried to lift the bag carefully. It slipped through her fingers, scattering more white.

Shit.

She immediately regretted that. Jerry's influence – dirty hands, dirty mouth.

She'd just managed to cradle the bag into the garbage when Jerry emerged. He held a stack of long cardboard rectangles, originally white but mildewed to cream.

"They're old, but they'll do."

"What are they?" In hopes he wouldn't notice the increased mess.

"New homes for our cute little friends. Move the dishes out the way."

Watching his giant hands perform fine motor skills was disconcerting, almost supernatural. "What are those?" she asked again.

"Come here," he said. He had assembled a box about the size of his palm, its two ends open so that it formed a squat tunnel.

"Put your finger in there," he said. "Go on now, it won't bite."

She gingerly touched the inside, felt a gummy suction instantly pull her finger down.

"Sticky traps. Had this problem couple years ago, goddam filthy neighbors piling garbage in their backyard. But that asshole moved, don't know why these little bastards are back."

It seemed to Nora he stared at her a second.

She tried to withdraw her finger. "Jerry, it's stuck."

"Couldn't get the plain glueboards to work." He let go of the trap, leaving it suspended from her finger as he began folding the next one. "Like roach motels – sticky all around, and the little bastards love to crawl through things. These cleared 'em out so well I had leftovers."

Nora tried to shake the box loose, but it clung as if part of her now. She gripped it with her other hand and pulled. Nothing, and then a sound like the air tearing, and her now-free skin throbbing.

"That hurt," she tried to demand.

"O come on," he smiled, "at least they still work."

He plucked the trap from her and placed it in the cabinet. In doing so he glanced in the garbage.

"Why'd you throw the sugar out?"

"I – I thought it was ruined." She hated herself for that stammer.

"Well it is now," he said, "now that it's in the garbage."

"I thought that's what you'd want me to do." And I always think wrong, sometimes I swear you do things just to contradict me.

"Well thank you Nora," he said, the way you'd thank a two-year-old who was trying to help but just making it worse.

And he went about cleaning up and setting his traps.

Nora left for the rest of the house, to fiddle with her figurine collection that had once held prominence in her apartment living room. It was now relegated to an unused guestroom.

Then into the bathroom to hunt for disorder – all the towels stained but none of them out of place, and the grime too deeply set in to launder.

At least there were dishes in the kitchen sink, something to occupy her when he took over the living room. But the dried food detached quickly, and soon she just stood in the lonely kitchen while his television chattered. Trying to be curious, she searched through the cupboards and under the sink, discovering Jerry's white little houses. They innocently waited amid bottles of cleaners, boxes of macaroni.

She picked at the tip of the finger she'd stuck in. Unnaturally smooth, as if she'd lost part of her fingerprint.

And then there was no where left to go except the small living room, as cramped as the rest of the house. She sat at one end of the couch, vacantly staring at the television in the dim lighting Jerry insisted on. He stretched his girth in his cracked leather recliner. At times he would encourage, almost demand, she "lounge" on the couch, not "sit like you got a rod rammed up your rear."

Nora didn't want to lounge, throw herself about like some limp doll. She wanted her own chair, her straight back rocker with the country blue seat cushions. The one shoved next to her figurine collection.

Nora vaguely recognized she could just as easily sit in her chair in the back room – she didn't even like television. Hadn't that been the whole point of getting married, though? To avoid being an old woman sitting in a room alone and lonely –

176

"What was that?" she asked.

She imagined Jerry heard similar sounds all day – caught gears and stuck belts giving off squeals. Once Jerry had muted the sports re-cap though, she could plainly hear the organic nature of the sound, the emotion eking from the kitchen.

Jerry smiled hideously as he began flinging open doors, searching. The noise jumped in volume as he opened the cabinet containing the sugar.

"Returned to the scene of the crime," he said to the box. The box fell silent as Jerry plucked it up and thrust it at Nora's eye level.

"Mickey, meet the missus."

The tiny creature inside was stuck in mid-crouch. The pose would have been cute if not for the frantic pistoning of its legs trying to run. Three long whiskers had become affixed to the side wall, and its pointy brown head jerked at them as if in seizure. It managed to wrench one free – free from its face, the whisker still quivering on the wall. The momentum sagged the creature back, planting its rear in the glue.

It can't shit now. This was not crude in her mind, simply a statement of basic need. For some reason that bothered her quite a bit, the thought of the mouse slowly poisoning itself with its own waste.

It began to squeal again as it struggled. A tinny litany of meeping, whining, crying.

"Enough." The hardness in her voice surprised her. "Kill it."

"Nah, I always let them starve."

The cries were growing louder, it seemed. "What? Why?"

Jerry shrugged. "Living off me, my food – just seems fair."

A nasty voice sing-songed through her head – it's just a mouse, it was in his house, don't be a louse…

"Jerry, please. Why should it suffer?"

He bit at his lip, and Nora believed for a second she'd won.

"You can do it," he said.

"What?"

He placed the trap on the kitchen floor. "Just step on it. One good stomp'll do it."

"I…why can't you do it?"

"Nora, you're the one worried about this varmint. You can take care of it."

Can you do that? Can you crush the life out of this helpless thing?

Very very quietly she said, "I don't want to."

"Well I don't either." Jerry opened the door to the garage. A metallic rattle as he dropped the trap into the garbage can.

"OK," he said. "Problem solved."

Night descended on the little house. Jerry was at the shop every morning by six, and so he went to bed early, and thus so did Nora. She could stay up, but what was the point? To wander some more around a house that wasn't hers?

I was too old to get married. The thought came unfettered, without the guilt that used to flood her. And he was too. She remembered the day they met, when she brought her sputtering car to his shop. He'd seemed – what? Confident. In control. She'd even admired his hands, those dirty hands that at the time she thought were the honor badge of a working man, someone dependable, who could provide a good life.

Their courtship had begun at his initiative, was practical and methodical, not at all the passionate swooping Nora had always hoped for. But those hopes had failed for over fifty years, and if the comfortable security Jerry exuded was the best she could do, then Nora jumped at it. It's better than being alone.

Nora bitterly twisted the bed covers in her fingers. Expecting two people with over a century of separate lives between them to blissfully meld was the height of foolishness. And Nora was the bigger fool, for she had expected him to want the same as her – a new life, a we-life. What Jerry wanted, though, and what he was perfectly clear on keeping, was his life, peculiarly neat and casually cruel, now just with the benefit of someone to eat with and lay next to.

The worst part was, Nora had known. Known almost immediately after the marriage that something was wrong, and yet she continued to tell herself that being with someone automatically prevented you from being alone, scared, trapped in the dark and just waiting for your time to end.

The mouse rose unbidden in her mind. How long does it take to starve to death?

She should have done it. Stomped down on that trap, silencing the hurt and fear in that tiny box. She tried to imagine the look on Jerry's face if she had done so. In the three years they had been together, she had never seen him surprised or confused.

And that's what got her out of bed.

She deftly slipped from under the covers. Years of insomnia had taught her considerable skill at working through the grey-black of a darkened house. Down the hallway, into the kitchen. One of the few trees still with leaves tapped at the small window over the sink. From the garage there came – nothing. No rattled struggle, no sad meeping. Nothing.

Autumnal chill curdled her bare feet as she stepped onto the concrete step. In spite of her terrycloth robe, a shiver passed through her.

The garbage can sat to the right of the stairs, its lid dully shining with a slit of street light reflection. It remained silent. Maybe it's already dead. Oh I hope so.

And yet, part of her needed it still alive, still struggling, so she could finish what he had started, so she could tell him in the morning, so she could see even just a flicker in the overly-controlled meat of his face.

Nora exhaled bravely and lifted the lid. A wet vegetable smell reared up at her. The little box was balanced precariously atop a mound of plastic blackness. Nora reached out, her fingers hesitantly touching it.

The trap lurched as if of its own accord and sidled down the garbage bag, disappearing to the bottom of the can.

"Shit," she hissed.

Each new step brought a fresh raw bite to her soles. She snapped on the garage light, whose sudden glare revealed her as wholly in Jerry's space now, its perimeter marked by long work benches with thick mounted vises. Jerry's hulking truck at her back, and rows of tools lined above the trashcan like torture implements.

Nora strained deep into the can, the metal harshly rubbing at her armpit. As her hand was swallowed by the can's darkness, an image invaded her – a sudden snap as something (a giant rat trap, or a rat itself) latched onto her hand.

Don't be stupid. Her words, but Jerry's voice.

Her hand closed on the slick box. As she lifted the box from the can, she was keenly aware of her feet planted solidly on the concrete floor. She felt firm, grounded.

I'm here to help, which sounded ridiculo–

The trap was empty.

Nora tilted the box, feeling (Jerry's voice again) stupid, like it was a magic trick she didn't get. Still, the feeling of being rooted to the spot. There was something in there, though not the mouse. A chunk, some garbage remnant maybe, grimy congealed dirt and hair with a bit of twine tangled in it, almost like a tail...

Not hair. Fur. And not like a tail –

That's part of it. It pulled and pulled and finally skinned itself alive, to get away. Its hindskin, its tail. And oh God, there's the starprint of a tiny tiny paw it left behind –

The box fell from her numb fingers. That sense of stuckness had thickened over her entire body. The garage seemed huge and echoing, and she was very small and frozen, a caught animal, unable to move except for the tide of nausea rapidly rising up in rhythm with it skinned itself alive, it skinned itself alive...

Nora turned to flee. Her legs remained anchored.

Only a frenzied flailing kept her balance. She felt dizzy, pitched out of control, but only from the waist up. When she felt she was able, she tried to walk again and found she could not.

It's alright, you can find it, put it out of its misery, but you've got to move first.

A few deep breaths. Ok, try it again.

Her feet would not move.

Nora bent her knees, feeling them brush against her nightgown and robe. She felt her hips pivot as she shifted. But the only sensation from her feet was that of being seemingly mired in quicksand.

She bolted in sudden panic. Tried to bolt – this time momentum threw her body forward even as he legs stayed locked. A terrific strain rippled through one knee. Something tore away in her other leg. The fall crumpled her ankles, breaking them both, breaking her free of this unearthly inertia for just a second, only to have it clutch even tighter at her as she – one shin and knee, the entire stretch of the other leg, and both hands – contacted the floor and became cemented there.

Nora thrashed just once, uselessly.

"Jerry! Jerry...oh Jerry please hurry!"

The call coming without forethought or intention, her bitterness toward him washed away in fear and need, need for him to understand what was happening, solve this problem, save her. That's what husbands did, right?

Finally, after seeming minute upon minute of yelling, she heard his heavy approach. "In the garage, the garage!" she keened.

Jerry emerged through the doorway like a policeman called to a disturbance – alert but unfriendly. "What the blue hell you doin'?"

"The floor." She had to crane her neck up at him. "There's something...something sticky all over the floor. I can't move."

He chuckled at the idea of an uncleaned spill in his garage. "What?"

"No, don't!" she said he came down the steps toward her. "Don't get too..."

Her words faded as Jerry approached her. Stood overtop of her. Paced around her, so close his slipper touched her immobile hand. She darted her head in disbelief at his easy movements.

"I...I don't understand –"

She tried her hands and legs again. Nothing.

He dropped onto his haunches, his slight pot-belly swelling his t-shirt toward her face.

"Nora, what's going on?" A tired voice, trying not very well to hide its annoyance.

"I – I can't get up," she repeated stupidly.

Jerry grasped her wrist and effortlessly lifted her hand off the floor.

"Oh Jerry thank you –"

He lowered her hand back down. "There, you're free. Now let's go back to bed."

Her hand was stuck again, even worse than before. "I – I can't."

"Nora," he blew out a harsh breath, "you're fine. Come on."

She squeezed her eyes against the embarrassment, the fear, his condescending gaze. "Can – can you help me up again?"

"Why do women do this?" Jerry asked himself. "Why do you invent ridiculous situa – Why's that laying out?"

His eyes had focused on the sticky trap by the garbage can.

"Jerry please, I need your help –"

"Oh hell Nora," as he looked the chunk of mouse on the board, "did you try to help it? Did you actually try to peel that little sonofabitch off there?"

The sob broke out of her like a betrayal. "Jerry, please –"

"Great, now it'll die in the walls. You know how that's gonna stink?"

Nora felt like she was back in the living room, trying to beg for help from the prattling television.

"I'm going to bed," he said disgustedly and got up.

"Jerry!" she panicked. Don't leave me out here like this…

"That's what this is, right? You knew I was gonna be pissed about the mouse, so you're trying to fake some problem? Turn yourself into the victim?"

"Jerry, I swear to you I cannot move."

One of his hands on her head, the other on her neck – smooth and gentle, like a parent's guidance but very fast, so that before she could struggle her face was touching the cold concrete floor.

"Jherrye!" she tried through the smushed left side of her mouth.

"God you're really gonna push this, huh? I'm going to bed. When you get tired of looking like some bowing A-rab, you come in and join me."

"Gad Jherrye dun gew, plea!"

"Goddam games." His voice floated away from her. Two or three footfalls into the kitchen, then a pause.

"Maybe this will move ya – I'd keep an eye out for that mouse. He's probably not real happy right now."

The garage door shut as the lights went out.

Nora tried to scream, but the sound just seeped from her glued mouth, pooled in her smeared nostril, collected in her snarled hair. Her right eye was tearing up, from both emotion and the eyelashes bent backward against her pupil.

The black washout from the sudden absence of light slowly eroded, her surroundings re-emerging by streetlight. The garbage can directly before her. To its side, the trap and its creamy almost-glow. One of Jerry's tools on the wall, a thing used for tightening or holding.

She thrashed whatever was mobile – her rear end, her elbows. The movements jarred her wrist, ached her knees. Her back began to throb, and her right arm quivered from the strain of holding most of her body weight. Her right breast brushed the ground, and it adhered as if the nightgown and robe were porous, or not even there. Nora imagined a squashed piece of gelatin, wobbling between her breastbone and the grabbing floor.

The absurdity of the image, of all of this, was like a weight draped across her shoulders. She sagged, her right side giving wholly to the demanding firmament. The quivering in her arm stopped but was replaced by an ache of contortion in her right shoulder blade. Only her left side was free now, from about the midpoint of her rib-cage. Everything else was trapped

If I lay down, I'll smother. It will grab my chest and not let me breathe.

She almost did it. Just let gravity take her, fate asphyxiate her. But that was her worst fear, what she had dreaded so much she had jumped into Jerry's half-open arms – dying unknown, in the dark and by herself.

Except now she was not alone.

At first she mistook the tremor for her still-twitchy arm. Then, as it purposefully, stumblingly traced a wet line from her right shoulder blade to left, fighting against the slight incline, gradually cresting her high arm, dangling over, searching for a descent route as it came toward her, she thought oh please, Jerry was right you're coming back for me and I'm sorry I wasn't braver before, I'm so sorry –

The mouse came down – not some ghostly tormenter, but like a suicide off a cliff. It landed with a wet smack on its side. The streetlight seemed to dance in the glistening across its skinned rear flank. A pudding drop of what Nora could only guess was intestine nested under the ragged start of its fur. The paw-less front leg scraped uselessly against the concrete.

It's slipping away, just like me.

"Hey," she called gently. The breeze from her breath bristled what was left of its fur, and its tiny head jerked toward her. Half its face hung from its chin. One eye was a blind wrinkled dot, like a bit of raisin surrounded by flecks of skull.

I've been a coward, all my life. She stared at the mouse's double visage – furry innocence and grim determination.

Her arm quit twitching. Her breathing slowed. Everything seemed to shrink upon itself until it was just her and this half-undead animal, taking each other in.

Nora could feel something gathering in the center of her gut, some energy beyond adrenaline, building, churning as she thought of this small creature, caught in circumstance, methodically dismembering itself to get free, break free, escape…

She had stopped breathing. She was utterly still. Her body waited for just one signal.

I'm sorry I didn't help earlier. I'm sorry that I didn't have your courage. But I need it now, and I'm not going to be a mouse anymore.

Now.

Her body sprang forward, hearing the ripping of clothes, flesh, most of her hair yanking out, her arms resisting for split seconds before breaking and tearing as well, long strips of thigh skin fluttering as her teeth closed on the tiny figure, bone and fur and juice bursting in her mouth, all around her and deep within her, like muscle clenching so strong all that escaped her teeth was a hiss…

Up the garage stairs. One. Two. Kitchen.

Her skin slick across the linoleum. Legs pushing, undulating like two separate tails. Arms – their remnants, really – more guidance than power.

Living room. Hallway. A bumped table drops a lamp.

"Nora?"

She keeps pushing toward his voice. Carpet itchy, wet with her passing. Just outside the bedroom door. She bangs it open with a half-hand.

He is raised up in bed, looking toward the doorway but not seeing her low form.

She settles back on her haunches. That low tickle, like before. She holds it tight as it churns faster, faster.

He finally catches sight of her. Freezes. "N – Nora?"

And she springs, clears the length of the room in one coiled jump, landing atop his chest. Her weight pops a gasp from him as she curls into a ball, sinking his ribs down. His stained hands just flap at her.

Wheezes now, trying for words. "I – I –"

She grinds deeper into him. Her lidless eyes don't blink. Not you. Me.

It takes a long time to work her mouth around his skull.

House Broken

James Reilly

Andrea peered out the window, but all she could make out through the frosted glass was the snow blowing furiously around the lone street light on the corner. The hail rattled against the windows like popcorn kernels in a frying pan, as the gusts of wind seemed destined to blow the house off of its foundation and send it sliding down the ice coated street and into the churning ocean at the base of the hill. She sighed as she stood back and looked at the clock on the wall.

Nearly 9:30pm; Dale was already two hours late, and he wasn't answering his cell. Her roommates had left earlier in the day, before the storm had gotten too bad. Andrea now wished she'd had done the same, as it was obvious that once Dale did get here – if he got here – she would be forced to spend Christmas Eve alone with her brother.

Andrea walked into the kitchen, filled a mug with hot water, and placed it into the microwave. Rummaging through the cabinets for a tea bag, she found an empty Lipton box, frowned, and tossed it on the counter, settling for a cup of cocoa instead.

She took the mug out of the microwave with thirty seconds left on the timer and dipped the tip of her finger in the steaming water.

"Fuck!" she cried, as she withdrew her hand and stuck her scalded fingertip into her mouth. Andrea dumped the contents of the envelope of cocoa into the mug, still sucking at her wounded digit. As she reached for a spoon, she paused when she heard a scraping sound on the roof.

She leaned against the small window above the kitchen sink, wiped her hand across the frost, and peered upward into the darkness outside. The sound grew louder, like the creak of a tree about to go over, and Andrea felt her heart start to race. A sheet of snow slid down in front of the kitchen window, slamming against the sill. Andrea leapt back, catching herself before letting out a scream.

The phone rang and this time she did scream.

"Jesus!" she cried, grabbing at her chest. She shook her head and grabbed the receiver off the wall.

"Hello?"

The phone clicked and crackled to silence, followed by a dial tone.

She hung up and the phone rang again.

"Hello?"

"Andrea? Can you…this…" It was her brother's voice, but the signal was weak and garbled.

"Drew? Thank God, I can…"

"Shit…I can't…you. I'm…stuck…Amhers…"

"What? Drew, I can't understand. You're breaking up."

"Stuck in Amherst!" he yelled. "Th…state police…closing… ways…driving ban…effect. I can't come…to…you!"

Andrea felt her heart sink, but was happy to hear her brother's voice, any voice.

"Look, don't worry. Just…just stay there. I'll be okay. Call me tomorr…"

The phone clicked again, but this time there was no dial tone, just silence. Andrea tapped the switch-hook, but the line was dead.

"Oh, great."

She looked around the living room; the tiny, sparsely decorated tree, dirty sweat socks jokingly hung from the mantle above the brick fireplace, and the small pile of presents she planned to take back to Derry for her family.

So this is Christmas, she thought.

The snow piled up to Barkley's knees, and the wind caked the rest of him with a thick layer of the stuff. He turned back toward

Leopard, still a half-a-block away, aiming the stolen palm sized camcorder at the sky.

"Leopard, move your ass you dumb 'spic!" Barkley shouted. His voice must have been lost in the wind as Leopard didn't move. Barkley shouted again.

"Leopard!"

"What?" Leopard cried back. "I'm comin', yo."

He held the camera in front of him, aiming it at Barkley, and trudged through the snow. He was taller than Barkley, and made it look easy.

"Bro, this thing is phat!" Leopard shouted. He aimed the camera at Barkley and Barkley swatted it away lazily.

"Man, get that thing out of my face already," Barkley said. "Cops see you with that shit and we're fucked."

Leopard scoffed at the idea. "Yeah, right," he said, smacking his tongue against the roof of his mouth. "Ain't no cops drivin' out in this shit. This city's ours tonight, bro."

Leopard's real name was Javier, but everyone called him "Leopard" on account of his fair complexion and the abundance of abnormally large brown freckles that dotted his face. He dropped the camera to his side and wrestled an overstuffed backpack off his shoulder. He dropped it into the snow in front of him, and unzipped it, revealing a bounty of watches, jewelry, prescription bottles, and liquor. He reached in and produced a liter of Wild Turkey, screwed off the cap, and held it up to Barkley.

"I feel like fuckin' Santa and shit," Leopard said with a grin.

"Yeah, just like Santa," Barkley said, taking a swig from the bottle. He winced as the whiskey burned its way down his throat and then handed the booze back to Leopard. "Half that shit you got in there's fuckin' worthless, bro."

"Nah, I got some good shit," Leopard said as he spun the cap back on the bottle of whiskey.

"Yeah? Good for what?" Barkley reached down into the backpack and grabbed a handful of the prescription bottles. "You even know what any of this shit is?"

Leopard shrugged. "Junkies'll buy anything, yo."

"Least the camera's worth a few bucks," Barkley said, dropping the pill bottles into the snow. Leopard sighed as he scooped them up.

"Why you gotta be like that, man?"

Barkley laughed. "We got a blizzard on Christmas Eve, with houses jacked with money, presents and shit, and you got us hittin' up houses of people poorer than us. That's all I'm sayin'."

"So, let's do another one then. You pick it this time!" Leopard said, heaving the backpack up onto his shoulder.

Barkley nodded as he reached inside of his jacket and pulled out a cigarette. He cupped a hand over it and turned his back to the wind as he lit it.

"C'mon," he said, tapping Leopard on the shoulder. He let out a stream of smoke that mingled with his hot breath and hung in the cold air long after he started walking. "I got a place."

Andrea dipped a facecloth into the water and wrung it out, then carefully draped it over her face as she rested her head against the curve of the tub. She took a deep breath and let it out slowly, letting her arms float to the surface. As the tension of the day flowed out of her, she felt weightless. Her knees and her toes breached the water as the base of her spine was now the only part of her touching the bottom of the tub. She arched her back and her body rocked gently. She slipped down further and the water pooled around her head, filling her ears. The music from the stereo down the hall became a distant, muffled rumble; as indistinguishable as rolling thunder. But then she heard something else; a rapping sound that made her sit upright. The face cloth slipped from her face and splashed in the tub between her thighs.

Someone was knocking at the door.

She stood and reached for her pink terrycloth robe. The cold air made her wet skin break out in goose pimples. She stepped out of the tub, wrapped the robe around her, and hurried out to the half-moon shaped window at the end of the hall. Andrea shielded her eyes from the light in the hall and peered out into the darkness. She could barely make out the lone streetlight, its glow diffused by layers of ice and snow caked against the window.

Someone pounded at the door again.

She ran back to the bathroom, slipped into a pair of tattered white slippers and hurried to the stairs. As she stepped down to the first landing, she could see a flash of movement through the small frosted glass panes at the top of the front door.

"Hello?"

Barkley stood in the middle of the intersection waiting on Leopard, who was taking a piss further up the road, swaying and shifting his hips in an effort to write his name in the snow. The plows had been by earlier, as they'd left a wake of heavily packed walls of snow three foot high on either side of the street. Even so, at least another three or four inches of fresh powder had fallen since. Leopard jogged down the street and slid into Barkley.

Barkley nearly fell over from the impact, and pushed Leopard hard, sending him teetering onto his backside.

"What the fuck?" Leopard sighed as he got back to his feet.

"Over there," Barkley said pointing to a rundown Victorian house sandwiched between two vacant buildings at the end of the street.

"What?" Leopard asked.

"That house. They rent it out to college kids," Barkley said, squinting through the snow. "It's Christmas, man. They're all gone for the holidays."

Leopard shrugged. "So?"

"So? That place is a goldmine. Computers, CD players, I betcha there's one in every bedroom."

Leopard's eyes lit up. "Shit, maybe they got Nintendo, yo?"

"Maybe," Barkley said.

He took a few steps down the street toward the house, and then froze.

"Shit," he muttered, as a stabbing pain shot through his head.

Leopard ran up beside him. "What?"

Barkley squeezed his eyes shut and shook off the pain. When he opened them again, he found himself staring up at a light in the second floor window.

"Nothin'," he said, rushing along and hoping Leopard wouldn't notice.

It was too late. Leopard grabbed his shoulder and pointed up at the light.

"Damn, bro. We can't hit this place," Leopard said. "Somebody's home!"

"Maybe," Barkley said, scanning the street. There wasn't a car on the block, and the driveway was empty. "Maybe not." He gave Leopard a pat on the shoulder. "But there's one way to find out."

Andrea crept to the bottom of the steps, and flicked the switch for the porch light before remembering that it hadn't worked since she'd moved in.

"Hello?" she cried. No reply, just the howl of wind forcing itself through the cracks under the door, sending a chill up her robe.

"Hello? Who's there?"

A muffled reply.

"What? Uh…yeah, hello?"

It was a man's voice; deep and throaty. Andrea pressed her ear to the door.

"What do you want?" she asked.

There was a long pause.

"Well?" she asked impatiently.

"Uh…can I use your phone…my car…I'm stuck!"

"I'm sorry…the lines are down."

Andrea brought her hand to her mouth, as if she could somehow stuff the words back in.

"Stupid," she whispered. She may as well have hung a sign in the window that said, YOUNG GIRL, ALONE & VULNERABLE.

She quickly regained her composure and shouted through the door.

"I can't help you right now," she said. "There's a gas station a few blocks north. I'm sure if you…"

"What?" the man asked. Andrea heard what sounded like another voice. Was that laughter?

"Is there someone else with you?" she asked, suddenly feeling a tingling in the pit of her stomach. She heard movement on the porch.

"No…no. It's just…I'm alone," he said. "Can I come in? It's…it's really bad out here."

"Look, I'm sorry. I…I can't. It's my…my boyfriend…he's…he's in bed…with the flu, so I have to go, okay. I have to…"

Andrea turned her head and yelled toward the stairs.

"What? I'm coming honey!" she yelled, and then turned back to the door. "He's really sick…I have…I have to go take care of him. I'm sorry!"

She waited for a reply, but got another long pause.

"Are you still there?" she asked.

"Okay," said the man. "Sorry…sorry to bother you."

"It's okay," Andrea replied. "The gas station…I'm sure…"

Her words trailed off as she heard the man loudly descend the steps.

Andrea slowly moved into the dark living room, and felt her way around the furniture to the bay window. She carefully peeled back the curtain, and leaned in toward the glass. It was too frosted over to make out much more than the distorted lights in the distance, but she stood there for a moment anyway, hoping to catch a glimpse of the man heading back up the street. Instead, she saw a blurred figure race quickly across the porch. Andrea fell back against the couch, gasping, and then raced back to the front door. The man began to pound on it again, this time more aggressively. She pressed her back to the door and held her hands to her ears.

"Go away!" she screamed. "Go away before I call the police!"

The doorknob rattled as the man on the other side tested the lock, and then the entire door shook as he threw his weight against it, sending Andrea tumbling forward to her knees. She scurried back to the door and pressed her back up against it, kicking off her slippers and wedging her bare feet against the cold, hardwood floor.

It was then that she heard the glass shatter in the kitchen.

"She's alone, man," Barkley said. "She's fucking alone!"

Leopard didn't like the look in his friend's eyes. "Still, bro, I ain't goin' in there," he said, pushing past Barkley.

"Come on, man. We'll be in and out," Barkley pleaded. He grabbed Leopard by his hood and tugged him back toward him. Leopard spun around and the two were face to face. "I promise," Barkley whispered.

"She'll see our faces, Barkley," Leopard said.

Barkley shook his head. "Nah, nah, man. Look."

He unzipped his coat and pulled his scarf out from around his neck and threw it around Leopard's shoulders.

"Wrap it around your face," Barkley said.

"What about you?" Leopard asked.

Barkley slipped out of his coat and started unbuttoning his flannel shirt, revealing a white t-shirt underneath.

"Fuck, it's cold," he said, his teeth chattering on cue. He peeled off the flannel, balled it up in his hand, and pulled his coat back on. "I'll use this."

Leopard shook his head. "I dunno, man."

Barkley folded the flannel and covered his face, tying it behind his head. Then he did the same thing with the scarf around Leopard's neck. Barkley looked Leopard up and down and nodded.

"You're all set," he said, placing a hand on Leopard's shoulder. "Trust me."

Leopard stood there, staring down at his feet. The blowing snow spiraled around his boots. He looked back up at Barkley and nodded. "Fine. But we're in and out."

"In and out," Barkley repeated.

They walked back to the front steps, and Barkley paused.

"Listen, gimme a second. I'm gonna run around the side. Start banging on the front door and get her attention and I'll come in the back. I'll let you in when I'm inside."

Leopard took a deep breath, and Barkley frowned.

"Ya hear me, Leopard?" he asked.

"Yeah, I hear ya," Leopard said. And with that, Barkley trudged off into the darkness around the side of the house. Leopard stared up at the front door, squinting through the snow. He paused and looked up the street. The house was book ended by a warehouse on one side, and a fenced-in clearing that sloped down into the ocean on the other. Across the street there was a boarded up old fishery, a small parking lot, and an empty garage. This was as isolated as a house could get in this city, and, on a night like tonight, it was even more so.

Barkley sure knew how to pick them.

Leopard let out another deep sigh and walked back up the steps. He balled his fist and brought it down, stopping just shy of hitting the door. What was he doing? He knew where this was going. He knew this could only end one way, and that scared him. It scared the shit out of him. But he thought of the look in Barkley's eyes. He'd seen that look before.

And that scared him even more.

The girl swung at him, but Barkley sidestepped her, and pushed her down. Her body slapped hard against the tile floor, and she let out a dazed groan, before regaining her senses and quickly rolling onto her back. She scurried across the floor until the refrigerator blocked her progress. Barkley stomped toward her and grabbed a fistful of her hair. He pulled her to her feet while the girl shrieked in protest.

"Shut the fuck up!" he screamed, pushing her into the next room. She started to run toward the stairs, but Barkley grabbed her by the back of her robe, tugging her back to him.

"Just relax," he said, wrapping one arm around her neck, "and you won't get hurt."

Barkley reached for the latch on the front door with his free hand, unlocking the door and pulling it open a crack. Leopard charged through, as if catapulted by the cold wind, and quickly turned and slammed the door shut behind him.

"Here, hold her," Barkley said, pushing the girl into Leopard's arms. "I have to close the back door."

Leopard held on to the girl, but his eyes told Barkley he wasn't comfortable with it.

"I'll be right back," Barkley said. Leopard said nothing.

Barkley walked back into the kitchen, the glass from the window he punched out crunching under his boots. He closed the door, peered out into the dark alley between the house and the building next door, and then turned back toward the kitchen, eyeing the faded bone white Frigidaire in the corner. He walked over to it, peeling off his bulky thermal gloves, and looked inside. There was at least a half-case of beer, a few wine coolers, and two pizza boxes. Barkley smiled and grabbed a couple of cans of beer and one of the pizza boxes, setting them down on the kitchen table. He flipped open the lid to the box, revealing three huge slices of dried out pepperoni and green pepper pizza. It didn't look too appetizing, but he was starving. He leaned to the side and peered into the living room. Leopard held the girl close to him, with one of his arms wrapped around her waist, and a huge gloved hand covering her face.

"Yo, what are you doin', bro?" Leopard yelled. She was fighting him, but he had it under control, whether she liked it or not.

"Gimme a minute," Barkley said, grabbing a slice of pizza and stepping out of their line of sight. He lowered the flannel he had wrapped around his face and took a series of huge bites. On any other day this pizza would have gone down like cold, wet cardboard, but not today. Today this was the finest pizza he'd ever tasted. He cracked open a can of beer, and suds flowed up his nose, and out over his hand, splashing on the floor.

"Oh shit," he said, laughing and spitting up chewed chunks of pizza.

"Yo! Hurry the fuck up in there!" Leopard yelled from the other room. "Let's fuckin' do this!"

Barkley nodded, taking a swig of the beer. It was foamy and the taste reminded him of stale cigarettes, but it washed down the rest of the pizza. He took another swig, slammed the can down on the table, and brought the flannel back up over his face. As he started into the other room, he saw the phone on the wall. He picked up the receiver and held it to his ear.

"Phones are dead," Barkley said as he put the phone back on the hook.

He walked back to Leopard, grabbed the girl's wrist, and pulled her toward him. Leopard held onto her.

"Let her go, man. There's beer and pizza on the table in there. Go get some," Barkley said.

"We don't have time…" Leopard started. Barkley cut him off.

"We've got plenty of time. Go have some."

Leopard sighed, and released the girl, and Barkley pushed her down on the couch.

"Please…please don't…" she cried.

"Just sit there and shut up and you won't get hurt," he said, walking around behind the couch. Barkley pulled back the curtains, and lowered the blinds on the bay window. "Where's the light in here?"

The girl pointed to the wall near the bottom of the stairs. Barkley walked over and turned the dimmer, recoiling as the ceiling fixture flooded the room with a harsh bright light. He dialed it down to a dim glow, and surveyed the room. Leopard came back in from the kitchen.

"Take a look around upstairs, I'll watch her," Barkley said. He then looked at the girl. "You got any money."

She shook her head.

Barkley leaned in toward her.

"You got any money?" Barkley yelled.

The girl winced.

"I...I...only have...I have a little in...in...in...."

"In...in...in," Barkley screamed in her face, raising the back of his hand. "Spit it out or I'll bust your fucking head open."

"My purse!" the girl cried out. "I have...some...money in my purse."

She pointed to a chair in the corner of the room. A long wool jacket was draped over it, and a small, red handbag poked out from underneath. Barkley charged across the room and grabbed the purse, opening it upside down, and letting the contents spill out onto the floor. He knelt and dug through them. There was a makeup bag, a tin of mints, and bunch of receipts, and a small, embroidered change purse. Barkley opened the change purse and produced a trio of crumpled ten dollar bills and a condom, and shook his head.

"Is that it?" he asked.

The girl stared down at the floor and nodded.

Barkley sighed and looked back up at Leopard who was still standing behind him. He was staring at the girl, eyes wide and full of fear. Barkley punched him in the leg and Leopard jumped.

"I thought I told you to look upstairs?" Barkley snapped.

"Yeah, okay," Leopard said, quietly. He drifted toward the steps and looked back at the girl one more time before disappearing around the corner. Barkley waited until he heard Leopard's footfalls on the stairs before he stood up and walked back toward the girl. He slid the coffee table aside and knelt before her. She was trembling. When he placed his hands on her knees, she gasped, and Barkley held a finger to her mouth.

"Shhhhh..." he hissed, sliding his other hand up her under her robe.

"Please, god, no...," she said, shutting her eyes and squeezing out a stream of tears.

Barkley pressed his finger against her lips, dragging it across them, and she started to sob as his other hand slipped further up her thigh. He forced her knees apart and felt the warmth between her legs. She squeezed them shut, clamping his hand between her thighs, and slapped at him. Barkley brought his hand from her mouth and grabbed her neck, squeezing hard enough to make his point. The girl's body shuddered, and he felt her legs relax, and slowly drift apart again.

As she loosened her grip, he loosened his, and, beneath his flannel mask, he smiled.

Leopard flicked on the light and looked around the first bedroom. There were posters taped all over the walls; pictures of shirtless actors, and magazine clippings of bands he'd never heard of. There was a nice television in the corner, as well as an expensive looking stereo, but both were too big to lug through the snow. He rummaged through the drawers of a tall dresser. The top drawer was full of panties, nylons, and paired-up socks, but, stashed deep in the corner, Leopard felt a rolled up plastic baggie. He smiled as he pulled it out of the drawer and held it up to his nose. The bag smelled of perfume, but what was inside was unmistakably weed. He shoved the bag into his hip pocket and worked his way through the rest of the dresser, but found nothing else worth taking.

He turned his attention to a small brass vanity on the other side of the room. There was a black jewelry box with gold dolphins painted on its side sitting in the middle of the table, surrounded by containers of nail polish, lipstick, and an oversized wood-handled hairbrush. Leopard walked over to the box, lifted the lid, and sifted through its contents. He settled on a few thin gold chains, a couple of rings, and a pair of small studs that may or may not have been diamonds, and stuffed them in his pocket with the bag of weed. When he closed the lid on the jewelry box, he noticed the pictures taped to the vanity's mirror.

The picture was of a pretty brunette with a young man in a Mets hat. Another picture showed the same girl holding up a bottle of beer while on a beach with palm trees behind her. She was wearing an oversized white t-shirt shirt that said "RELAX" in huge black letters and was playfully flipping the bird at the photographer. Below those there was a bigger photo of her with two other girls sitting on the front steps of a house. Leopard recognized the one in the middle as the girl who was now downstairs with Barkley. In the picture, she was smiling. Her bright and friendly eyes seemed to stare right through him. He stared at the picture, studying the pretty girl's face, and suddenly felt sick to his stomach.

He'd seen this face before.

Many times before

And when he heard the scream from downstairs, he knew what had to be done.

Barkley turned the girl around and pressed her head into the couch cushions. He couldn't look at her face. He could never look at their faces. It was just easier this way. He peeled off his flannel shirt mask, and threw it on the floor next to him. The girl fought, slapping back at him, and he leaned forward, pressing his elbow into the base of her neck.

"Stop moving," he hissed.

Barkley grabbed one of her wrists, and bent it behind her back. She let out a muffled cry, reaching around her back with her free arm.

"Fight me and I swear to fuckin' Christ, I'll break it," he said as he lifted her robe.

The girl's free arm flailed about, and her fingernails gouged into his cheek, just missing his right eye.

"You fuckin' bitch!"

He bent her arm up far and fast; so far, in fact, that the back of her hand touched the base of her skull. A sickening popping sound echoed through the house as her arm popped out of its socket. Barkley let go of her wrist when he heard a deep, guttural sound emerging from her. The girl seemed energized by the pain, and threw herself backward so hard that she sent Barkley tumbling into the coffee table. As she stood, she screamed, and charged toward him. He lifted his leg and kicked her in the stomach, sending her flying across the room, and crashing into the brick fireplace.

Barkley jumped back to his feet and charged across the room, but before he could get to her, he felt a pair of arms around his chest, and soon he was back on the floor, facedown in the carpet. Barkley rolled onto his back and stared up at Leopard.

"What the fuck are you doing?" he asked.

Leopard shook his head.

"It's over. We're going," Leopard said.

Barkley sat up, slowly rising to his feet.

"What? What did you say?" Barkley asked.

"I said it's over," Leopard said. His voice was softer, and his gaze wavered.

Barkley shook his head. "I'll say when it's over. You…you just go back upstairs and do what I told you to do. And don't come down until I…"

Leopard's pale grey eyes suddenly grew very wide, and he grabbed Barkley by his shoulders, tossing him back to the floor. Barkley's nose hit the ground, and a burning pain spread across his face, right through to the back of his skull. As he pushed himself to his feet, drops of blood fell from his nose, rhythmically tapping against the carpet below. He stood, clenching his fists.

"Youfuckinsonofa'..," Barkley's voice trailed off as he turned and saw them standing there.

Leopard was staring down at the girl, and she back up at him. His face was pale, his mouth was moving but there were no words, just quick breaths that grew steadily shorter, and a deep rattling sound coming from the back of his throat. Barkley looked down at the iron fire poker sticking out of his friend's stomach and watched as the girl's hands slowly fell away from it. She stepped backward, shaking her head, her unblinking eyes locked with Leopard's.

"I'm…I didn't mean to…I didn't mean…"

Leopard dropped to his knees, and Barkley ran to his side to catch him, lowering him slowly to the ground. Leopard looked up at him and a faint smile spread across his face.

"It's over," he said.

Barkley lowered his head, and squeezed his eyes shut. He smeared blood and snot across his cheek with the back of his hand before wrapping his hands around the fire poker. He pressed his knee against Leopard's chest, and pulled. The head of the poker scraped against something hard inside of the body. Barkley twisted the poker, and tugged again. Leopard's body jerked forward like a fish on a hook, and Barkley pulled harder, finally tearing the poker free.

And then he looked back at the girl who sat motionless in the corner. She stared at Leopard's body. Barkley stood and walked toward her, but her eyes remained fixated on the dead man in the center of the room.

Barkley brought the poker above his head and brought it down upon her. The skin on her head split down the middle, peeling like an orange, as a spray of warm blood splashed into Barkley's face, but she didn't scream. She didn't even move.

She was broken.

She was done.

But he wasn't.

Not by a long shot.

He hit her again and again. He kept swinging until his palms ached so bad he couldn't hold the poker any longer. It dropped from his hands and into the dead girl's lap. He stepped back and stared at the unrecognizable lump of pulverized flesh and shattered bone that lay crumpled before him. He felt dizzy and bile crept up the back of his throat. Barkley stumbled back a few steps and doubled over as the cold pizza and beer in his stomach burst forth with such force that he could feel the blood vessels popping in his cheeks. He fell to one knee and struggled for balance. He wiped his mouth with his sleeve, swallowed hard, and turned to where Leopard's body lay.

But it was no longer there.

Barkley fell back on his haunches and backed himself against the wall. He looked at the corner where the girl was, but she was gone, too.

Not only were they gone, but the room...

It changed.

There were pictures on the wall that weren't there before. The sofa was different. The coffee table was gone. There was a TV where the armchair was, and the fireplace...

Where's the fireplace?

There has to be a fireplace!

That's how I get rid of…

Pure panic washed over him. His arms and legs suddenly tingled and his mind raced. He remembered it all; the cracking of bone, the wet snapping of blood on burnt embers, the smell of roasting flesh.

But how could he?

It hadn't even happened yet.

The pounding on the front door stopped, and Andrea ran for the closet in the front hall. She threw open the door and dug through a pile of blankets and shoes, until she felt the rubber grip of the aluminum softball bat. She pulled it out and stared at the thick barrel, took a deep breath, and held it aloft as she made her way to the kitchen. She darted across the dark living room and crouched as she peered around the corner. The back porch light cast a sea of shadows across the kitchen floor and small shards of glass shimmered like diamonds against the dark tile.

Andrea bit her bottom lip and slowly leaned into the kitchen, looking at the back door. There was a fist sized hole in the glass panel closest to the doorknob, but the door was still closed, and, other than the swirling wind and snow, there was nothing outside. She stepped over the glass, switching off the porch light, and bent down and peered out through the broken panel.

The stiff, frigid breeze made her eyes tear, as a blinding beam of light cut through the darkness. Andrea shielded her eyes from the glare, and stumbled backward. She let out a cry as glass crunched under foot, digging into her heels. She fell to her knees. The bat slipped out of her hands, rolled across the kitchen floor and into the shadows.

Barkley tried to open front door, but it wouldn't give. Much like the door in the kitchen, as if it were frozen shut. He peeled back the curtains and tried the windows but the snow seemed to be piled as high as the window pane. They wouldn't budge. He punched at the glass, but his fists hit the glass with a dull thud, leaving behind nothing more than smears of blood and skin from his raw knuckles.

"What the fuck is going on here!" he cried out. Except, as each moment passed, he knew what was going on; it was coming to him.

He just didn't want to admit it.

You never did…

Barkley paced back and forth and he suddenly felt very cold. He wrapped his arms around himself and tried to rub the chill out of his body. As he did, he felt something trickle down his cheek, wiped at it, and then examined his hand.

"Blood?" he asked aloud.

He ran his fingers along his face, feeling the rough patch of dried blood around his nose, then traced along his lips and cheeks, until he found something warm and wet in the center of his forehead. He pressed it, but felt no pain, just a dull pressure in his head. He ran his finger around the wound. It was small and round, and raised on the edges.

No bigger than a dime.

No bigger than a bullet hole.

"Are you okay, miss?" asked the older policeman.

Andrea nodded as the officer finished wrapping gauze around her feet.

"You're cut pretty bad," he said. "I wrapped 'em up, but we're gonna have to get you to the hospital. There's glass in there, and you're definitely gonna need stitches."

Andrea winced at the suggestion, and the young cop smiled as he stood up and carefully peeled off his rubber gloves.

"Burt, you wanna call it in?" the young cop asked.

"Huh?" Burt asked.

"An ambulance?" the young cop asked.

Burt nodded slowly. "Yeah, Danny," he said. "I'll call it in."

Burt scanned the room, his face ashen and eyes hollow. He shook his head and reached for the door handle. Andrea could see his hand trembling.

"I'll call it in," he said again softly, as he opened the door and slipped out into the howling storm.

"Is he okay?" Andrea asked.

Danny took a deep breath and frowned.

"Sure…I guess. I mean considering the circumstances," he said.

"What circumstances?" Andrea asked.

Danny cocked his head. "You're not from around here, then?"

"No, I'm from New Hampshire. I just…"

"You just go to school here," he said. "Sorry, somethin' like this you just figure everyone knows about."

"Something like what?" she asked.

Danny sprang from the arm of the chair, and nearly slipped on the floor, as Burt hurried inside, and forced the door closed behind him. His dark blue uniform half white, coated with windblown snow.

"Jesus, Burt," Danny said, hand over his heart. "You scared the shit outta me!"

"Ambulance…won't…be here," he said, trying to catch his breath. "We…gotta bring her in…ourselves."

Danny nodded. "Okay, let's get you in something…where's your coat?"

Andrea pointed at the closet as she tried to stand up. The pain shot through her, and she fell back into the chair.

"No, no. You stay there, I'll get something," he said.

Andrea sucked at the air through her teeth. "Thank you," she said. "There are extra blankets upstairs, at the end of the hall."

Danny nodded, and jogged up the stairs.

Burt's face grew as pale as the snow on his uniform. He cleared his throat, and reached for the doorknob.

"I'll wait outside," he said, and, before Andrea could reply, he was swallowed up by the snowy night.

Who were these people? Where did they come from? Barkley knew one of their faces. The old cop at the door; he'd seen him around, he was sure of it. But who was this girl? Where was he?

When was he?

He stepped across the room and looked at the old cop. He was standing toe to toe with him, but the man just stared right through him.

"Look at me!" he cried. "Can't you fucking see me?"

The cop just stood there, his gaze drifting back and forth around the room. He seemed to look everywhere except at Barkley. And then he finally did look at him, and when their eyes locked, Barkley saw it all again.

He saw the pieces of Leopard mingling with the pieces of the girl. He saw the bloody kitchen knives and the flimsy saw with the broken blade. He smelled the burning flesh in the fireplace, and heard the wet popping sounds it made as it was devoured by the flames.

And then he heard the door creak and snap.

And felt the cold air rush past him as it burst open.

And then he saw him. He was younger, but it was him. He knew it was him.

The fear in his eyes. The look of absolute horror.

It was the same.

The cop raised his weapon, and Barkley stood, raising his own.

And with a sound no louder than a firecracker he felt the life drain from him.

Again.

Now, the older version of the cop turned away, and walked out the door. Barkley started to call after him, but stopped himself. There was no point. The other cop came and wrapped the blankets around the shivering girl, and, as they left the house, and the memories started to fade, he wondered…

How many times had he lived this?

How many times had he killed that girl?

How many times had he watched Leopard die?

The snow piled up to Barkley's knees and the wind caked the rest of him with a thick layer of the stuff. He turned back toward Leopard, still a half-a-block away, aiming the stolen palm sized camcorder at the sky.

The Woman Who Coughs Up Flies

David Turnbull

Her entire world is hemmed in by the narrowly defined boundaries of her armchair. She has been unable to move since she collapsed there and felt its enveloping softness wrap around her like a glove. It seems to her that she might eventually become one with the upholstery. Her frail body feels like it has moulded itself to the yielding contours of the cushions. The joints in her knees seem frozen in place, as if they will never allow her to stand straight again. She wonders if she is fading to the colour of the fabric?

She watches the clock on the wall, following each circuit of the hands from twelve to twelve and back round again. She counts off each click to the minute, takes mental stock of each turn of the hour, and sees day turn into night and back again.

Her grandson, who left her this way, has been back to the house several times now. She hears him crashing around upstairs as he searches for her jewellery. She hears him unplugging her appliances in the kitchen and struggling with them along the corridor. She hears him emptying out the garden shed, hauling away the lawnmower and the hedge trimmer and the shears and the shovel.

He hasn't yet had the courage to return to the living room. But soon he will have no choice. There are too many valuable things in this room. There's a terrible hunger that drives him. It won't let him rest till he's had the lot.

She feels an itching sensation at the back of her throat. She knows what is coming and she tries to swallow it back. Her mouth is far too dry, she can't produce enough saliva to lubricate her tongue. She coughs and the thing that she dreads arrives in her mouth like wet phlegm. A small and dark object goes zipping past her lips as fast as a bullet from a gun.

Half way across the room the projectile halts in mid air. It turns and comes back in her direction, flitting and weaving this way and that. Before her eyes hovers a plump, black fly with quick, transparent wings that she has somehow brought up from deep inside her.

This is the fourth of its kind to have come tumbling out of her mouth. She has never known anything like it. She feels embarrassed, somehow unclean, mortified by the inference. She has a theory as to why this is happening. But she doesn't dwell upon it. The implications are too terrible.

The fly settles on the light shade above her head, fidgeting and fussing alongside its three cousins. She hears them buzzing in unison and the sound is like some distant, spiteful conversation. She imagines them gossiping about the state she's in, looking down upon her and casting aspersions.

After a while one of the flies dismounts the light shade and goes spiralling down to settle on a picture frame that sits on her mantelpiece accumulating layers of dust that put her to shame. The picture is of her grandson, Martin. When he was younger. When he was her beautiful, blue-eyed boy. When he showered his unconditional love upon her and she smothered his head with her kisses. When his visits brought the sunshine into her day and made her sing with the joy of life.

Martin is lost to her now. His eyes no longer sparkle. His hair no longer shines. He has been replaced by a half dead beast that exists in a permanent drug induced stupor and only comes fully awake when it explodes into a blood spitting rage. The thought of what he has become makes her want to cry. But even the ability to carry out such a simple act has been robbed from her. Her eyes have become as arid as dried out riverbeds.

"Martin." She whispers his name and her voice rasps like that of an acute asthmatic. The hands of the clock jump to another minute. The three remaining flies corkscrew down and cavort around her head. "Martin." His name is like a wish upon her lips. In spite of what he has done and what he has become, he is the one that she waits for as she sits motionless inside the pliant folds of her armchair.

The fly on the mantelpiece launches itself from the picture frame and comes pestering around her head with the others. She would swat them away if her hands would move when she tells them. They are like hunks of lead on the end of her flaccid arms. Not even a finger will budge. The fly lands on her chin and rubs its legs together. Her eyes follow its twisting, erratic route across her face.

She watches the clock. Each second seems to take an age to tick off. Eventually another minute goes by. Old forgotten songs go lilting around her head. Matt Munro and Al Martino. Trini Lopez and Tony Bennett. They form the soundtrack to fragmented slices of her life. She recalls better days, coloured yellow by the sun. She sees Martin, as a small child, dropping the needle to the record and dancing with her across the floor, giggling and squealing with delight. A minute drifts to fifteen, fifteen drags to thirty, thirty heaves its weary way to the hour.

Her throat starts to tickle again. She coughs and this time two flies come buzzing out of her mouth. They caper around the room for a while before settling themselves amongst the pleats of her mouldering curtains.

The curtains are closed. Even during the daylight hours the room is shrouded in a cold and murky gloom. Martin pulled them shut after she'd fallen back into the armchair. He didn't want anyone peering in through the windows and discovering what he had done.

He needn't have worried. No one is likely to come looking for her. Her husband died long before Martin was born. Her daughter and son-in-law no longer have any contact with her. They fell out with her when they tried to take a hard line with Martin and she allowed herself to become the soft touch. In their eyes she undermined them and her betrayal sent Martin spiralling further down into his decline.

She remembers how he'd come to her begging to borrow some money because his parents had left him short for this or that, a CD or a book or the latest brand of trainers. He'd look at her with those sad blue eyes and take her in a big bear hug and before she knew it her purse would be out and half her pension would fall into his greedy, expectant hands.

She remembers the arguments with her daughter.

"Do you know what he does with the money you give him?"

She would defend him, take his side, make excuses for him. "He's young. He'll learn how to manage his money. You were the same at his age."

"Your money goes straight to those filthy dealers," her daughter would yell down the phone. "You'd be as well buying the stuff for him yourself."

"I'm sure it's not as bad as all that," she'd reply.

"He's an addict." Her daughter would be crying now, pleading with her. "Please, Mum. Don't give him any more money. You have no idea what this is doing to him. Promise me."

And she would promise.

But when Martin next came to visit all she could see before her was her little soldier. The boy who used to help her with her household chores. The boy who'd sit on the floor with his shoulder against her leg and his head on her lap. The boy who was her only companion on long, lonely winter nights, laughing with her at comedy shows on TV as she stroked his hair. She couldn't bring herself to believe that her boy, her only grandchild, was the same person her daughter worried so much about. So she would give him her money and he would go and buy what he needed.

When his parents finally gave up on him and threw him out on the street she let him move in. She cleaned up after him, ignoring the bloodstains on the sleeves of his shirts and the dried vomit on the collars. Pretending that she hadn't seen the little packages of white powder that were pushed to the back of his sock drawer or the used needles that poked dangerously out of his paper bin. She gave him more and more of her money. She started dipping into her savings. She turned a blind eye when little things went missing from the house.

She had a final blazing row with her daughter, defending him to the last. Her son-in-law came on the phone and hurled abuse at her. "You stupid old woman! He's going to wind up dead in the gutter somewhere and it'll be all your fault!"

For a long, long time she remained intentionally blind to what was going on around her, telling herself it wasn't true, it couldn't be true. Not Martin. Not her Martin. Not her boy. Not her beautiful blue-eyed boy.

Then one day something clicked in her head and cleared the fog from her eyes. She saw Martin for what he had become. The spark had gone from his eyes, the shine had gone from his hair, his complexion had become grey and deathly. His hands trembled when he tried to lift a cup of tea to his mouth. He'd been wearing the same clothes for a month. She couldn't remember when he'd last had a bath. There was a bad smell about him. It was like the smell of death, clinging to him, waiting till it sank right through him.

He asked her for money. She had her back to him, furniture polish in one hand and a dusting cloth in the other. "No," she said. The word came out as a whisper.

"Pardon?" She knew from his tone that he couldn't believe what she'd just said.

"No," she said again, this time louder. "I'm not giving you any more money till you promise to stop taking that terrible stuff."

"I need money!" She heard him stand to his feet.

She turned to face him.

"I can't afford it," she said.

"Of course you can," he told her. "You're loaded."

"You've had all I can give you for this week."

His face turned red. His eyes seemed to roll crazily in their sockets. He clenched his teeth together and stepped menacingly towards her.

"Give me some fucking money!" he demanded.

She was stunned by his language and the threatening pitch of his voice. But she stood her ground, reminding herself that it was the drugs and not Martin that was talking to her this way.

"No!" she said again, her knuckles turning white as she clutched the furniture polish.

She saw him close his fist and raise his arm. She looked into his eyes. The fury that was in them terrified her, but she didn't blink. The old Martin was in there somewhere. He had to be.

They stood like that for a long time, his cold blue eyes staring into hers. She could feel her knees trembling and her heart racing far too fast. After a while he bowed his head and dropped his arm. For a moment she thought that she'd somehow gotten through to him. Unfortunately his anger was far from spent.

He brought his heel down onto her foot with such force that she felt sure some of the bones cracked. The polish fell from her hand and clattered to the floor. A moment later she fell too. She bit her tongue with the jar of the impact. She watched as, without a second glance, he turned from her and picked up her handbag. The pain in her foot was excruciating. She could taste blood in her mouth. Through floods of tears she watched him help himself to the last money in her purse. Then in a blink of her eye he was gone, slamming the door so loudly that the walls shook.

She didn't see him again for ten long days. She hobbled around the house on her swollen foot, afraid to go to the doctor in case he asked too many questions. She managed to live on the few bits and pieces of food that were left in her fridge and cupboards. At night she lay awake, listening for the turn of his key in the door, part of her wishing he'd come home, part of her hoping that he wouldn't.

When he finally came slouching through a hole in the fence and into the back garden her foot had almost healed and she was walking a bit steadier on it. He looked at her through the kitchen window and his face was etched with guilt and sorrow. The first thing he said to her was: "Sorry." A tear went rolling down his face. She forgave him instantly.

She told him that she needed him to take her to the supermarket to buy some food. She put her arm through his for support as they walked down the High Street. He cracked a joke and she laughed. He whistled the chorus to one of the old songs from her record collection and she hummed along. It felt almost the way it had once been with him.

She withdrew some money from her account at a cash dispenser. When they came back home she cooked him a hot meal. Grilled chicken, chips and peas. His favourite when he was a boy. Sadly she watched him trying to force the food down, barely chewing, swallowing awkwardly as if he was being compelled to eat cardboard. He had no appetite whatsoever. Her heart sank with the realisation that he was still hungry for one thing only.

When the meal was over a cloud seemed to have descended over him. His face was sullen. His eyes seemed to have submerged into their sockets. He asked her for the last £20 out of the money she'd withdrawn. His hands were jittering across the tabletop. His breath came out of his mouth in an eerie, fluttering staccato. She didn't dare say no. He left without saying goodbye.

In the weeks that followed he hit her again, even when she agreed to his increasing demands for money. He was no longer in control of his actions. He was as taut as a length of wire ready to snap at the slightest touch. He always apologised. She always forgave him. And when she did the words of her son-in-law would ring in her ears. "He's going to wind up dead in some gutter somewhere and it'll all be your fault." But she couldn't help herself. She was as much addicted to him as he was to the drugs. It was better to have him that way than not to have him at all.

She hears him now, the impatient roughness of his key in the lock, the opening and slamming shut of the front door, his heavy feet clomping along the hallway.

The flies launch themselves from the light shade and curtains. They dodge around the room, buzzing past each other. She feels the familiar itching at the back of her throat. She coughs twice. Two flies roll over her tongue. Both take off from her brittle lip to join the aerial antics of the others.

She hears Martin on the stairs. She hears him enter her bedroom. She hears his frantic, fruitless search. She hears him go into the small room that once was his. There's nothing there for him to find. He'd sold all of his own belongings long before he started on hers. She hears him grunt with frustration and kick the wall. She hears him as he comes crashing back down the stairs.

The tickle in her throat has become impossible. She coughs and coughs and coughs and fly after fly after fly comes somersaulting out into the room.

She hears Martin in the kitchen. The rage is building up within him again. He's yanking open the cupboard doors and smashing crockery against the tiled floor. Around her the room is alive with the sombre droning of the flies and the dizzying dash-dash-dash of their intersecting flight paths.

Now she hears Martin in the hall again. She hears him stop outside the living room door. There is a long, long silence. She imagines him hesitating, swallowing hard, breaking into a cold sweat, not sure if he's desperate enough yet to come through the door.

One by one the flies descend and settle upon her. Some on her hands and arms. Others on the wiry strands of her grey hair. Most alight upon on her face like a dark, undulating mask. She feels a sensation as if she's about to sneeze. A fly comes crawling cautiously down the inside of her nose.

On the other side of the door she hears Martin take a deep breath. She sees the slow turn of the door handle. She hears the creak of the hinges. The door is edged slowly open. The flies sit still and patient. Their wings quiver. They crouch on tiny legs.

The door is flung wide. Martin steps in. The flies explode away from her like a flock of startled birds evacuating a rooftop. Martin jumps slightly when he sees this.

He is wearing one of those hooded sweatshirts that he has a penchant for. The hood is up around his head. His left hand has a dirty bandage wrapped around it. She can't see his eyes, but she can tell from the way he sways from side to side that he is high. Stupefied and only just aware of where he is and what he's doing.

He avoids looking over at her chair. He fumbles in the pocket of his jeans and brings out a handkerchief to hold against his mouth and nose. The smell in this room must be terrible. The shame of it gnaws at her. She hears the flies gossiping around her head.

Martin walks purposefully towards the cabinet that stands in the far corner of the room and opens the glass doors. One by one he begins to transfer her collection of ornamental silverware from the cabinet to a small, battered sports bag.

Determinately she curls the frail joints of her fingers around the armrests of the chair and slowly pulls herself to her feet. Parts of her that could not move before move now with the slow, faltering motion of a long disused engine. Her knees grind like badly oiled hinges. She strains against their stubborn resistance. Flies dance up and down the walls and hurl themselves about the room. She forces herself forward, step by deliberate step. The old, worn floorboards creak and groan under her lumbering weight.

Martin turns to the source of the noise. His jaw drops. His eyes pop wide with horror. The ornament in his hand falls and rattles across the floor. Half a dozen flies descend on him and fidget around his head as he steps away from her.

"How?" is all he can manage to say.

He pulls back his hood and looks from her face to her stomach and back again. Slowly she follows his gaze. The front of her dress is ripped and caked in thick, dried blood. Under the tattered shreds there are three festering wounds, rotted black as liquorice. Martin's cruel handiwork. He finally progressed from kicks and punches to a weapon. A kitchen knife she seems to recall.

She had been dicing carrots in the kitchen when the argument started. As usual it was about money. Somehow all of their arguments seemed to start in the kitchen. As if fate was circling bleakly above them in that room like a murder of crows ready to swoop down.

She turned away from him when he began to rant and rave and throw foul-mouthed insults in her direction. When she turned back the knife was already in his hand. She saw it glint once, twice, and thrice as he plunged it into her belly. She staggered backwards and caught him looking at the blood that dripped from the blade as if he had no idea where it had come from.

Crying and whimpering he helped her to the front room and lowered her into the armchair. What he said next was ridiculous. "I'll get you a drink of water."

"Phone for an ambulance," she managed to groan.

He left the room. She felt her eyelids close. For a while all she was aware of was darkness and the dull, throbbing pain of the stab wounds. When her eyes flickered hesitantly open once more Martin was hovering over her. She saw her purse in his hand and the cold, remote look in his eye. He closed the curtains and engulfed her in darkness. He turned from her and left the room. She watched the door close behind him. She waited for the door to open again. It never did.

Until now.

Now her wounds ooze and drip with the foul and fetid fluids of her decomposing body. Within their putrefying hollows hordes of pink maggots squirm and writhe, gorging themselves on her decaying flesh. Some of them are in the advanced stages of transformation. She understands now exactly where the flies come from. She feels the tickle of their feet against her windpipe. She coughs again and another fly blunders out of her mouth.

The sight of this spurs Martin into action. He turns to run. Not realising that the door has swung backward he runs straight into it. The rebound sends him crashing down onto the floor.

She shuffles to where he lies and looks down on him. A purple bruise begins to form on his forehead. Flies fall upon his face and scurry around on their wiry legs. He lets out a yell and swats them away.

"I've been waiting for you," she whispers. "You've been gone such a long, long time." With each word another fly falls from her mouth.

Martin tries to scramble to his feet, but she curls her cold, reanimated fingers around his neck. He struggles, attempting desperately to pull her off. He is no match for her. Her dead hands are far, far stronger than they ever were in life.

"Come back to me, Martin," she croons. "Be mine once more." She squeezes tighter at his neck. His eyes bulge. His complexion becomes as purple as the bruise on his forehead. Then, as he slips into unconsciousness, his face relaxes and his drug addled features soften. She sees him once more as her beautiful, blue-eyed boy. She squeezes a little harder. Her touch is almost tender. The last breath rattles slowly from his mouth.

Somehow she manages to drag him back across the floor to her armchair. She settles back into it. Her body melds with its gentle contours. She arranges Martin so that he is sitting on the floor, his shoulder leaning against her leg, his head upon her lap. Tenderly she strokes his hair. The clock ticks to the minute. The hint of an old nostalgic song is playing distantly somewhere in her subconscious. Martin is by her side. All is well. The day becomes as yellow as the sun.

Her eyes fall shut. Her head lolls to one side. Her jaw drops open. She is free now to pass over. For a long time afterwards black flies with quick, transparent wings emerge from the hollow cavern of her mouth and skit this way and that across the room.

Special Offer

John Llewellyn Probert

"We're going to take a short break now, but don't forget our switchboard will be staying open to take orders for that lovely diamante-encrusted globe of the world, that superb scale model of the Eiffel tower made out of pewter, and all the other fantastic items I've been showing you over the last two hours in our special after midnight Sit 'N' Shop Bazaar of the Bizarre. When we come back it'll be subscribers only so make sure you've got your PIN number ready!"

Tony Chivers breathed a sigh of relief as he received the signal to say they'd cut to the ad break. He loosened the knot of his 'genuine imitation silk of polyester' blue and black striped tie (a bargain from Sit'N'Shop at half the price you could expect to pay in a store), popped open the collar of his white button-down collar cotton shirt (available in packs of three for the price of one but hurry! Only a few left!) and took a cigarette from the crumpled packet of Benson & Hedges he kept off camera. He lit it and inhaled deeply, his muscles relaxing as three hours of nicotine deprivation were assuaged. He was alone in the studio – the camera operated by a remote control timer that switched to the ads as necessary and was responsible for the encryption between 3.00am and 4.30am – but he still made sure to smoke behind the camera in case the fumes could be spotted when he went back on air.

This was his only break of the night. By all rights 'Sit'N'Shop' wasn't supposed to stop broadcasting this long for a commercial break, but it was hardly as if the channel would be getting many casual viewers at 2.45am on a Tuesday morning, let alone any who would consider complaining to consumer watchdogs. Of those who were awake at this time, the market research had shown that the lonely were watching porn, the young some MTV chill-out thing, no doubt with the aid of a little chemical enhancement, and the elderly a news channel, something like CNN. Tony imagined them smirking as they munched on tea-sodden Digestive biscuits, their eyes glued to the endless replays of people younger than themselves who had made it to the grave before them. Besides, he thought, he needed this. When he started up again it would be his busiest hour and a half of the week.

Sit'N'Shop's encrypted slot.

Hardly anyone knew that the channel had ninety minutes of late night programming not available to the general public. But a few did. Those special members of the viewing audience who even now were getting ready to watch and participate. He could just see them having set their alarms for this time, dragging themselves out of bed to come downstairs and switch the television on, sitting there in the flickering darkness readying themselves to key in series of codes which were changed on a daily basis to prevent unwanted spectators. On the other hand perhaps they didn't try and sleep beforehand. Perhaps they just waited up nervously, flicking through all the other crap that was on at that time with increasingly jittering fingers. Well, he thought, they had good reason to be afraid. After all, they wouldn't be tuning in if they weren't in serious trouble.

Tony knew for a fact that the only adverts being played before the show would be for 'low-cost loans'. The knowledge always raised a tired smile. Eddie Vincent, his producer, always called it 'the glorious circle'. It was so easy these days for people to get into debt. Some even seemed to manage it just through buying too much of the sort of crap the Sit 'N' Shop Channel peddled twenty two and a half hours a day. Then when the limits on all their credit cards were exceeded they could organise a loan to consolidate their debts. Even at this stage, an unlucky few seemed to deal with the crawling, nagging feelings of desperation that they owed such a huge amount of money by spending even more cash they didn't have.

His earpiece hummed. Sheila, the only other person within a five mile radius of where he was standing, told him from her position at the switchboard that they already had a couple of calls waiting. Tony stubbed out his second cigarette just as the little red light flashed on top of the camera.

Here we go again, he thought.

"Good evening, or rather good morning ladies and gentlemen, and welcome to the special part of our transmission. I'm reliably informed that we already have a couple of calls waiting and I believe the first is from Angela. She's thirty two and if I could remind her no surnames on air please just to maintain confidentiality, the same goes for the actual amount you owe. The details you've given our switchboard are just between you and us. Angela, could you tell us what we can do for you, please?"

There was a pause. There always was with the first one. Tony let it ride. They always managed to get going in the end. After all, they didn't have much choice. The female voice trembled in a way he knew some of his bosses found unaccountably thrilling.

"Hello Mr Chivers."

"Tony, please." It wasn't his real name so he didn't care.

"Sorry – Tony. Well, I'm thirty two and my problem is that the overdraft I have at the bank is getting a bit uncontrollable."

"It's coming up on the screen now," said Tony, looking at the monitor positioned to the left of the camera which was now displaying the amount she owed. Compared to some of the debts Tony had to deal with it wasn't too bad at all.

"It was much higher," Angela explained. "I've managed to pay some of it off, but I can't see myself managing to clear much more. The problem is that if I don't do something now the interest will just cause the amount I owe to go up again and everything I've paid back so far will be for nothing. I talked to someone who told me about your programme and gave me the number."

Tony nodded sympathetically, doubting that talking was all she had needed to do to get access to the codes.

"I can understand. So what you're saying is you need a quick and easy way of earning the outstanding amount?"

A pause.

"Yes."

Tony rubbed his hands together and assumed the air of a shop-keeper trying to help a customer.

"Well I wouldn't have thought that should be too much of a problem. The autocue is bringing up a list of possible options, and I can see from the picture you've sent to us on the Web Cam that you're quite an attractive girl."

"I don't know about that."

Tony marvelled at how she could sound so coy at a time like this. He turned to look at the monitor again. Now a list of items, white letters on a black background, was scrolling up the screen.

"Well Angela, we've got quite a few choices here. First of all, can I presume you would prefer an option that involves a minimum of physical pain to either yourself or anyone else?"

"Yes please. None at all if possible."

No pause this time. Tony smiled. This one would be easy.

"I see from your details on the screen that you live in Chiswick?"

"That's correct."

"Fine. Well this Saturday night there is going to be a meeting at a private gentleman's club located close to junction 2 of the M4. We'll give you the details once you're off air. All you have to do is turn up, do whatever they want for the course of the evening and we will ensure that your debts are settled."

This time the pause lasted twenty seconds.

"Is that the only option?" The tremor in her voice was stronger now...

"Not the only one my love but believe me it's the quickest and least painful. If you stay tuned in for the rest of the show I think you'll realise some of our customers don't have the luxury of getting off quite so lightly."

"I see."

Her voice was barely a whisper, and there was another long pause before she gave him her decision.

"Okay."

"I'm sorry my love could you speak up a little? Just so we can get it on tape for confirmatory and contractual purposes?"

She repeated her reply and he could hear the shame in her voice. If only she knew what some people had to do, Tony thought.

"Thanks very much Angela. Like I said, our switchboard operator will give you the details and explain the small print. As with all our customers tonight, I would seriously suggest that you listen to that part very carefully." In the bright light of day it was not unusual for customers to consider reneging the deal. Some of them even thought about going to the police. The small print put a stop to that. Which, of course, is what it was there for.

The next customer was through.

"Hello David from Abertillery. What can we do for you?"

"I need some money quickly to settle some debts, provide me with safe passage out of the country and the setting up of a new identity in–"

"That's all right David. We don't need a justification of the amount, just how much you need. The options are running past me now. Okay. I see from the file we have on you that you've spent some time at Her Majesty's Pleasure?"

"Yes."

"For armed robbery?"

"Yes."

"So you know how to handle a firearm?"

"If it's a job taking someone out I'd be happy to do it."

"It's a man, his wife, and his daughter actually, but if that's all right then we can provide you with the details. We'd like the job done by next Wednesday please, after which you will receive the necessary sum and also at no extra charge the services of our emigration department."

"I don't know if even you can help me," said the next male caller.

"We'll be the judge of that my friend," said Tony. "If it's a financial matter we can usually do something. It's Chris isn't it? I'll just have a look at the monitor Chris."

It was a considerable amount of money.

"Quite a few pounds, and I dare say a few pence as well." Tony's quip failed to elicit a reaction, but he was doing it for his own morale rather than that of any of the poor souls he was trying to assist this evening. The autocue didn't need to scroll this time. Once you started owing that sort of money the options for a quick and easy fix were limited.

"I take it you've liquidated all your assets?" Tony asked. Sometimes the callers were so distressed, or so brainwashed by a culture in which the immediate solution to a problem was to borrow more money, that they hadn't even thought to do that.

"Everything," was the reply. "They're gambling debts you see and unless I pay up they've said that–"

"We're not interested here in what will happen to you, Chris. We know you wouldn't be ringing unless the situation was desperate. Have you sold your house?"

"We rent."

"I see. Sorry about that. You'll be pleased to hear we do have a couple of options, though. I see that you're married?"

"Yes."

"Any children?"

"Not yet."

"But no reason why you can't have them?"

"No."

There was the briefest of pauses after that last reply but Tony ignored it. It wasn't his fault these people got themselves into so much trouble.

"What I'm trying to say here Chris is that if your lovely wife was to become pregnant and to deliver a full-term normal baby then that could probably just about write off the amount you owe."

"You mean you–"

"Our service is very discreet, and the baby would be retrieved by our agents while it was still in the maternity unit. Saves us all the trouble of going to a customer's house. You wouldn't believe the out of the way places some people choose to live."

There was silence.

"You might like to think it over," said Tony. "People in your situation often do. Could I just add that the price quoted is for a healthy full-term male Caucasian boy. If it were to be a girl or any other race variant we would need to renegotiate on the basis of current international demand. I'm sure you understand."

Chris rang off without saying anything further. Tony knew Sheila would be giving him a contact number and a series of passwords should he decide to take the company up on its offer.

Other than that it was a fairly quiet night. All the other amounts asked for were considerably smaller, and could be solved by the agreement to perform various illegal or sexual acts. In fact by the time they went off air most of the requests from the company's customer base had been fulfilled, right down to that rather odd one for certain household pets.

Tony picked up his mail on the way out. There were two envelopes, one of which contained his pay slip. He looked at the tiny amount of his salary that had been transferred into his bank account for him to live on. The rest, of course, contributed to paying off his and his wife's debts. The second contained a sachet of white powder and a slip of paper on which was written today's date and a time which was an hour from now. He almost vomited when he saw it.

Oh no, he thought. Not again.

One of his first questions when he had started working for his employers had been why they felt it necessary to broadcast the deals he made on behalf of the company. His answer had been a warning that if he asked any further questions they would have to find someone else to take his place. He had kept quiet after that. Perhaps the moneylenders liked to see their problem cases being sorted out. Maybe there were even some weird people out there who got a kick out of watching the sheer desperation and misery of people who had got themselves up to their necks in debt.

Or even over their heads.

The night sky over the horizon was the pale indigo of approaching dawn as Tony parked his rusting Ford Fiesta in the driveway of his bungalow. Before he went into his house he paused for a moment and looked up and down the road in which he lived. The neat rows of single storey dwellings side by side looked so innocent in the early morning twilight. But who knew what might be going on behind those brightly-painted front doors, those front room curtains that doubtless matched the carpet and three piece suite bought on the never-never? He took a deep breath and the ozone in the air stung his nostrils.

He slammed the front door to announce his arrival. From the living room, to the right of the entrance hall, his wife Paula gurgled a greeting. He ignored her and went straight into the kitchen, passing the now-empty crib that sat next to the bare telephone table.

He boiled some water in a saucepan and made himself a mug of tea. He spooned instant coffee into Paula's cup, added powdered milk, water and the contents of the sachet he had been sent. He snapped on the cup's special plastic top with its straw attached, and carried the drinks into the front room.

Bright yellow sunlight glowed through the crack in the frayed curtains, but Tony didn't draw them. The living room hadn't seen daylight for several months now. He took a sip from his mug, put it down on the stained carpet, and turned to his wife. She was seated in a worn, stained armchair, the dull brown colour of which had become darker in places recently. It was the only piece of furniture in the room apart from the dialysis machine the company had thoughtfully provided after her second kidney had been removed. Not, of course, because of any compassion on the company's part – they had just been protecting their investment.

"I've brought you some coffee," he said, switching on the battered electric fire.

She gurgled in reply and waved the stump of her right arm at him. Where it ended just above the elbow the crude bandage Tony had made out of an old flannel had oozed a little fresh blood overnight. She couldn't press on it because her left arm had been taken off at the shoulder a month ago.

Yet even those losses, along with her tongue, had still not been enough.

He would never be able to come to terms with it. He had tried so many times not to blame himself, not to feel as if he was somehow responsible for his wife's spending addiction. After all, it was she who had taken the loan out in the first place. He still couldn't believe how quickly the interest rate had rocketed. And the living hell to which he was subjecting her had been her wish, after she had tried all those oh-so desperate measures to pay everything back, culminating in the day when he had come home to find that she had given them their son. His boy, Max.

"They say this should be the last time," he said. As she tried to mouth words that sounded like 'Are you sure?' he pushed the straw between her lips, tipped up the cup and squeezed the sedative liquid down her throat.

Through the crack in the curtains he could see the private ambulance that had pulled up outside to take his wife away again and remove God-knows-what from her this time. Remove it so that it could be transplanted into someone who had sufficient will to live, sufficient funds, and most of all sufficient lack of morals not to care where the donor tissue came from.

Her eyelids began to flutter as he undid the restraining straps.

"Probably," he whispered in her ear as he carried what was left of her to the door.

"Probably."

Body Hunt

Chet Gottfried

"**D**ad! Dad! Dad!"

Woken by his son's shouting, Sid jumped out of bed and raced down the stairs to the basement while flicking on light switches. He stopped in front of the tear-stained Danny – and saw the three naked bodies hanging upside-down and dripping blood.

"You promised!"

"Okay, okay, Danny, I know. I promised. Now stop crying. It's going to be all right."

"You promised!"

"I left a note with Oscar. You know Oscar. He's pretty reliable. I bet he's going to return."

Danny pointed to the third body. "That's Oscar."

Sid approached a step closer. "Well I'll be! I wonder if anyone took over his route? Oscar's assistant might have grabbed it. Business is getting very fierce. I warned Oscar that he better watch out. You can't go hiring clever help."

"Daddy!"

"It's only a mistake, son. Mistakes happen. I guess the assistant read the note wrong." Sid placed his right hand on Danny's shoulder, but Danny shook the hand away.

"But you know that I need the blood for school. Mr. Jenkins said I had to bring the blood from at least five bodies. Look! Just look! There's only three. Everyone's gonna know that I don't have enough. The whole ceremony is gonna be a bust, and they'll blame me! I'll get left behind in fourth grade, and you know what that means."

"I left a note…"

"Daddy!"

Sid grabbed Danny's shoulders. "Listen: we have four hours before I take you to school. I'll get two bodies." He let go of Danny and yawned. "I have to eat something first. I can't go body-snatching without breakfast."

"There won't be enough time to drain them," Danny whimpered.

"Not completely," Sid admitted, "but you have plenty of blood already, and you'll have your five different bodies in case the school has a pop DNA readout. We can save time if you begin bottling the blood now in those one-gallon containers. Besides," Sid added with a touch of bravura, "I'll get an extra body, so the draining factor won't be as important."

Danny hugged his father around the waist. "You'll do that, Daddy? You'll get extra bodies for me?"

Sid roughed up Danny's hair. "Don't worry. You'll have your blood."

Letting go of his father, Danny began gathering the plastic containers and siphons.

"And don't forget to have a bath when you're done," Sid cautioned. He clunked up the stairs and thought, Where am I going to get three bodies at this time in the morning? Damn school projects.

Sid went to the bedroom and dressed. Jeans, a gray turtleneck, and a dark cotton sweater seemed appropriate. He noticed that his wife Milly wasn't in bed. If home, she'd come running on hearing Danny scream. And if not home, where? He mused bitterly that she could have gone to Sergei again. Sid could never understand her attraction to werewolves. The pills afterward were frightfully expensive.

He sat on the bed to pull on a pair of socks and saw himself in the mirror opposite. My hair is thinning, he thought, but were-wolves always have such an abundance of hair. I should grow a moustache. People wouldn't notice that my nose is a bit off to the side. He opted for running shoes, instead of boots. Less noise.

In the kitchen, he started a pot of dark coffee and put a couple of pieces of bread in the toaster. He opened the refrigerator and took out a container of apple juice. Milly glided into the room.

While pouring the juice, he said, "I wondered where you were."

An unfamiliar voice said, "Theosebia is here."

Sid looked at her. Milly was wearing her favorite sheer nightie and levitated about an inch above the floor.

He said, "You've screwed another pentagram. How many times have I warned you about that?"

"We seek the emerald tablet and the holy stone Kyphi."

"If you paid more attention to your drawing, we wouldn't be having this conversation. A proper pentagram takes at least an hour to prepare. You must have rushed through it again." Jealousy nagged him. "You're trying to cover the fact that you were out tonight, aren't you?" The bread popped out of the toaster, and he began buttering it.

"We need gold and silver. Forget not the chesteb and mafek either."

The coffee was ready, and Sid sat down at the table and began eating his breakfast. Looking at Milly-Theosebia, he said, "You're becoming smaller." She was clearly less than five feet tall.

"It is written that hertes is the catalyst."

"I don't suppose you know of any nearby bodies fit for snatching?" Sid asked. "You sound like a visionary, and Danny needs bodies. I have less than four hours to come through for our kid."

Milly-Theosebia glided next to him and held out her arms. "Make love to me. Only in that manner can we share power with a mortal."

Swallowing the last piece of toast, Sid said, "Who am I going to find this early in the morning? The pimps, whores, and muggers must have staggered to bed. The werewolves and ghouls would have finished prowling. Maybe I can get lucky and find a drunk or a jogger." He gulped down the remainder of his coffee and stood up.

She grabbed him around the neck and screamed into his mouth, "Love me!"

Sid freed himself, took her by the waist, and sat her on the table.

"You're less than four feet tall now. Not that I have anything against midgets, but I can see that loving you could lead to a painful trap. More important than either your feelings or mine, our son has to finish his class project. If he doesn't, whatever part of you is Milly must realize that he'd flunk out and go to summer school. If summer school, no camp. No camp, and we have him underfoot for over two months. Do you remember last year? Do you want to repeat that again? Of course not. We need bodies. Can you tell me where to find any?"

Milly-Theosebia said, "A male is taking out garbage. He is alone and defenseless."

"You know how strict the condo management is about snatching residents. What with all the riffraff living here, no one would be left if we didn't have discipline."

She shut her eyes, leaned back, and hummed a little. "I sense a human, alone and on foot, one whom no one would miss. About four blocks away and outside the condo border. Where Green Street runs into Cleveland Avenue."

"I'm on it!" Sid said. "By the way, while I'm away, go easy with Danny. I don't think he's ready for you."

"Hurry," said Milly-Theosebia. "We've only until midday before oblivion."

"No problem," said Sid, who kissed her but wondered whether she meant oblivion for Theosebia, Milly, himself, or a third party.

Jupiter was setting in the November sky, and the Pleiades were overhead. Dawn wouldn't begin for another hour. Sid got into his hatchback, which could accommodate four bodies in the back. He didn't turn on the headlights.

Driving along Green Street, he came across a person carrying a large flashlight. Sid eased his car close to the curb, about a hundred feet away from his target. He took out a crowbar and quietly tailed the woman, who didn't notice him. She was in her late fifties, wore a raincoat and low-cut tennis shoes.

It couldn't be, he thought as he caught up with her. But it was. Sid hastily concealed the crowbar between his arm and his body.

"Hello, Sid," she said, noticing him. "Raggs got out again, and I want to find him before I go to work."

"I'd like to help you, Karen," Sid replied, "but I'm looking for stuff for Danny's class project."

They were next-door neighbors. Even without the condo rules, Sid could never harm Karen. Her daughter was a particularly vicious ghoul. Six months ago he saw her rip the arms off a deliveryman. Sid made it a point to stay on her good side.

"What kind of stuff?"

He shrugged and smiled guiltily. "You know. Stuff."

"Something like this? I found it on the lawn."

It was an emerald tablet, which he gratefully accepted.

"That will do very nicely. Thanks, Karen."

"I could help you look!"

"No thanks. You better find Raggs. You know what a commotion Raggs caused the last time he got out."

Sid returned to his car. He wondered whether he should drop off the tablet before proceeding.

From Green Street, he switched to the tree-lined Foster Road, and then drove south on Derby. It led to a small park that used to be a teen hangout – until the vampires discovered it. And no one had repopulated the park either. He was the only one in the parking lot.

Driving north on Derby, he turned back on Foster, which led to crowded housing and various rental units. Near Southside Boulevard, Sid realized that he was being followed by a Ford Explorer. If someone wants to chat, he thought, I'm willing. He stopped in front of a street lamp. The Explorer parked a few car lengths behind him. He got out, concealed the crowbar behind him, and strolled over. The SUV's windows were dark-tinted, and he rapped lightly on the driver's side.

The window rolled down.

"Hello, Sid."

"Why, howdy, Naomi. What brings you out?"

"I'm lonely."

231

They had first met earlier in the year at a PTA dinner. Her daughter Tyla was in Danny's class. Sid and Naomi had hit it off immediately but never had much opportunity to do anything about it. Nevertheless, there sat Naomi, and the street lighting, as dim as it was, showed her to advantage. Her blouse was open to her waist, exposing her black leather bra, and her skirt had risen high along her thighs. The dagger earrings piercing her plump earlobes excited him the most. He imagined them in his mouth.

He sighed. He had no time. "Danny has this class project, and he has to bring the blood of five—"

"Bodies," finished Naomi.

"You too!?"

"It's the swimming pool rite."

"I haven't thought of the pool rite for years. That was fun! Did your school have one?"

"No. I went to private school. I didn't have my first blood rite until college."

"That's too bad."

"Tyla didn't tell me until yesterday." She drummed her fingers on the steering wheel. "These kids! How does she expect me to come up with five bodies in one night? Well, two bodies. I got three so far." She looked at him wistfully. "I hoped you'd be my fourth."

"I haven't had any luck."

Naomi said, "I've been up the whole night. And there are only two hours left before schooltime. You know the penalty for not bringing enough blood."

Sid nodded. "I'm the same with Danny."

She exhaled sharply. "There's no reason that both kids should flunk. Give me your bodies!"

"Wait a minute, Naomi. Fair's fair. Give me yours. You have three?"

She tossed a plastic cover from behind her.

"Wow! Did you get Sergei? I wouldn't have minded coming across him."

Opening the car door, Naomi got out of the Ford, wrapped her arms around him, and slammed his body against the SUV.

After the second kiss, Sid said, "Frank deserted you. But what am I going to tell Milly?"

She pulled his head against her chest and began pushing his head down. His chin hooked over her bra, which came loose. Naomi said, "I'll make it worth your while. Give me your bodies!" Sid's lips were level with the silver camel fetish in her navel when they were illuminated by a passing car.

They both stood up.

Naomi said, "That's Annie. Her kid is in the same class as ours. I recognized the license plate."

"Is she cruising for bodies too?"

"No," Naomi laughed. "The lucky bitch drives an ambulance. I should have flagged her down."

"An ambulance driver . . ."

"So you have wandering eyes!"

"Did Frank ever finish your pit?" Sid asked.

She softly touched his face and then let her purple-black nails slide along his jaw line. "Yes," she whispered.

Taking her hand, he licked her nails. "You've serrated the edges."

"No," she said. "I put on Ares' Favor. The polish includes steel filings. Us or the kids?"

"Their bodies. Their blood. Their pit."

They shared a lingering kiss.

Naomi asked, "How soon can you bring Danny?"

❧

Sid admired Naomi's basement. Whatever kind of werecreature her ex happened to be, his workmanship was first rate. Frank had completely finished the basement. Soft rugs decorated the floor, a miniature bar with four stools highlighted one corner, and the classy school rite wallpaper was an adaption of Bosch. However, without any doubt, the basement was dominated by the pit.

Twelve feet in diameter and eight feet deep, the pit had a stainless steel mesh lining. The mesh allowed water and silt to fill in during rainy weather while keeping stones and larger rocks out.

Whatever the season, groundwater always covered the bottom, forming a viscous mud. Surrounding the pit was a low picket railing, which had two openings on opposite sides. Each entrance led to an aluminum ladder by which a participant descended to the mud below.

"Wow!" Sid said before Naomi and he sat down on the brown velvet sofa in front of the pit. "Too cool."

"Would you like a drink?" She had changed into a cloud-print lounge gown, but Sid was happy that she kept on her dagger earrings.

"Later maybe. We should let them get started."

The two children, Danny and Tyla, stood glumly in front of the sofa. The kids wore old sweats, since their clothes would likely be ripped off, but were disarmed.

The parents frisked their respective children.

"What do you call this, Danny?" asked Sid.

"Geez, Dad, my brass knuckles aren't really a weapon. Everyone has at least one."

Naomi found a necklace garotte around her daughter's ankle.

"Those are the rules, son," Sid said. "And you're lucky we have rules. If Tyla kept her garotte, you'd be in trouble, with or without brass knuckles."

Naomi made Tyla take off the razor earrings.

"You always let me fight with my razor earrings in the pit," Tyla complained. "I don't see why this has to be any different."

Petting Tyla, Naomi said, "Darling, you're not trying to make your mark on the pack. All you want to do is knock Danny unconscious for a tiny bit. You'll have all the blood you need for school." She pushed Tyla forward. "Now stop whining and get into the pit."

Each child went to a ladder.

"One, two, three – and down you go!" Naomi cried.

As each kid scrambled down, Naomi winked at Sid. Both parents jumped up, and they pulled out the ladders. Standing at the edge of the pit with her hands on her hips, Naomi said, "First one out wins. If no one shows up in half an hour, we'll see who's standing. If no one's standing, well, let's hope it doesn't come to that."

Danny and Tyla began circling each other, and Sid and Naomi returned to the sofa.

"We can't see them from the sofa," complained Sid.

"There's a mirror on the ceiling."

"Well look at that! I wonder where Tyla hid the blackjack?"

Naomi shrugged. "I didn't notice Danny wearing an Xacto ring."

They laughed. "Kids!" After their laughter faded, Naomi whispered, "Excited?"

He grabbed her by her shoulders, pushed her down, and bit her left earlobe. Sid whispered intently, "Did Frank do it?"

Twisting free, Naomi yanked his pants down to his knees, and something clattered on the floor. She pointed. "What's that?"

Sitting up, Sid said, "It must have fallen out of my pocket. It's—"

"My emerald tablet!" a high-pitched voice screeched. A nine-inch-tall Milly-Theosebia materialized next to the tablet and grabbed it. "We're saved! The world is saved!" Then tablet and materialization vanished.

"Who or what was that!?" Naomi had not recognized the miniature Milly.

Sid shrugged and smiled self-consciously. "Something about oblivion."

"I'll give you oblivion," said a disembodied voice.

Sid blinked and found that he was hanging upside-down in his own basement. Next to him, also upside-down, was Naomi. They were both leaking blood.

Smoothing Danny's hair, Milly stared at the two of them. "Danny won," she said, "but I had a better idea." She turned and went upstairs. "I've a pentagram to finish."

"Hey!" Sid shouted.

"Relax, Dad," Danny said. "With all the bodies I got, all I need is a quart from you. Or not more than two."

The Place of Revelation

Ramsey Campbell

At dinner Colin's parents do most of the talking. His mother starts by saying "Sit down," and as soon as he does his father says "Sit up." Auntie Dot lets Colin glimpse a sympathetic grin while Uncle Lucian gives him a secret one, neither of which helps him feel less nervous. They're eating off plates as expensive as the one he broke last time they visited, when his parents acted as if he'd meant to drop it even though the relatives insisted it didn't matter and at least his uncle thought so. "Delicious as always," his mother says when Auntie Dot asks yet again if Colin's food is all right, and his father offers "I expect he's just tired, Dorothy." At least that's an excuse, which Colin might welcome except it prompts his aunt to say "If you've had enough I should scamper off to bye-byes, Colin. For a treat you can leave us the washing up."

Everyone is waiting for him to go to his room. Even though his parents keep saying how well he does in English and how the art mistress said he should take up painting at secondary school, he's expected only to mumble agreement whenever he's told to speak up for himself. For the first time he tries arguing. "I'll do it. I don't mind."

"You've heard what's wanted," his father says in a voice that seems to weigh his mouth down.

"You catch up on your sleep," his mother says more gently, "then you'll be able to enjoy yourself tomorrow."

Beyond her Uncle Lucian is nodding eagerly, but nobody else sees. Everyone watches Colin trudge into the high wide hall. It offers him a light, and there's another above the stairs that smell of their new fat brown carpet, and one more in the upstairs corridor. They only put off the dark. Colin is taking time on each stair until his father lets him hear "Is he getting ready for bed yet?" For fear of having to explain his apprehensiveness he flees to the bathroom.

With its tiles white as a blizzard it's brighter than the hall, but its floral scent makes Colin feel it's only pretending to be a room. As he brushes his teeth the mirror shows him foaming at the mouth as though his nerves have given him a fit. When he heads for his room, the doorway opposite presents him with a view across his parents' bed of the hospital he can't help thinking is a front for the graveyard down the hill. It's lit up as pale as a tombstone, whereas his window that's edged with tendrils of frost is full of nothing but darkness, which he imagines rising massively from the fields to greet the black sky. Even if the curtains shut tight they wouldn't keep out his sense of it, nor does the flimsy furniture that's yellow as the wine they're drinking downstairs. He huddles under the plump quilt and leaves the light on while he listens to the kitchen clatter. All too soon it comes to an end, and he hears someone padding upstairs so softly they might almost not be there at all.

As the door inches open with a faint creak that puts him in mind of the lifting of a lid, he grabs the edge of the quilt and hauls it over his face. "You aren't asleep yet, then," his mother says. "I thought you might have drifted off."

Colin uncovers his face and bumps his shoulders against the bars behind the pillow. "I can't get to sleep, so can I come down?"

"No need for that, Colin. I expect you're trying too hard. Just think of nice times you've had and then you'll go off. You know there's nothing really to stop you."

She's making him feel so alone that he no longer cares if he gives away his secrets. "There is."

"Colin, you're not a baby any more. You didn't act like this when you were. Try not to upset people. Will you do that for us?"

"If you want."

She frowns at his reluctance. "I'm sure it's what you want as well. Just be as thoughtful as I know you are."

Everything she says reminds him how little she knows. She leans down to kiss each of his eyes shut, and as she straightens up, the cord above the bed turns the kisses into darkness with a click. Can he hold onto the feeling long enough to fall asleep? Once he hears the door close he burrows under the quilt and strives to be aware of nothing beyond the bed. He concentrates on the faint scent of the quilt that nestles on his face, he listens to the silence that the pillow and the quilt press against his ears. The weight of the quilt is beginning to feel vague and soft as sleep when the darkness whispers his name. "I'm asleep," he tries complaining, however babyish and stupid it sounds.

"Not yet, Colin," Uncle Lucian says. "Story first. You can't have forgotten."

He hasn't, of course. He remembers every bedtime story since the first, when he didn't know it would lead to the next day's walk. "I thought we'd have finished," he protests.

"Quietly, son. We don't want anyone disturbed, do we? One last story."

Colin wants to stay where he can't see and yet he wants to know. He inches the quilt down from his face. The gap between the curtains has admitted a sliver of moonlight that turns the edges of objects a glimmering white. A sketch of his uncle's face the colour of bone hovers by the bed. His smile glints, and his eyes shine like stars so distant they remind Colin how limitless the dark is. That's one reason why he blurts "Can't we just go wherever it is tomorrow?"

"You need to get ready while you're asleep. You should know that's how it works." As Uncle Lucian leans closer, the light tinges his gaunt face except where it's hollowed out with shadows, and Colin is reminded of the moon looming from behind a cloud. "Wait now, here's an idea," his uncle murmurs. "That ought to help."

Colin realises he would rather not ask "What?"

"Tell the stories back to me. You'll find someone to tell one day, you know. You'll be like me."

The prospect fails to appeal to Colin, who pleads "I'm too tired."

"They'll wake you up. Your mother was saying how good you are at stories. That's thanks to me and mine. Go on before anyone

238

comes up and hears."

A cork pops downstairs, and Colin knows there's little chance of being interrupted. "I don't know what to say."

"I can't tell you that, Colin. They're your stories now. They're part of you. You've got to find your own way to tell them."

As Uncle Lucian's eyes glitter like ice Colin hears himself say "Once…"

"That's the spirit. That's how it has to start."

"Once there was a boy…"

"Called Colin. Sorry. You won't hear another breath out of me."

"Once there was a boy who went walking in the country on a day like it was today. The grass in the fields looked like feathers where all the birds in the world had been fighting, and all the fallen leaves were showing their bones. The sun was so low every crumb of frost had its own shadow, and his footprints had shadows in when he looked behind him, and walking felt like breaking little bones under his feet. The day was so cold he kept thinking the clouds were bits of ice that had cracked off the sky and dropped on the edge of the earth. The wind kept scratching his face and pulling the last few leaves off the trees, only if the leaves went back he knew they were birds. It was meant to be the shortest day, but it felt as if time had died because everything was too slippery or too empty for it to get hold of. So he thought he'd done everything there was to do and seen everything there was to see when he saw a hole like a gate through a hedge."

"That's the way." Uncle Lucian's eyes have begun to shine like fragments of the moon. "Make it your story."

"He wasn't sure if there was an old gate or the hedge had grown like one. He didn't know it was one of the places where the world is twisted. All he could see was more hedge at the sides of a bendy path. So he followed it round and round, and it felt like going inside a shell. Then he got dizzy with running to find the middle, because it seemed to take hours and the bends never got any smaller. But just when he was thinking he'd stop and turn back if the spiky hedges let him, he came to where the path led all round a pond that was covered with ice. Only the pond oughtn't to have been so big, all the path he'd run round should have squeezed it little. So he was walking round the pond to see if he could find the trick when the sun showed him the flat white faces everywhere under the ice.

"There were children and parents who'd come searching for them, and old people too. They were everyone the maze had brought to the pond, and they were all calling him. Their eyes were opening as slow as holes in the ice and growing too big, and their mouths were moving like fish mouths out of water, and the wind in the hedge was their cold rattly voice telling him he had to stay for ever, because he couldn't see the path away from the pond – there was just hedge everywhere he looked. Only then he heard his uncle's voice somewhere in it, telling him he had to walk back in all his footprints like a witch dancing backwards and then he'd be able to escape."

This is the part Colin likes least, but his uncle murmurs eagerly "And was he?"

"He thought he never could till he remembered what his foot-prints looked like. When he turned round he could just see them with the frost creeping to swallow them up. So he started walking back in them, and he heard the ice on the pond start to crack to let all the bodies with the turned-up faces climb out. He saw thin white fingers pushing the edge of the ice up and digging their nails into the frosty path. His footprints led him back through the gap the place had tried to stop him finding in the hedge, but he could see hands flopping out of the pond like frogs. He still had to walk all the way back to the gate like that, and every step he took the hedges tried to catch him, and he heard more ice being pushed up and people crawling after him. It felt like the place had got hold of his middle and his neck and screwed them round so far he'd never be able to walk forward again. He came out of the gate at last, and then he had to walk round the fields till it was nearly dark to get back into walking in an ordinary way so his mother and father wouldn't notice there was something new about him and want to know what he'd been doing."

Colin doesn't mind if that makes his uncle feel at least a little guilty, but Uncle Lucian says "What happens next?"

Colin hears his parents and his aunt forgetting to keep their voices low downstairs. He still can't make out what they're saying, though they must think he's asleep. "The next year he went walking in the woods," he can't avoid admitting.

"What kind of a day would that have been, I wonder?"

"Sunny. Full of birds and squirrels and butterflies. So hot he felt like he was wearing the sun on his head, and the only place he could take it off was the woods, because if he went back to the house his mother and father would say he ought to be out walking. So he'd gone a long way under the trees when he felt them change."

"He could now. Most people wouldn't until it was too late, but he felt…"

"Something had crept up behind him. He was under some trees that put their branches together like hands with hundreds of fingers praying. And when he looked he saw the trees he'd already gone under were exactly the same as the ones he still had to, like he was looking in a mirror except he couldn't see himself in it. So he started to run but as soon as he moved, the half of the tunnel of trees he had to go through began to stretch itself till he couldn't see the far end, and when he looked behind him it had happened there as well."

"He knew what to do this time, didn't he? He hardly even needed to be told."

"He had to go forwards walking backwards and never look to see what was behind him. And as soon as he did he saw the way he'd come start to shrink. Only that wasn't all he saw, because leaves started running up and down the trees, except they weren't leaves. They were insects pretending to be them, or maybe they weren't insects. He could hear them scuttling about behind him, and he was afraid the way he had to go wasn't shrinking, it was growing as much longer as the way he'd come was getting shorter. Then all the scuttling things ran onto the branches over his head, and he thought they'd fall on him if he didn't stop trying to escape. But his body kept moving even though he wished it wouldn't, and

241

he heard a great flapping as if he was in a cave and bats were flying off the roof, and then something landed on his head. It was just the sunlight, and he'd come out of the woods the same place he'd gone in. All the way back he felt he was walking away from the house, and his mother said he'd got a bit of sunstroke."

"He never told her otherwise, did he? He knew most people aren't ready to know what's behind the world."

"That's what his uncle kept telling him."

"He was proud to be chosen, wasn't he? He must have known it's the greatest privilege to be shown the old secrets."

Colin has begun to wish he could stop talking about himself as though he's someone else, but the tales won't let go of him – they've closed around him like the dark. "What was his next adventure?" it whispers with his uncle's moonlit smiling mouth.

"The next year his uncle took him walking in an older wood. Even his mother and father might have noticed there was something wrong with it and told him not to go in far." When his uncle doesn't acknowledge any criticism but only smiles wider and more whitely Colin has to add "There was nothing except sun in the sky, but as soon as you went in the woods you had to step on shadows everywhere, and that was the only way you knew there was still a sun. And the day was so still it felt like the woods were pretending they never breathed, but the shadows kept moving whenever he wasn't looking – he kept nearly seeing very tall ones hide behind the trees. So he wanted to get through the woods as fast as he could, and that's why he ran straight onto the stepping stones when he came to a stream."

Colin would like to run fast through the story too, but his uncle wants to know "How many stones were there again?"

"Ten, and they looked so close together he didn't have to stretch to walk. Only he was on the middle two when he felt them start to move. And when he looked down he saw the stream was really as deep as the sky, and lying on the bottom was a giant made out of rocks and moss that was holding up its arms to him. They were longer than he didn't know how many trees stuck together, and their hands were as big as the roots of an old tree, and he was standing on top of two of the fingers. Then the giant's eyes began to open like boulders rolling about in the mud, and its mouth opened like a cave and sent up a laugh in a bubble that spattered the boy with mud, and the stones he was on started to move apart."

"His uncle was always with him though, wasn't he?"

"The boy couldn't see him," Colin says in case this lets his uncle realise how it felt, and then he knows his uncle already did. "He heard him saying you mustn't look down, because being seen was what woke up the god of the wood. So the boy kept looking straight ahead, though he could see the shadows that weren't shadows crowding behind the trees to wait for him. He could feel how even the water underneath him wanted him to slip on the slimy stones, and how the stones were ready to swim apart so he'd fall between them if he caught the smallest glimpse of them. Then he did, and the one he was standing on sank deep into the water, but he'd jumped on the bank of the stream. The shadows that must have been the bits that were left of people who'd looked down too long let him see his uncle, and they walked to the other side of the woods. Maybe he wouldn't have got there without his uncle, because the shadows kept dancing around them to make them think there was no way between the trees."

"Brave boy, to see all that." Darkness has reclaimed the left side of Uncle Lucian's face; Colin is reminded of a moon that the night is squeezing out of shape. "Don't stop now, Colin," his uncle says. "Remember last year."

This is taking longer than his bedtime stories ever have. Colin feels as if the versions he's reciting may rob him of his whole night's sleep. Downstairs his parents and his aunt sound as if they need to talk for hours yet. "It was here in town," he says accusingly. "It was down in Lower Brichester."

He wants to communicate how betrayed he felt, by the city or his uncle or by both. He'd thought houses and people would keep away the old things, but now he knows that nobody who can't see can help. "It was where the boy's mother and father wouldn't have liked him to go," he says, but that simply makes him feel the way his uncle's stories do, frightened and excited and unable to sepa-rate the feelings. "Half the houses were shut up with boards but people were still using them, and there were men and ladies on the corners of the streets waiting for whoever wanted them or stuff they were selling. And in the middle of it all there were railway lines and passages to walk under them. Only the people who lived round there must have felt something, because there was one passage nobody walked through."

"But the boy did."

"A man sitting drinking with his legs in the road told him not to, but he did. His uncle went through another passage and said he'd meet him on the other side. Anyone could have seen something was wrong with the tunnel, because people had dropped needles all over the place except in there. But it looked like it'd just be a minute to walk through, less if you ran. So the boy started to hurry through, only he tried to be quiet because he didn't like how his feet made so much noise he kept thinking someone was following him, except it sounded more like lots of fingers tapping on the bricks behind him. When he managed to be quiet the noise didn't all go away, but he tried to think it was water dripping, because he felt it cold and wet on the top of his head. Then more of it touched the back of his neck, but he didn't want to look round, because the passage was getting darker behind him. He was in the middle of the tunnel when the cold touch landed on his face and made him look."

His uncle's face is barely outlined, but his eyes take on an extra gleam. "And when he looked…"

"He saw why the passage was so dark, with all the arms as thin as his poking out of the bricks. They could grow long enough to reach halfway down the passage and grope around till they found him with their fingers that were as wet as worms. Then he couldn't even see them, because the half of the passage he had to walk through was filling up with arms as well, so many he couldn't see out. And all he could do was what his uncle's story had said, stay absolutely still, because if he tried to run the hands would grab him and drag him through the walls into the earth, and he wouldn't even be able to die of how they did it. So he shut his eyes to be as blind as the things with the arms were, that's if there wasn't just one thing behind the walls. And after he nearly forgot how to breathe the hands stopped pawing at his head as if they were feeling how his brain showed him everything about them, maybe even brought them because he'd learned to see the old things. When he opened his eyes the arms were worming back into the walls, but he felt them all around him right to the end of the passage. And when he went outside he couldn't believe in the day-light any more. It was like a picture someone had put up to hide the dark."

"He could believe in his uncle though, couldn't he? He saw his uncle waiting for him and telling him well done. I hope he knew how much his uncle thought of him."

"Maybe."

"Well, now it's another year."

Uncle Lucian's voice is so low, and his face is so nearly invisible, that Colin isn't sure whether his words are meant to be comforting or to warn the boy that there's more. "Another story," Colin mumbles, inviting it or simply giving in.

"I don't think so any more. I think you're too old for that."

Colin doesn't know in what way he feels abandoned as he whispers "Have we finished?"

"Nothing like. Tomorrow, just go and lie down and look up."

"Where?"

"Anywhere you're by yourself."

Colin feels he is now. "Then what?" he pleads.

"You'll see. I can't begin to tell you. See for yourself."

That makes Colin more nervous than his uncle's stories ever did. He's struggling to think how to persuade his uncle to give him at least a hint when he realises he's alone in the darkness. He lies on his back and stares upwards in case that gets whatever has to happen over with, but all he sees are memories of the places his uncle has made him recall. Downstairs his parents and his aunt are still talking, and he attempts to use their voices to keep him with them, but feels as if they're dragging him down into the moonless dark. Then he's been asleep, because they're shutting their doors close to his. After that, whenever he twitches awake it's a little less dark. As soon as he's able to see he sneaks out of bed to avoid his parents and his aunt. Whatever is imminent, having to lie about where he's going would make his nerves feel even more like rusty wire about to snap.

He's as quick and as quiet in the bathroom as he can be. Once he's dressed he rolls up the quilt to lie on and slips out of the house. In the front garden he thinks moonlight has left a crust on the fallen leaves and the grass. Down the hill a train shakes itself awake while the city mutters in its sleep. He turns away and heads for the open country behind the house.

A few crows jab at the earth with their beaks and sail up as if they mean to peck the icy sky. The ground has turned into a single flattened greenish bone exactly as bright as the low vault of dull cloud. Colin walks until the fields bear the houses out of sight. That's as alone as he's likely to be. Flapping the quilt, he spreads it on the frozen ground. He throws himself on top of it and slaps his hands on it in case that starts whatever's meant to happen. He's already so cold he can't keep still.

At first he thinks that's the only reason he's shivering, and then he notices the sky isn't right. He feels as if all the stories he's had to act out have gathered in his head, or the way they've made him see has. That ability is letting him observe how thin the sky is growing, or perhaps it's leaving him unable not to. Is it also attracting whatever's looming down to peer at him from behind the sky? A shiver is drumming his heels on the ground through the quilt when the sky seems to vanish as though it has been clawed apart above him, and he glimpses as much of a face as there's room for – an eye like a sea black as space with a moon for its pupil. It seems indifferent as death and yet it's watching him. An instant of seeing is all he can take before he twists onto his front and presses his face into the quilt as though it's a magic carpet that will transport him home to bed and, better still, unconsciousness.

He digs his fingers into the quilt until he recognises he can't burrow into the earth. He stops for fear of tearing his aunt's quilt and having to explain. He straightens up in a crouch to retrieve the quilt, which he hugs as he stumbles back across the field with his head down. The sky is pretending that it never faltered, but all the way to the house he's afraid it will part to expose more of a face.

While nobody is up yet, Colin senses that his uncle isn't in the house. He tiptoes upstairs to leave the quilt on his bed, and then he sends himself out again. There's no sign of his uncle on the way downhill. Colin dodges onto the path under the trees in case his uncle prefers not to be seen. "Uncle Lucian," he pleads.

"You found me."

He doesn't seem especially pleased, but Colin demands "What did I see?"

"Not much yet. Just as much as your mind could take. It's like our stories, do you understand? Your mind had to tell you a story about what you saw, but in time you won't need it. You'll see what's really there."

"Suppose I don't want to?" Colin blurts. "What's it all for?"

"Would you rather be like my sister and only see what everyone else sees? She was no fun when she was your age, your mother."

"I never had the choice."

"Well, I wouldn't ever have said that to my grandfather. I was nothing but grateful to him."

Though his uncle sounds not merely disappointed but offended, Colin says "Can't I stop now?"

"Everything will know you can see, son. If you don't greet the old things where you find them they'll come to find you."

Colin voices a last hope. "Has it stopped for you?"

"It never will. I'm part of it now. Do you want to see?"

"No."

Presumably Colin's cry offends his uncle, because there's a spidery rustle beyond the trees that conceal the end of the path and then silence. Time passes before Colin dares to venture forward. As he steps from beneath the trees he feels as if the sky has lowered itself towards him like a mask. He's almost blind with resentment of his uncle for making him aware of so much and for leaving him alone, afraid to see even Uncle Lucian. Though it doesn't help, Colin starts kicking the stone with his uncle's name on it and the pair of years ending with this one. When he's exhausted he turns away towards the rest of his life.

What Betty Saw

Joel Jacobs

B etty saw things. Good things, bad things, all sorts of things. Betty saw the sweetness, the adoration, the commitment of lovers, the strength of new mothers, the grit of construction workers, the will of politicians. She could measure those things.

Betty saw the abusers and the abused, the beaters and the beaten, the batterers and the battered. She saw this physical evil through the body language and the emotional auras projected by the people who were hurt, and who committed the hurt, no matter how well they disguised it.

She knew which of the teenage girls walking to school past her porch each day were virgins and which were not. She saw the sperm on the ten year old neighbor girl's cheeks long after it had been wiped away. And she saw the fear in the youngster's eyes that could never be expunged.

Betty also saw secrets, like past abortions, illicit desires, regret, hate and the hidden personifications of the seven deadly sins brewing below the skins of their possessors. She saw the congealing of criminal thought before the crimes were performed.

Betty saw the lottery numbers that would be drawn and the winners and losers of horse races, boxing matches and popular sporting events. She felt the rumble of earthquakes before the movement of the tectonic plates and the gush of volcanoes on the verge of spewing steam and lava.

She did not predict the weather. She knew it and dressed accordingly.

What Betty saw did not disturb her or alter her joi de vivre. It was her gift, not her burden, and she was happy to have it. She enjoyed knowing the sex of babies in utero, for instance. Life went on, shit happened, people lived and died and Betty saw it all, at least all of it that she wished to see.

Her stockbroker father had provided for her. She never married because she was aware that she would not be able to deal with the prescience of the sickness and health of a spouse and children, or their deaths. She didn't want that kind of foreknowledge so she didn't allow it to happen.

Betty was a perpetual bystander, a seer, a watcher, a stoic. The good, the bad, the ying, the yang, it all made sense to her.

Betty saw the supernova 36 hours ahead of its burst. She resolved not to experience the pathos of those millions of screaming souls enduring their last few seconds. She took the bell collar off the cat and let it out. She treated the dog to all the left-overs in the fridge. She opened a window and freed the canary.

Then, she changed the answering machine tape to say, "Betty has embarked on a long journey… Please, don't bother to leave a message…" and swilled eight Benedryls with her favorite sipping whiskey. This she followed with Black Forest cake and jasmine tea laced with arsenic. The flavor of almonds in chocolate was the last thing she perceived.

That was yesterday.

Endpiece

Ramsey Campbell

S hall we emerge blinking from the confines of the book? Too bright! Too bright!

Thank heavens, it was only a story. Don't worry. It's still dark. The only light belongs to the tales, which illuminate this structure we're still in. What is this place? Will the labyrinth of rooms and corridors ever end? Perhaps it's a cinema complex – surely those views of landscapes swarming with monsters are on screens, not through windows. It contains apartments too, some of them as extensive as houses, all of them occupied by lonely tenants and their nightmares. Stay out of there, and avoid those steps that lead into underground darkness. Don't speak to anyone you see in the shadows, and be glad you can't see them more clearly. We seem to have been wandering for longer than a night. Will it never end?

Surely that's the exit. The ushers are beckoning us towards it. They seem eager to be rid of us; perhaps they're hungry, not having dined for all this time. How thin they are! They deserve to be fed. It must be cold outside for their teeth to be clicking so much. At least we can't mistake the gestures of hands as long as those. Where does the door lead? It must be the dawn, which is all that matters, and a colourful one too. We can see it now. We can see something red that's coming for us.